GRAPES FROM THORNBUSHES

Alissa Ordabai was born in Almaty, USSR. She studied art history at the Courtauld Institute of Art in London and popular music and sound technology at the Liverpool Institute for Performing Arts before graduating with a law degree from the University in London in 2006. She is a staff writer at Russia's *Rockcor* magazine and a contributor to *www.crushermagazine.com*. She lives in London.

Alissa Ordabai

GRAPES FROM THORNBUSHES

Merodach Publishing

Merodach Publishing
27 Old Gloucester Street
London
WC1N 3AX
UK

ISBN: 978-0-9559826-0-6

Cover design by Juno Enkidu

My thanks:

Chip Stern

Alexey Boldov

Christine Natanael

Alexander Rappaport

Sophie Arkette

By their fruit you will recognise them. Do people pick grapes from thornbushes, or figs from thistles?

Matthew 7:16

I

DIRTY SECRETS

Ed Sunders sat across from me in his trendy ripped Levi's jacket, a size too small, oozing the smell of Lynx Alaska, sweat, and cigarette smoke, telling me about my old band the Storm Angels getting a record deal with Global Union Records. His skinny face kept breaking into his usual tense grin, each time showing his yellowing teeth and bringing out crow's feet around his small brown eyes. He was constantly touching his hair. I could have lived with his peroxide-blond jacked-up hair, if only it didn't contrast so disturbingly with his brown eyes and his black moth-eaten eyebrows.

'Joe, you wouldn't believe it,' Ed was saying to me agitatedly, spilling some of his pint on his skin-tight grey jeans. 'The boys have finally made it! Going from playing clubs to signing a major record deal, all in the space of twelve months! Has this ever happened before? Since Hendrix?'

'Didn't take him long to start comparing this band to Hendrix,' I thought, cringing inside. 'Sums up his brand of music journalism to a tee.'

'They are flying to LA next month to record with Global's biggest producer,' Ed was carrying on, oblivious of my internal commentary. 'The same guy who worked with all the legends back in the Seventies. I'm hoping to fly in too for a couple of days to do a feature on them while they are recording.'

'Big labels only give access to the journos they know,' I said deliberately.

Ed looked at me as if to say, 'What do *you* know about big labels,' but quickly grinned again and asked the barman for a packet of cheese and onion crisps.

We were sitting at the bar of a spit-and-sawdust pub in Northwest London, a place where no wannabe rock star, no matter how heavy their eyeliner or how over-bleached or over-teased his hair, would ever feel out of place. I was listening and watching Ed, thinking he wasn't getting any younger, and that now that he's turned thirty-five, which made him ancient in comparison to everyone else on the scene, the best thing he could do was to stop trying to break into the upper echelons of music journalism, stop writing exaggerated reviews that no one reads for online music mags that don't pay, stop hanging around young wannabes in the hope that one of them becomes a star and helps his career, and that he could begin with stopping to grin so enthusiastically while telling me how my ex-bandmates were going to become millionaires by the end of this fiscal year.

Ed is crap at trying to look laidback when he's breaking important news, and I could tell he was scrutinising my face trying to spot any sign of irritation, so that he could later report to every musician and every small-time groupie on the unsigned London scene how Joey Mormile is incredibly jealous of his old band getting signed to a big label. But you'd have to be an idiot to instantly believe everything Ed Sunders told you. And even if this time he was telling the truth, it didn't bother me too much. Knowing the Storm Angels, they were going to get dropped as easily as they got signed. That I was certain of because I knew their dirty secret, the dirtiest secret a rock band could ever have: *They didn't write their own songs.* Their manager, a beefy-faced, slimy excuse for a human being called Doug Scrivener did it for them. I knew this because up until a month ago I myself have been spending five hours a day rehearsing sleek, upbeat Eighties-style glam metal tunes written for the Storm Angels by Doug. Doug was bargaining on the fact that Eighties rock was making a comeback. Now I knew he's been guessing right.

Ed had just finished his second pint and was waiting for me to buy him the next, but all I did was carry on looking at him sideways from under my newly cut fringe pretending I was bored and about to take off.

Having realised he wasn't getting anything out of me – no reaction to the news and no drink – Ed got slightly annoyed, and the way he showed it was by telling me all over again, this time in more detail, how he bumped into Doug at Astoria last night and has been told everything about the record deal.

'Doug says the promotional budget is going to be phenomenal. And there will be a world tour once the album is out. They will even go to Japan. Classic rock is on the up there too, as you know. Doug is also hoping to win the best newcoming act award from one of the big mags.'

'Yeah, and then they will win ten Grammys,' I thought to myself. 'And will all marry porn stars and retire in mansions in Malibu once they turn thirty. And then, out of sheer boredom, they will make a habit out of playing Russian roulette with each other on weekend nights after they've run out of cocaine and Dom Perignon.'

Meanwhile Ed was carrying on with the same gusto, 'I'm so glad I was among the first to notice you guys back then! It adds to my standing, don't you think?'

'Standing,' I thought. 'Good god.'

While Ed was babbling, I sat there thinking how much I hated my former band and how I hated that old tosser Doug Scrivener. If there was one person on the London underground circuit who deserved to be tarred, feathered, and then paraded through the streets of London, it was him. A greasy, creepy, fifty-two year old geezer always on a lookout for young naïve musicians willing to sell their soul for a piece of paper with "Record Contract" typed at the top. They'd sell their souls and he'd take all the money. He wouldn't even run. He'd take the money and then sit there and smile, and give the boys a lecture on how their dreams of stardom have come true because of his incredible entrepreneurial talent and vision. And he'd continue taking their money and milking them until they were dead either of exhaustion, drug abuse, or pure disgust at being his puppets. Doug Scrivener, the Master of Puppets.

I was finally getting up to leave when I caught Ed looking at me with what I interpreted as a plea.

'Joe…' he began hesitantly.

I sensed something awkward was coming up. Was he going to ask me to take him with me to the Silver Cats aftershow tomorrow? I hoped not. Because I wasn't sure I myself was invited. And I didn't want him to know that.

'Joe, don't get upset or anything, but I've asked Doug if he'd take you back…'

'You did what?!' I glared at Ed, instantly wanting to smash his ugly little face, break his pimply nose and his yellow teeth, rip the bleached hair out of his skull, and to continue battering his face until he was on the floor in a pool of blood and vomit. I almost saw him crawling on the floor, trying to shield his smarmy face from my kicks.

'I thought you wouldn't mind, Joe. You know I always said you were the best guitarist on the scene, better than that geezer Doug had to draft in after you've left… It's an opportunity of a lifetime, Joe, you deserve it.'

'Since when are you representing me, Ed?' I said. 'I thought you were just a fanzine writer.'

I deliberately called him a fanzine writer. Then I got up, turned around and began walking towards the door. I was glad I was wearing my cowboy boots that day. Cowboy boots give your walk a kind of swagger that you can't imitate in any other footwear. I knew Ed was watching me as I was leaving, I even heard him carry on talking, saying that he just thought he'd ask for my own good, but I pretended I didn't hear.

It's easy for me to lose it, but I cool off just as quickly. As I was walking up Camden High Street, all I was thinking about was who old Douggie Scrivener had to blow to get a deal with Global. I remembered how when I was about thirteen, the phone rang in our house one day, my dad picked up and then shouted, 'Joey, for you!'

I was practicing guitar upstairs in my bedroom, so I shouted back, 'Who is it?'

'Global Union Records,' my father yelled back as a joke.

This memory made me smile. I knew I was going to get my own record deal when the time was right. A proper big label deal with quarter of a million advance, the one where my band would be writing its own material. Sold-out stadium shows, my face on the cover of Rolling Stone, platinum albums on the walls of a house in St. John's Wood, flats in New York and LA, movie stars for friends and models for girlfriends – this was the future I've been imagining for myself since I was thirteen. I could have it all if only I was given half a chance. All you need to succeed in this business is to be in the right place at the right time. And I knew that I was. I was in London and classic rock, the kind of music I loved and knew how to play, was topping the charts again. I just didn't want any deception, secrets, or ghost songwriters. I wanted my win to be clean.

Looking back, I couldn't believe I managed to end up in a band which didn't write its own material. We must have been the only band on the London unsigned scene where this was going on. Practically no one knew about this, but we constantly worried someone would find out. I wondered if Global knew what the real deal was with the Storm Angels. I really wondered. There was no way in hell people at Global would have offered a record deal to a band they knew wasn't writing its own songs. Suddenly I was struck by a thought that made me stop on my tracks. I stood on the side of the pavement for a while, not being able to carry on walking or to do anything else for that matter. I needed a cigarette, but I didn't have any with me, and I couldn't afford to buy a new packet.

I looked around trying to figure which direction to go in.

I finally remembered that there was an internet place near Chalk Farm tube, and once I did, I instantly started walking again, this time briskly and confidently. I loved the sound the heels of my boots were making against the pavement. A couple of teenage girls turned to look at me as I passed by them, and I was convinced it was because of my new haircut that I've spent all of this week's dole money on. I didn't look back because I knew that if you acted like a rock star, you were more likely to become one.

Camden is more or less tolerable on week days. It's still full of tourists, but not as jam-packed as on weekends, where you can't swing a guitar case without hitting a group of foreign students hanging in Camden "to experience the alternative culture". To them the experience usually starts with buying an overpriced Hendrix t-shirt from the market and ends back at their B&B in Edgware with examining the contents of a small plastic bag, which is actually nothing but five or six crushed Aspirin tablets, but which a sixteen year-old hoody on the corner of Arlington Road and Inverness Street described as "Columbian finest" before flogging it to them for forty quid. But once they are back to their home town of Catania, Sicily, or Moll, Belgium, wearing their new t-shirts, and brandishing used tickets to a Kaiser Chiefs gig like some kind of trophy from a place more culturally advanced than their won, they will, of course, by default become heroes to all other students at their local provincial uni, who will then be told stories about "hanging with really cool creative people in Camden", meaning the bloke with long grey hair who sold them the shirts and told them he used to share a flat with Pink Floyd in 1966, or the guy with dreads who plays bongos by the entrance to the market, who told them that he was a musician, an artist, and a Reiki healer. Once back, they will even talk about taking a year off and going to London to work behind the bar of one of Camden's pubs "to find myself" because "I don't want to end up in a dead-end job like my dad without experiencing the world". These are the kind of people who sure as hell will end up with a dead-end job, a mortgage on a suburban three-bedroom house, a revolting wife, and a couple of bratty kids by the time they are thirty.

What a lot of people don't know about Camden though is that if you can get past all the trashy shops and all the show that the locals are putting up for the tourists, you can come by truly great stuff there, if you know where to look. You can even meet some really cool people, not tourists, or maniacs, or teenage drug dealers, or spaced out old hippies. Because no matter what we, London musicians, say when we feel snobbish, Camden clubs is where you will hear all the new rock trends first. And if you know where to look, this is also where you can get any bootleg that's ever been recorded, or buy the coolest vintage clothes from any decade of rock – from the early Sixties to the late Eighties, usually for peanuts.

Quarter of an hour later I was in the caf, in front of a computer screen, searching for the phone number for Global Union Records Artist and Repertoire Department. Half an hour later I had it scribbled down on the back of my tube ticket. I went out into the street and was about to make the call when my phone rang first. I recognised the number immediately and stared at the screen of my Nokia with thoughts running through my head at one hundred miles an hour in all kinds of crazy directions. It was Doug fucking Scrivener calling me.

I took the call and heard Doug's smooth cheery voice sounding like piss mixed with honey, 'Hey, Joey, how are you doing, mate?'

I was so spooked by getting a call from him when I least expected it, that I mumbled back something incoherent. The last time Doug and I spoke was five weeks ago when I called him a cunt and he called me a "wannabe with no talent and no future".

'Listen, mate, I need to talk to you,' Doug was saying. 'As you probably know, something very important has come up. We are about to sign a deal with Global. I want you to come down for a chat. What are you doing tonight?'

Under the usual circumstances when anyone asks me this, I always say that on that particular evening I'm busy. And so far acting like a rock star has only won me points. In this business, if you are important, you are always busy. And rarely available. This is what Doug himself has always been telling us. But this time I was so gobsmacked, I suddenly forgot all the lessons of the last twelve months that we've been managed by him. I agreed to be at Doug's flat at seven.

After I clicked off, I contemplated going home to change into my Rock and Republic jeans and Fixel t-shirt, but then realised that this, after all, wasn't an audition, and that Doug probably knew me better than I knew myself. So I decided to hang in Camden until half six and then catch the Northern Line tube to Balham where he lived.

I went to a pub on Kentish Town Road which is always full of goths and emo kids, and where you can sit with a pint for as long as you like without being harassed by anyone, watching guys in platform boots and makeup, all dressed in black, and women in PVC and black lace.

What I don't get about the goth scene is why almost all the girls are so unattractive. Maybe they are goths because they are ugly? I have a theory that good-looking people, regardless if they are male or female, very rarely follow extreme fashion styles, unless they are paid good money for it. The way I explain it is that good-looking people are always popular, and when you are popular, you don't feel pissed off, or depressed, or anxious, or troubled enough to start dressing in a truly weird manner. As for myself, I've always been a musician first and everything else second. I don't have to wear ripped jeans and band t-shirts to show everyone that I'm a rocker or a bohemian. The reason why I do wear ripped jeans, and wear band t-shirts, and have long hair, is rather to conform to the circle of people I interact with every day – other musicians, managers, promoters, music journos. After all, these are the people my career depends on, and I don't want to look like I don't belong. Plus my shoulder-length hair really suits me. Young girls stare at me in shops and in the street all the time, and sometimes I wonder if they would if I had a crew cut.

I picked that particular pub to kill time at before going to Doug's because goths are completely unobtrusive, so I could sit there all day if I wanted to without anyone paying any attention to me. Even though it's a myth that goths don't judge you. The way I see it, of all counter-culture tribes, goths are the most opinionated and bigoted. They'd judge a bee for being too eager to make honey. To them, all other people are either too "chavvy", or too "emo", or too "cock-rock", or too whatever. But a goth would never say anything to your face. That's how a lot of people are mislead into thinking that goths are intelligent. People who don't say much are thought of as smart for some reason. It's not real intelligence with goths though, it's timidity, because a goth would never rise to a challenge. He'll walk away and moan about it to his mates. I've never seen a goth stand up for himself or his girlfriend when confronted. A goth will always walk away from a fight.

Thinking about fights, the last time I got involved in one was about a year ago after a couple of chavs started shouting unimaginative insults at me and my mate Pete at West Croydon train station as we were waiting for the last train to Victoria. Don't ask me what brought us to West Croydon train station that night. At the end of the incident I had a bruised eye, and Pete had a broken nose, and I had to go to an A&E with him. I'm not sure what was the exact damage the chavs have suffered, but I remember booting one of them in the stomach a couple of times when he was already down. I know this is out of order, but it's hard to control yourself when provoked by particularly moronic specimens of Southeast London lowlife who think that any male with hair long enough to touch his ears and jeans that actually fit, is a class enemy.

While I sat at one of the tables watching goths having their quite conversations (I'm sure about something utterly empty but pretentious, like how emo is inferior to the new wave, or the other way around), I was trying to think what I was going to say to Doug in a few hours' time. I knew what he was going to ask me. Since I left the Storm Angels, I've been on a lookout for a band that would take me on as a lead guitarist and let me practice writing my own material. I write a bit – a bridge here and a chorus there – but I've never written a complete song in my life. But I figured that I'm only twenty-two and it's not too late to start learning at my age. I've been looking to join or to form a band for over a month now, but so far nothing has panned out. None of the more established bands on the scene needed a lead guitarist, and all the new bands were so terrible the guys there didn't know how to play three chords in a succession.

The reason why I quit the Storm Angels was because Doug was a complete control freak. He was constantly telling us what to wear and how to look, he'd tell us who to talk to on the scene and who not to, and he'd decide on every small detail that concerned the band, down to the order of the songs for our shows. On tour, if he decided that we were going to drive to the next town at midnight straight after the show, then that's what we were doing. I've overheard a girl from a Brazilian mag saying to Doug once, 'You drive them like plantation slaves,' and Doug answering, 'Sure, there is no other way.' The fucker didn't even have the decency to smile or to make a joke about it. That's the thing about Doug – he's always been so deadly serious about things, never had any sense of humour. I'm thinking that if he did, maybe people wouldn't hate him so much. At the moment it seemed though that everyone did, either openly or secretly – fellow band managers he'd piss off by slagging off their acts in public, journalists he wouldn't let interview the band, promoters he'd cheat out of their fee, and even his own band.

But I guess I could still deal with all that, no matter how suffocating and soul-destroying Doug's approach to managing us was. What really made me quit was the material that Doug was writing for us. I love classic rock, sure, hell, I grew up listening to Aerosmith, and AC/DC, and Deep Purple and all those bands, but Doug's songs took the soul out of the classic rock style and turned it into a dead formula. His songs were like wax figures at Madame Tussauds – instantly recognisable as inspired by the classic bands, but with no life of their own. Doug's material just didn't give you the thrill that the real stuff did, didn't have that magic that grabs you and makes your heart beat faster. It was lifeless and insincere, even though well-written. He is a pro songwriter, I have to give him that. What utterly escapes me is how Global could have decided that Douggie's sanitised conveyer-belt tunes had any potential. I guess it just shows how weird the situation is in the music business right now. Or how shallow the music fans have become. I think people these days would buy into any trend once it's "in", no matter how artificial or cynically fake it is. And imitations of classic rock are now "in", apparently. Doug's always had a nose for trends.

Once I left the band, I felt great. For a few weeks. I was even proud of myself. I had to be, otherwise what would have been the excuse for me leaving a promising band just before they were supposed to get signed? To be honest, I didn't know Douggie had a record deal coming up. If I did, I'd probably stick around for a bit longer just to see where the whole thing was going. I would, of course, still quit, and sooner rather than later, but it would still be amazing to go to LA to record with a producer who's worked with all the legends. Which again made me think that I knew what Doug was going to ask me. So what the hell was I doing going here? Shouldn't I have just gone home and not returned his calls? Or should I call him and tell him I can't see him this week, something's come up? And once I'm there, what am I going to say to him? I mean, I know what I'm going to say, but what words should I use?

At quarter past seven I was on Doug's doorstep ringing his bell. Once the door opened, I instantly regretted ever coming down to see the guy. He was wearing a blue shell suit with trousers sagging around his knees, his thin greasy hair in a pony tail, and his face puffier than I've ever remembered it. He was beaming from ear to hear.

'Joey, come on in!'

I stepped in feeling utterly miserable. I suddenly remembered reading an interview with Nikki Sixx in some old Eighties mag, where Sixx was saying, 'I never go back to what I've left behind. I never even call my ex-girlfriends.'

I was now in Doug's undersized sitting room I knew so well. This time the ceiling seemed even lower, the yellowish curtains even dirtier, and the smell of dust and cheap apple air freshener all of a sudden really got to me. In one corner there was an old PC and a synth, in the other – an old beat-up stereo with two antiquated speakers, and to the left from the door – a grubby brown Argos foam sofa I ended up sitting on, with about half a dozen or so tablature books scattered on the stained coffee table in front of me: Cinderella (which really amazed me), Aerosmith, Led Zeppelin, Free, Cream, Deep Purple, UFO... This was where Doug's been nicking ideas from for his songs. I wished the guys from Global saw this pile of creative props – the inspiration behind the Storm Angels' music... It probably wouldn't bother them though. The audience they were going to sell the band's music to have never heard of Free or Cream. Even if the Storm Angels were to rip *All Right Now* or *Tales of Brave Ulysses* note for note, the fans wouldn't know it. Because they've never heard the original. If it dates further than five years back, the kids wouldn't know anything about it these days.

'What are you drinking, Joe?' asked Doug.

'I'm fine, Doug, cheers,' I heard myself say, even though what I really was going to say was, 'I'm not drinking tonight, thanks.'

'You are not driving, are you?' he asked.

The fucker knew too well I didn't drive. I didn't drive and I didn't have a car. I pretended I didn't hear that last thing he said and took my phone out of my pocket as if I've just received a text. In fact, my phone's been switched off all this time.

Douggie went to the kitchen and returned with two wet whiskey glasses and a bottle of Jack.

'No ice, mate, sorry,' he said.

Once he poured the glasses, Doug looked at me very seriously, with the kind of expression he's always been giving us in the band when he was going to tell us that we needed to practice more, or that we where putting on weight, or that if our parents were coming to any of our shows, they weren't supposed to say who they were to the fans in the audience.

'Joey, listen,' started Doug. 'I'll be very straight with you this time. As you know, Global are about to sign a deal with us and this is as serious as it gets. I am prepared to give you a second chance because I care about you as a human being. After all those months I've worked with you, and all I've invested in you, I wouldn't feel comfortable with myself just throwing you out. I'd feel bad to do this to you. You're a young lad and we've all made mistakes when we were young, so I'm prepared to take you back. But you've got to promise that all nonsense stops here. From now on it's serious business, no more tantrums.'

I sat there motionless, my glass untouched, while Douggie continued, 'Do you want to know what Global have planned for us? We're flying to LA next month to record an album with their best producer, and then there's a world tour. I've had a meeting with their A&R man last week, the contract is on the table. In fact, we could have singed already, but I thought I'd talk to you first because, as I said, I don't feel comfortable leaving you behind. Your real career could start here, matey. I think it's time to get serious and get to work. You'll be a rock star in less than a year from now.'

I sat looking at Doug thinking that this morning I would never have thought he and I would ever speak again, let alone negotiate my return to the band. There was something very fishy

13

about the whole thing. But I still didn't know why Douggie was so keen to have me back. It wasn't like I was Joe Perry and the band were Aerosmith.

'What about the new guy you've hired in my place?' I asked.

'Bobby?' Doug suddenly looked surprised as if I've asked him about his cat. 'I've hired Bobby just to fill in temporarily, you know. But we all kind of liked him, so he stayed on. He's a good kid, he'll understand.'

It occurred to me that I should have asked to see a copy of the contract, but that would have meant that I've already agreed. And I wanted to know why Doug needed me back first. I knew he didn't give a toss if I lived or died and that there must have been a good reason why he wanted to have me back. But Doug was a clever old cunt and he wouldn't have told me anything even if I asked.

'Did you speak to Ed Sunders?' I said.

'Who?' Doug suddenly stared at me as if I've just said "Mark Chapman", not "Ed Sunders".

'Ed Sunders, a journo. I was having a drink with him this afternoon.'

'I don't know an Ed Sunders. What does it have to do with this?'

Doug was lying. He knew perfectly well who Ed was. A few months back Ed wanted to interview the band for one of the online mags he was writing for, and Doug didn't give him access because he thought Ed was going to ask questions about how songwriting worked in our band.

'He said he saw you at Astoria last night and you were telling him about the deal.'

'I've been talking to dozens of people at Astoria last night. The editor of Global Rock was there and he congratulated me. We had a good chat, Global Rock wants to do a big feature on us. Anyway, that's beside the point. What are you going to do, Joe?'

As much as I wanted to tell Doug to shove his deal up his fat hairy ass, all I did was take my phone out of my pocket again.

14

'I can't give you an answer right now, Doug,' I finally said. 'I have to think about this one. It's not like you are asking me to lend you a guitar case.'

'I am not asking you, mate, I'm giving you a second chance,' said Doug. 'What's there to think about? I know it hasn't been easy lately, and I've been putting a lot of pressure on all of you, but it has all been for your own good. I always knew that if we all worked hard enough, we'd get somewhere. And here you are.'

'I'll be able to give you an answer by the end of the week,' I said.

All I wanted now was to get the hell out of Doug's flat, go home, have a spliff and take serious stock. Maybe call a few people.

Doug shook his head and gave a little laugh like he was dealing with an unreasonable and stubborn child.

'Great,' he finally said. 'I'll speak to you on Friday. Think about it, Joey. This kind of opportunity only knocks once.'

On my way home all I could think about was how I'd hate to work with Doug again. Doug was the kind of person who never cared about anything else apart from his own gain. Once he saw an opportunity, he grabbed it and didn't let go no matter what. He's always been convinced that you have to fight for the good things in life, that access to success was limited and that once you saw your chance, you had to make the best of it, no matter how many people got hurt, exploited, or deceived along the way. He spent so many years going nowhere in life that at this point all he wanted was this deal. Suddenly it was all within his reach – the money, the acclaim, the success. I just didn't know what my role was supposed to be in all this.

Doug played bass in a third-rate glam rock band here in the UK at the end of the Eighties. I've seen pictures of them on the internet, and they looked hilarious. They all had permed puffed-up hair, wore tight leather jeans and ripped polka-dot and fuchsia shirts, wore loads of make-up and pouted into the camera trying to imitate that insolent look Poison and Ratt always had on their promo shots. Only here you could tell right away this was a poor man's English version of the Hollywood glam metal scene. While Ratt and Poison always looked like millionaires, these guys looked like a Sunday band of your local cab drivers. The band was signed for a short time to a small indie label that dropped them after their first EP flopped. That was in 1989. I guess at that time music fans could still tell a fake from the real thing.

Doug had enough savvy to quit the band almost immediately after it got dropped and not waste any more time trying to become a rock star. He probably had a good look at himself in the mirror, realised that he was thirty-six, overweight, and ugly, and concluded that his chances of making it in the show biz as a performer were next to zero. He then hung on the fringes of "the biz" for fifteen years making money as a small-time promoter, a second-hand instrument shop owner, and even a wedding photographer, until a year ago he met me and Andy, our bass player, at a gig in Camden, and told us he had some tunes he wrote back in the Eighties that would sound very "in vogue" now, given the return of all things Eighties and Seventies in general, and classic rock in particular. He said he already had "a killer singer" and a drummer, and was looking for a guitarist and a bass player. This is how our band the Storm Angels started out. I would never have thought that this chance meeting would lead to me having to struggle with one of the biggest dilemmas of my life.

I couldn't remember when was the last time I had an issue I needed to brainstorm. But what I did know was that a spliff helps you think like nothing else. The fact that all the music I've ever written was the product of a good ganja session, is a proof to that. So on my way home all I've been thinking about was if I had to buy a packet or Rizla in my corner shop, or if I was going to make a bong. I finally decided against a bong because I knew it would knock me out before I had a chance to think of anything properly. And the whole point of getting stoned that evening was to think.

When I got home, none of my flatmates were in. Since I quit the Storm Angels, I've been sharing a flat in Ealing with two sound techs, Ben and Dave. Before all five of us in the band were renting a three-bedroom flat in Kensal Green, but once I quit the band, I moved out. I found Dave and Ben through a friend who's been with them at LIPA, the Liverpool "fame school" which had some A-list patrons. Both Dave and Ben graduated from LIPA last summer, both with degrees in sound engineering, and both were still on the dole, like me. I wonder what they teach them at LIPA if you can't find a job once you graduate. Ben's mother who ran a fish and chip shop in Southampton was sending him money now and then, and Dave was getting packages from home in Liverpool with canned sausages and pasta once a fortnight. I guess his parents thought that if they sent him cash, he'd spend it on booze and drugs. I suppose they were guessing right.

My own parents didn't know I was signing on. If they found out they'd be seriously disappointed. Both my parents worked all their lives, my father as a chef in an Italian restaurant, and my mother as an architect's secretary. They both work, as they are still relatively young, and neither of them believes in going on the dole without a good reason.

When I first moved to London from Colchester, my hometown, I began working in a guitar shop on Charing Cross Road, but after I met Doug and joined the band, I couldn't hold down a job and do all the rehearsals, gigs, and tours. I tried it for a while though. I'd finish work at six and would then rehearse with the band from seven to ten in a tiny stinky rehearsal room in Morden Doug's been renting for three quid an hour. It was small and completely bare. All it had were electricity sockets and a soiled carpet on the floor. It didn't even have any windows. We had to bring all our gear up each time in Doug's van. We could have found a place where we could rehearse and store the gear, but Doug thought it wouldn't hurt us to drive every evening to Morden, unload and set it up each time all over again. That didn't matter much as far as my main job went, but we'd go on tours quite often, and the owner of the shop where I worked was at first fine with it, he even encouraged me, but once we went on a two-week UK tour supporting the Silver Cats, a very cool Eighties band from LA, and when I got back, I was told that the business was suffering because I was taking too much time off, so I had to quit to be able to continue touring. I've been signing on for eight months now. I've said to myself that unless I found a decent band to join within the next four weeks, I'd get a job, most likely in a music shop again, at least this way I'd be more likely to meet other musicians who may need a guitarist. The circle I'm moving in is pretty wide, but it's still impossible to know all London rockers because there are thousands, and the fact that someone doesn't belong to my circuit doesn't mean they are bad musicians. In fact, it could be the opposite. To be honest, I think that if any of the London classic rock revivalists or glam bands are going to break into the mainstream in the future, it is going to be a band completely unknown to any scenesters. At least to the scenesters I hang with.

As I sat on my living room floor rolling a spliff, I realised that unless I had some inspiration, being stoned wasn't going to help me think. So I stuck one of my old T. Rex DVDs into the player. A second later I wished I haven't done that, as I remembered that Marc Bolan had always had a totally mesmerising effect on me, especially when I was stoned. It turned out that I remembered right, because the DVD completely distracted me from my own situation I was meaning to contemplate, leaving me sitting on the floor leaning against one of the armchairs, taking one drag of the joint after another, and staring at Marc Bolan dancing, singing, playing guitar, and shaking his "corkscrew hair", hypnotised like a teenage fan.

The thing about T. Rex is that I would never say they are my favourite band or that they are even in my top ten, and I can go for years without listening to them, but every time I do get to hear them on the radio or see them on TV, they completely blow me away. Every single time. It's that rock star magic all of us on the unsigned scene are so desperately trying to imitate. I guess that if Bolan wore a bin bag instead of his suits, played the banjo instead of a Les Paul, and sang country-and-western tunes instead of his amazing songs, everyone would still instantly recognise him as a rock star. Sometimes I can't believe that with some people it's innate. Some people are so damn lucky. I remember once I even wanted to have my own hair permed to look like Bolan's, but then had enough sense to realise that no matter what I did, or how I dressed, or how hard I tried, I would still end up looking like his caricature at best. This kind of stuff always has to come from within. I wonder if it can be acquired in any way. If so, then how? Marc Bolan, the son of a lorry driver from Hackney...

So I sat there watching T. Rex videos overwhelmed by mixed feelings of adoration and jealousy, getting more and more stoned, and suddenly realised that if I really wanted to help myself with coming to a right decision on what to do with Doug, the record deal, and my old band, I had to talk to someone who'd take a look at my situation from a more or less detached perspective. And then I realised that not only didn't I have any close friends I could speak to, but I didn't even have anyone I could confess to that the band wasn't writing its own songs. I instantly felt depressed and sorry for myself, thinking that my best option was to just call Doug tomorrow morning and tell him I was in.

Half of me though still couldn't believe that I didn't have anyone to talk to. I took my phone out of my pocket and started going through all the names in the address book. I became even more depressed when I realised that almost all of the people I had numbers for were either other musicians who I obviously couldn't say anything to, or girls who would listen to me and offer lots of sympathy, and probably say "go for it, it's a chance of a lifetime", and who would later tell everyone what a pathetic loser I was.

Then I looked at the last entry in my phonebook and nearly jumped. How could I have forgotten about Zara?

Zara was the coolest girl I knew. She was a photographer who freelanced for some of the biggest rock magazines, and she was the nicest, most sincere, and intelligent person I knew in London. We haven't spoken for months, in fact, I remembered that she hasn't replied to my last message I sent her through MySpace. Maybe she was busy, or maybe she didn't get it, but I remembered being vaguely annoyed at her for not writing back. That didn't matter now in the slightest, as I realised that I've missed her, and that she was the only person I knew who would genuinely try to help me. So I dialled her number right away.

Her phone rang twice and then she answered. There was noise and music in the background.

'Hi, Joey,' she said. 'Haven't heard from you for ages!'

'Hi, baby, how're you doing?' I said, trying to sound relaxed and happy.

'You don't have to call me "baby", I'm not one of your groupies!' she laughed.

'I'm sorry, Zar, it's just…'

'You sound stoned!' Zara said all of a sudden.

'I'm not!' I protested, 'I'm definitely not. Not as stoned as you may think! In fact, I'm completely focused, and I'm phoning to find out how you are and if you'd like to go see Silver Cats play in Camden tomorrow night. I'm on the guest list and you could be my plus one.'

'I could be your plus one!' she laughed again. 'I was, actually, planning to be there too. Are you going to the aftershow?'

'Sure, we'll go to the aftershow if you want,' I said. 'I just haven't heard from the guys yet.'

'Oh, it will be in Soho,' Zara said. 'We can go together if you like. So where do you want to meet me tomorrow?'

'Well, let's meet in the upstairs pub at six,' I said. 'We'll have a drink there before the show starts.'

'I'll see you then,' Zara said. 'Great that you called.'

I sat on the floor feeling tired, but much better now that I've spoken to Zara. I don't know what it is with the girls on the underground rock scene, but I can hardly stand any of them. Half of them are stuck up and pretentious with nothing to validate the arrogance, and the other half are so easy they'd shag anyone with long hair. Zara is different. To start with, she has a cool job, so she doesn't have to put on a big-headed act to prove anything to anyone. Secondly, she's friendly because people she works with – A-list bands and big international magazines – are friendly people, at least until you do something to piss them off. In this respect there is a huge difference between the unsigned scene and the big leagues. What I have recently discovered is that the rudest, most self-important people in the music business are always those who have failed. I guess you need to compensate for the lack of success, and on the rock scene the only way people know how to do this is by constantly telling themselves they have more talent and so-called "dignity" than the rest, no matter how badly things go for them. I've never seen an underdog show any generosity, cooperation, or sense of humour. Maybe because their situation is too dire to allow for any kindness or sense of comedy. And in a way I can understand this. Nothing can be worse in this little world than being a loser. Where Zara works, all is supposed to be different. Everyone is an international star, and she's been telling me that successful people living their dreams are almost always genuinely nice. I suppose all people tend to relax once they get what they want and once they know that their career is really worth something. And I don't care if that worth is calculated in sales figures, I'd still rather hang with successful chilled out people than a bunch of angry losers. I don't know how it is with all the acts that have become famous within the last few years, I have no idea what they are like, but Zara tells me that all the A-listers she's ever worked with – the kind of names who headline big summer festivals – are all very cool people. Sometimes I really envy her job.

Getting sleepy and thinking that I was probably going to wear my St. John t-shirt to tomorrow's gig, I stumbled into my bedroom and crashed out on the bed forgetting to take my clothes off. As I was drifting off to sleep, a cannabis-induced thought occurred to me that Marc Bolan's charisma probably stemmed from the fact that he was somehow completely devoid of the usual angst and insecurity the majority of young guys suffer from. In that way he was almost like a woman. Was it because he was bisexual? That was my last thought.

II

THEODORA

$\mathbf{M}$y mobile phone was showing quarter to eleven when I woke up and took it out of the back pocket of the jeans I was still wearing. I stayed in bed for half an hour thinking about yesterday's events, the Global Union deal and my conversation with Doug. I now knew that I shouldn't have gone down to his place. I should have told him to say whatever he had to say to me over the phone. I should have told him I didn't have time to meet him, never mind going to his place.

I have now decided that whatever my decision was going to be (I wasn't absolutely certain, but I had a hunch that I would accept), I wasn't going to call him and was going to wait until he rang me. And, again, I wished I knew why he needed me back in the band.

Having thought of all that, I finally got up and went straight to the fridge. There was nothing in there except for two cans of Stella, half an onion, and two eggs. I thought about frying an egg (even though the eggs weren't mine, they were either Dave's or Ben's), but then decided against it because it began to seem to me recently that I was beginning to put on weight. I put on weight as soon as I start eating as much as I really want to, something Doug has been reminding me about all the time while I was in the Storm Angels. So what I usually try to do is not to have breakfast at all, have something light for lunch and then have a couple of cans of beer instead of dinner. I know there are loads of calories in beer, but it still seems not as fattening as food. And I have to admit that so far it's been working for me. I don't have a twenty-inch waist like Randy Rhodes used to have when he was playing with Ozzy, but I'm close. And girls definitely dig that.

I decided that instead of frying an egg I was going to practice. I try to practice every day for at least three hours, but I've been slacking lately because there was nothing to practice for – I still couldn't find a band to join. But when I sat down with my Strat in my room, I was surprised how all of a sudden I came up with a really good riff, something that didn't happen to me very often. I even wanted to write a chorus and some lyrics to go with it, but couldn't concentrate on thinking about the words. So I focused on polishing the riff and didn't notice how it became nearly three o'clock – time to finally eat something and to begin thinking about my outfit for tonight.

To get food I had to go out and buy some, so I went though the pockets of all of my clothes that lay in a pile on my bedroom floor. Having put together all the coins I managed to collect after rummaging through three pairs of jeans and a jacket, I knew that I had five pounds and sixty-seven pence to last me until the end of the week. It was Thursday. I seriously began thinking about getting a job. I also wondered how big an advance the Storm Angels were going to get from Global. Given Douggie wasn't going to confiscate the money once the band got paid.

As I was about to leave the flat to get some crisps and a Lucozade from the corner shop, I saw Dave coming out of his room looking sleepy, his long, curly hair a mess, making him look like a character out of a Greek drama.

'Alright,' he mumbled. 'Heard you play that T. Rex tune, wassi' called, *Jeepster?*'

'*Jeepster?*' I stared at him for a few seconds, couldn't comprehend what he was on about, and went out.

As I was paying for my drink and crisps at the counter, I finally realised what Dave meant. The new riff that I thought I wrote this morning was, in fact, a slightly impaired version of Marc

Bolan's riff in *Jeepster.*

'Congratulations, Mr. Mormile,' I said to myself. 'You're a songwriting genius. You, like no one else, deserve a record deal.'

I had my lunch in the living room, while listening to Ben and Dave tell me about going up to Islington last night to this girl's flat they've been at LIPA with, who's invited all the people she was friends with at college to celebrate her birthday. They said that some people from their course had pretty cool jobs by now. One girl called Maria even got a traineeship at one of the oldest UK studios that has recently bought a custom-made desk for just over two million.

'No matter what they tell you at LIPA, it's still not what you know, it's who you know in this business,' Ben was saying.

'And who does Maria know in London?' asked Dave. 'She's Mexican, for god's sake.'

'I don't know,' said Ben, 'But she must know someone, otherwise how did she get that job?'

What I understood from the conversation was that it *was* possible to get a job with a LIPA degree. I wondered why I always got stuck with losers though. Why couldn't I share a flat with someone who had a serious industry job? Someone who could introduce me to a big name producer? Or at least someone who could give me some free studio time?

I sat listening to Ben and Dave for half an hour until I realised that it was almost four and time to start doing something about my hair before I went out.

To style my hair properly after it's washed takes an hour and a half. Thankfully I can do it myself now and don't have to go to the hairdresser's for a wash and a blowdry like I used to when I was in the band. Douggie had a friend who was a hairdresser and who would sometimes do the hair of all the guys in the band before our London shows almost for free. Before our first tour she showed us how to do it ourselves and I picked it up pretty quickly. I had to because I had no choice. We had neither the time, nor the money to have our hair professionally done while on tour, so I had to learn.

My hair style is quite clever, I think. It looks a lot like Brian Connolly's when he was with Sweet the Seventies – shoulder-length and straight, with a long fringe, but my style is lifted at the roots so that it has a slightly punky feel to it, not too feminine and not too retro. Or maybe just slightly retro, because classic rock is popular again and all that, and I have to look the part. I dye my hair too. It's naturally brown, but I dye it black.

I walked through the door of the pub Zara and I agreed to meet at wearing my Antic Denim jeans and an AC/DC t-shirt, with half a tube of gel in my hair. The gel went to the roots though to give it a lift, so I didn't look like a prat with wanky, over-processed hair. A lot of people were having their pre-gig drinks, and almost everyone was playing the game called "I am more important than you". There were musicians dressed in tight jeans and band t-shirts, almost all of them – naïve young wannabes, all imagining themselves to be rock stars, but, of course, totally unknown outside of their circuit. There were girls in their early twenties wearing mini-skirts, skimpy tops, thick black eyeliner, and red lipstick, posing in front of the musicians, but never making eye contact, obviously imagining themselves to be some sort of super-groupies. And then there were fanzine writers, small-time promoters, amateur photographers, street team kids and merch mamas, thinking of themselves as "belonging to the industry", even though most of them were either on the dole, or had day jobs that had nothing to do with music. Everyone in the room tried to feign casual indifference towards each other, but there was no disguising the fact that their top concern was what all others thought and said about them. To conceal that, they all stuck religiously to the peculiar etiquette this crowd knows better than the ten commandments – never approach anyone first, always act like you don't see or recognise the others, never smile at anyone, never let your guard drop. Each rule, of course, based on insecurity, envy, and fantasy-fuelled childish grudges.

I scanned the crowd, noticed a couple of people I wanted to say hi to later on and a lot of people I was going to try my best to avoid (Ed Sunders one of them), and then went to the bar to get a Diet Coke, as this was the only drink I could afford that evening. While I was waiting to be served, I noticed Tracy Huggins standing next to me, the editor and sole contributor of an online fanzine called Rocktastic Rockin' Review, gulping from a pint of cider black currant, looking glum and particularly gross on the night. A wrongly sized Bon Jovi 1989 tour t-shirt was straining on her torso, ending just above her fake leather studded belt, exposing the grey skin of her belly. Her hard, pained expression was making it hard to believe that Tracy was actually only twenty-one. The spots on her face adjusted her age though, adding to the severity of her look, along with her thin, bleached-out waist-long hair with two inches of dark regrowth at the roots. Her gloomy expression made me snigger. She heard me, looked at me, and instantly turned away like she never saw me.

Tracy hates me for a particular, rather disturbing reason. She was once infatuated with Billy, the Storm Angels singer, who never once bothered to say hi to her. After he once snubbed her after a Storm Angels show in front of everyone in the band and a couple of her teenage mates, all of us in the band instantly became her enemies. These are the kind of grievances people harbour against each other on the scene where a small occurrence can become a major factor in deciding who becomes your enemy or who becomes your friend. Your best friend is often someone who hates your enemies, usually for his or her own petty reason.

Tracy's fanzine is a desperate bid for popularity. It gives her an excuse to approach musicians who otherwise would never want to be seen talking to her, each on this circuit a self-taught elitist concerned with nothing else but how their associations, no matter how fleeing, reflect on their image. What the guys on this scene try to avoid the most is being seen with an unattractive girl, even if only for a few moments. So a prospect of a badly written piece about their band posted online usually doesn't make people change their mind about Tracy. But she is never downhearted. She asks all musicians she fancies for an interview. And she fancies just about everyone who has long hair and knows two and a half chords. A band with any chance of being written about by any other web site would as a rule decline, but those who can't get any other publicity usually agree and consequently have to meet up with Tracy to be subjected to an array of questions starting with "Where did you guys meet?" and ending with "What does the future hold for your band?", the whole interview tiresome as hell and ultimately unreadable, so no wonder Tracy's fanzine gets no more than eight clicks a week.

Tracy's so-called "reviews" are even better. For her, bands fall into two categories. Those who are nice to her are either "bloody ace", "shit-kicking", or "blinding", and those who don't want to have anything to do with her become described as "tuneless" and "boring".

I stood at the bar sipping my Diet Coke, when a grinning, tense, yellow-toothed face suddenly appeared in front of me. It was Ed Sunders, wearing exactly the same clothes he wore yesterday. Judging by the smell, he probably slept in them too.

'Joe, mate! Good to see you again!' His voice was deliberately loud, an attempt to draw everyone's attention to the fact that we knew each other. I instantly gave him a cold shoulder. There was no way I was going to be associated with a loser like Ed Sunders, a so-called journalist who by the age of thirty-five still hasn't written once for a decent publication. I just didn't want anyone to think that Ed and I could have anything in common.

'Hey, how are you,' I said coldly to him, and then added, 'I need to answer this text.'

I then slowly walked away, taking my phone out of the back pocket of my jeans, pretending I've just received a message.

I was going to text Zara and let her know I was already there when I saw her coming in through the door. She looked cute in faded jeans and a t-shirt that said "Wacken Open Air 2007". Wacken is an annual German heavy metal festival Zara goes to every summer to shoot for the magazines she contributes to. I was pleased to see her, instantly forgetting about everyone else in the room, glad to be seen with a pretty, smiling girl who also happened to be one of the few people here who did what they loved for a living.

Zara isn't tall, but cute. Her hair is naturally blond, but she dyes it black. I don't know any other girl who does that. Usually it's the other way around. Her eyes are grey, and she has a lovely face with features that at certain angles resemble Winona Ryder's. I was just hoping I didn't look too much like Edward Scissorhands.

Zara approached me smiling, saying, 'Hello, Mr. Mormile! How are you?'

She actually pronounced my name the way it should be pronounced – Mor-MEE-lee, not MOR-mile, as almost everyone else does.

I leaned over and kissed her on both cheeks.

'Pretty good,' I said, 'How was Wacken?'

'Wacken was great,' she said. 'The line-up was fantastic this year! And it was the first time I got to use my new Mamiya.'

'Wow!' I said, not having a clue what a Mamiya was.

'I've been saving for it for years,' she said. 'It's the best camera you can get.'

'Wow!' I said again. 'How much does it cost?'

'I got it second-hand,' she said. 'Eight grand.'

'Eight fucking grand?!' I stared at Zara who was smiling, perfectly aware of the impression she's just made.

'What does it do?' I asked moronically.

'Everything I want it to,' she replied, and let out a small, tinkling laugh.

As we were talking, I suddenly noticed Tracy Huggins staring at us from the corner of the room where she stood with a stick-thin, pale chick with long brown hair I didn't know but saw a couple of times before hanging with Tracy. Tracy didn't know who Zara was, and if she found out, she'd immediately start hating her just for the fact that Zara had a career in the business and was pretty. Or maybe she was hating her already for the fact that Zara was talking to me. Or simply for the fact that she was pretty.

I wanted to get away from Tracy's creepy stare, so I suggested we made our way to the club. The time was half six. We went outside and I went up to the ticket window, telling the girl behind the glass my name and that I was on the guest list "plus one". I got two passes, and let Zara go through first, down the stairs past two oversized doormen.

The reason why I was on the guest list was because tonight's headliners have put me on it. The band was called Silver Cats, and the Storm Angles supported them on their UK tour the year before. We've had a great time on the road together, despite the fact that we weren't attracting any huge crowds and mostly played small clubs.

Silver Cats are an LA glam metal band who had a platinum album in 1989, and a few number one hits in the next few years. After the music industry revolution of the Nineties their brand of rock became, obviously, redundant, and just like dozens of similar acts they faded into obscurity. Now that classic rock and glam were on the up, a lot of those bands were beginning to tour again, Silver Cats among them.

We didn't have any parties that were too wild while on tour, but we'd go out with them every night after a show, get plastered and wind up in one of our hotel rooms continuing to drink and would sometimes share a spliff or two. There weren't even that many women around. Doug wasn't letting any near us, and as far as Silver Cats went, they all had wives and kids waiting for them back in the States. They'd take girls to their hotel rooms after shows, but I had no clue if any of them stayed the night or not. Doug's been telling us to hit the sack not later than two a.m., and that was when the Americans were still up partying. So we had no way of knowing what exactly went on. If anything was going on, they were very discreet about it.

Still, I think that these days you can't hide what happens on tour. Girls will always kiss and tell on one groupie board or another.

And everyone knows that wives and girlfriends check groupie boards several times a day while their boyfriends or husbands are on tour. And especially after the tour ends.

The bar downstairs was already full of people, most of them – the same faces who a few minutes ago were having drinks upstairs. I was going to spend the last money I had on buying Zara a drink, but she beat me to it. She asked what I was drinking and I said 'JD and coke', figuring that it was going to be my last drink that night, as I was then going to buy Zara a drink in return, spending my last money on it, and that would have been it.

We found a place to sit in one of the alcoves, and I began asking Zara about her trip to Wacken. I didn't want to start going on about my own problems right off the bat.

'Wacken was excellent this year,' Zara said. 'Much nicer than Download. Kind of cleaner and nicer, and the crowd was definitely nicer.'

'Did you hook up with any rock stars?' I asked, smiling.

'Hooked up with any rock stars!' she said in a low-pitched voice, mocking me and laughing. 'No, I was there to work.'

'Do you get to talk to musicians at all at festivals?' I asked.

'Sure,' she said. 'They stop by the press office, and then there's always a VIP bar and a restaurant where you sit right next to them.'

'Do they ever try talking to you?'

'Sure,' she said again, 'All the time.'

'And you never had a relationship with a rock star?'

'No.'

'I don't believe you,' I said.

'You don't understand, Joey,' she said. 'I could have had hundreds of one night stands, but this is not what I want or what I need. All big stars are either married or they have girlfriends back home, so they are not looking for a relationship. If they are looking for anything at all, it's only a one night stand. And I'm not into that.

Not into that at all. I don't go to festivals and shows to look for a boyfriend or a husband. I go there to work so that I can pay my bills.'

'Every single woman in this room would kill for your job,' I said, feeling smug that I was talking to a real show biz insider in full view of everyone who knew me.

Zara looked around as if only now becoming aware of the other people in the room. In front of us there was a group of four women in their late thirties, all wearing open-toe high heel shoes, black fishnets, mini-skirts and tons of makeup – white powder, black kohl and red lipstick. One was wearing a blond wig. These were small-time groupies who back in the Eighties struck it lucky a few times managing to sleep with one or two B-list musicians, and who to this day hoped that their luck hasn't completely run out and that if they stood out enough from the crowd, had a chance of spending this night with someone from the headlining band. Their main problem was that half of females in the room were dressed exactly like them, and the majority were much younger. The young ones wore cheaper clothes, but looked eager, hungry, constantly looking around, trying to see if they could spot a sound tech, a journo, or anyone who they thought would have access to the Americans and could get them backstage.

'Sure,' I thought. 'Zara's right. A really cool girl would never be impressed by a man simply because he's in a band. Even if it's a famous band. But really cool girls are scarce on this scene, just like really cool musicians.'

'Say one of them gets backstage,' Zara said. 'Say she even sleeps with someone in the band. Then what? The guy wouldn't bother to remember her name once he's back to San Diego, California, to his wife and kids. He can't divorce his wife even if he wants to because divorce is expensive, plus he adores his children.'

As I was listening to her, I suddenly felt someone grab hold of my left arm. I looked up and saw Shawna, our drummer Johnny's ex-girlfriend. Johnny split up from her two months ago, and that was his only big achievement in life so far. Shawna was giving me a fake smile, her white teeth glowing spookily in the semi-darkness of the room, and she wasn't letting go of my arm.

'Joey!' she half-screamed, half-purred. 'Joey, it is *so* good to see you, babes! How *are* you?'

She was completely ignoring Zara. In fact, she cut into Zara talking mid-sentence, but still wouldn't acknowledge her presence. I said nothing, but gave Shawna one of those stares I've picked up from Douggie, the one he'd give to people who he wanted to go away immediately. The look wasn't working on Shawna though.

'You look so *good*!' Shawna continued in a sugar-sweet voice.

She was wearing baggy jeans (she always did because she had footballer's legs), but her pink sleeveless top was half unzipped so that everyone could see her newly bought boobs. I squirmed when I remembered Johnny begging Doug to lend him cash to pay for Shawna's boob job. Doug didn't lend him the money, because, according to him, Shawna wasn't the kind of girlfriend Johnny should have been spending any money on, because she was "trashy" and "ruined the band's image". Johnny then borrowed the money from this mother telling her he needed it to buy a new amp. Now that they've finally split up, Shawna was looking for a new boyfriend. Or maybe even a husband. She was twenty-nine. I just hoped she wasn't considering me as a potential partner.

'Joey, are you going to the aftershow later on?' Shawna whispered hotly in my ear as she leaned over, giving me the full view of her boobs and making me smell Dior's "Poison" she always sprayed in her mouth before going out. Why couldn't she just use a menthol mouth spray? Why did it have to be perfume?

I didn't reply this time either, just shook my head.

'Are *you*?' Shawna suddenly turned to Zara. 'I love your top. I'm Shawna, by the way, what's *your* name?'

Zara looked at Shawna not knowing what to say or how to react, but I saved her: 'Zara's got sore throat. She can't talk.'

'Oh,' said Shawna, getting the message this time. 'I'll see you later then.' She then flicked back her blond hair and walked away, swaying her broad hips and carrying her oversized boobs as if they were some kind of prized possession. To think about it, to her, they certainly were. They were probably the most expensive thing she owned, and definitely the most expensive gift she's ever received.

Shawna's main problem was her figure, and she knew it. She was too short and she had bowed legs. If she had a nicer body, she'd be married to some kind of C-list musician by now, because she had an OK face. Or maybe it was the fact that she was a bitchy, controlling, and manipulative little creature, boring and empty, that was preventing her from fulfilling her dream of marrying someone with money and a bit of fame. She just wasn't fun to be around, insecure, jealous, and shallow. All she cared about were clothes, restaurants, and cocaine which she loved but couldn't afford, as well as gossip about which of the groupies was saying what about whom, to whom, and when. In fact, she herself was a groupie, the one who maybe didn't sleep around too much, but who would go out with a guy only if he was in a band that had a potential. As she herself couldn't tell which band had a potential, she relied on the numbers of hits and comments bands were getting on MySpace. If it was in the region of fifty hits a day, she thought a band was showing promise. I wonder if this is how A&R people operate too.

All Shawna wanted in life was a glamorous lifestyle. As well as that, she also wanted to be famous by association with someone famous. She knew all too well that she couldn't bag a premier league footballer or a high-earning actor, because on that level the competition among potential girlfriends is fierce, so she hung on the unsigned music scene thinking she could hook up with someone who would later become a star.

The lifestyle Shawna wanted – restaurants, sports cars, trips abroad, shopping, and drugs – is all about money, and that's what she was after, although she's always been saying that it was creativity that she found attractive in men above anything else. And as she abhorred work, all she could offer in exchange for what she wanted was sex. That in my eyes made her no different from any groupie, and to me groupies and whores are the same thing. If you use sex as a bargaining tool, then you are prostituting yourself. That much I know. It's funny though how Shawna would always bitch about "fucking groupies" who, she feared, were going to sleep with Johnny and, god forbid, make him split with her before the band signed a record deal and before she had a chance to have his baby. In the end her fears came true. Johnny was now dating a presenter from a soft porn cable channel. Last time I spoke to him he was saying that they paid her four quid an hour, but she was still doing it "to advance her career". If I was her, I'd rather flip burgers. Or maybe I wouldn't... I've heard if you work at a fast food joint, you gain two pounds a week in weight.

Once Shawna left, Zara lifted one eyebrow and looked at me with a smile, but had enough tact not to say anything, which I was grateful for.

'Tell me how you've been, Joey,' she suddenly said. 'I heard you've left your band.'

I laughed nervously and said, 'Well, news sure travel fast...'

'I hope you don't regret it,' said Zara.

'Why?'

'Because Doug Scrivener is a nasty old dog. Everybody knows that.'

'How do you know?'

'Well, wasn't he trying to manipulate you guys all the time?'

'Oh yeah...' I began, but she interrupted me.

'Wasn't he trying to make you play the music he wrote back in the Eighties?'

I stared at Zara. I didn't know that she knew.

'How do you know that?' I finally asked.

'It's true, isn't it? I was wondering if it was... I read about it on one of the online boards.'

'Well, you see,' I said, 'this is the reason why I left, but now something's come up that makes me wonder if I should go back.'

'Go back?' Zara looked at me as if I was a mental patient.

'The thing is,' I said, 'Global Union have offered the Storm Angels a record deal.'

Now it was Zara's turn to stare.

'No way,' she said finally. 'I don't believe this.'

'It's true. Doug is saying I should come back.'

'Do you know what kind of deal it is?' she asked. 'Because you know, they have all kinds of deals these days – development deals, trail deals, one-album deals…'

'I haven't a clue,' I said. 'I haven't seen the contract yet.'

'That's typical of Doug, isn't it?' Zara asked.

'I guess,' I replied. 'But I know I won't be getting much money from this because all the songs are written by Doug anyway, so I guess he'll end up getting most of the money. What I'm thinking is that I should probably go back because this way at least I'll get my foot through the door. I could quit after the first album and join a much better band.'

'Oh, no,' Zara said. 'No. If you accept, this deal will ruin your career before it starts. Don't do it, Joey. You'll create a bad reputation for yourself from the very beginning. No one would want to work with you after they find out that you guys didn't write your own songs. And they *will* find out. The info is already out there.'

'You're probably right,' I said. 'I just don't understand why all of a sudden Doug wants me back, after the row we've had when I was leaving.'

'You had a row?'

I was going to say, 'Yes, we had a row and I called him a cunt,' but instead I whispered, 'Who is *that*?!' staring at a girl who had just walked past our table. The girl, who, the moment I saw her, I knew was the most beautiful woman I've seen in my life – either in the flesh, on screen, or on photographs. Her simple knee-length dress revealed a perfect, beautifully proportioned figure with long, slender limbs and a narrow waist, but it was her face that completely spellbound me. Delicately defined high cheekbones and deliciously sexy, full lips was what I noticed first. Her nose would have been slightly too big, if it wasn't balanced by a pair of magnificently, large brown eyes that looked with supreme confidence, almost a triumph, as she stopped her gaze on me for half a second while passing by our table. I turned to look at her again, and saw immaculately styled brown hair reaching to the middle of her perfectly straight back, so shiny it was like liquid glass reflecting the light. She had dark skin, or maybe it was a tan, but that was the last thing I noticed about her.

I sat there, helpless and pathetic, completely stricken by this beauty that all of a sudden appeared in a place where you'd hardly hope to find any good looks at all. What was someone like her doing at a place like this?

She already walked past us, and now I could see her standing at the other end of the bar, talking to a guy in his thirties in a beige linen suit. I was unable to stop staring. She turned her face in our direction once, and I saw her radiant, happy smile. She wasn't smiling at anyone in particular, rather at the room, and this amazed me, because no one else around her was looking particularly joyful. There was ease and confidence about her that no other woman in the room had. She wasn't trying to make an impression or a statement, but was simply enjoying the moment. The contrast between her effortless confidence and neediness written on faces of almost all other women who surrounded her, made me want to know who she was.

Zara was saying something to me, but I couldn't hear her.

'What?' I said finally, after the girl disappeared from my view at last.

'She's studying art history at the Courtauld.'

'Who?'

'Theodora.'

'Who's Theodora?'

'The girl you've been staring at!' Zara was losing patience with me. 'Aren't you listening?'

'Do you know her?' I asked.

'Yes, I know her, I've just told you! I was lending her some of my photogprahs for her course project.'

I looked at Zara, not knowing what to say, still trying to get over the shock of seeing the most beautiful woman in the world.

'She's beautiful,' I finally said.

'She is,' said Zara. 'Beautiful and rich.'

'Why is she rich?' I asked.

'Her father is a record label executive.'

'Which label?'

'Oh, all major labels at one time or another. You know how they rotate all the time. They live in LA. She is finishing her degree at the Courtauld this spring.'

'Is she American?' I asked.

'Yes.'

'What's her name?'

'I told you!' Zara exclaimed in exasperation. 'Why don't you listen? Theodora. Her name is Theodora.'

She sat and watched me for a while, and then said, 'Come on, I'll introduce you.'

'No way!!' I yelled. 'No fucking way. I'm totally not ready. Next time. Introduce me to her next time.'

Zara laughed. 'Don't be silly,' she said. 'She won't bite. She's nice.' And she practically dragged me from our table to the dancefloor in front of the stage where the first support band was getting ready to play.

We couldn't see Theodora, and I felt both relieved and anxious.

Zara said, 'Maybe she's gone backstage. I think her dad is friends with Silver Cats.'

'Maybe she's gone home?' I squealed.

'No, she couldn't have,' she said. 'We'll find her later.'

At that moment, Dirty Lick, the local support band, have launched into their first song.

Dirty Lick were four geezers all well over thirty (even though the band's MySpace page said their ages were between twenty-four and twenty-six), who have been playing shoegaze indie all their lives without much success. They have now decided to change their image and jump on the glam bandwagon hoping to get signed because glam was becoming trendy again.

The longer I watched them, the more obvious it became that no matter how hard they tried, they didn't know the first thing about glam. Even though they were all wearing PVC and makeup, their songs had that familiar lacklustre, depressive shoegaze quality, regardless of how much they tried to imitate Motley Crue or LA Guns. My guess was that they simply took the songs they wrote in the Nineties, changed the characters of their lyrics from "my neighbour in brown Dr. Martens" to "stripper wrapped in leather", doubled the tempo, persuaded their singer to go topless, and crossed their fingers in the hope that this time around they were going to get noticed.

After the first three songs I knew they couldn't be a glam band even if their lives depended on it. Their guitarist had a moustache and a full beard (has there ever been a glam band in the history of rock with facial hair?), but that wasn't half as bad as the fact that they all remained completely motionless throughout their set. The singer was glued to his mic stand, clearly embarrassed about having to stand in front of the audience topless, and the guitarist and the bass player evidently couldn't play and move at the same time. And not once did they look up from the fretboards of their instruments into the audience. Not a single time. I wasn't sure if it was their inability to multi-task or their timidity. It looked like it was both.

I can watch any band, no matter how awful, for as long as they keep playing because I like to know what other people can and can't do, how people on this scene progress (or regress, for that matter), and what ideas everyone's working on. But Zara got bored with Dirty Lick after the first few songs and asked if I wanted to go back to the bar. I went with her because I didn't want her to think I was a geek (although all professional musicians are geeks, some just know cool ways of disguising it).

Back at the bar, I came face to face with Sandy, the guitarist from Lightning Blast, the band who were on next. He looked great, with multi-coloured streaks in his dark-blond hair that got longer since I last saw him, biceps showing through his Ramones t-shirt (Sandy was obviously working out) and a hint of a stubble on his handsome face. Sandy looked good and he knew it, but for some reason he still didn't have much confidence. Maybe it was because he changed his image, straightened his hair and gone blond only recently and wasn't completely comfortable with his new look yet. Just a few months ago Sandy had black curly hair and flab on his stomach and forearms. Something, or someone, must have made him go for a drastic change.

'Joe, how're you doing, mate?' he said, slapping me on the back.

'Great, great!' I replied, wanting to sound relaxed, upbeat, and positive.

'I heard you've left your band,' Sandy said.

'Ah, I just needed a break,' I said vaguely. I didn't want him to know all the details of my career.

'Check out our show,' Sandy said before walking off. 'We've got some new material. We're off to Japan next week to showcase for some labels over there.'

'Wow, cool!' I said. 'Hope it works out for ya!'

Lightning Blast were the Storm Angels' number one competitors on the unsigned scene. Or at least that's what Doug has constantly been telling us. He was probably right because Lightning Blast could write amazing tunes if they felt like it. The problem was that they felt like it only once or twice a year. Some of the songs they've written were pure genius and made me suffer from bona fide jealousy. Sandy could write beautifully crafted potential hits with stunning melodies that qualified for radioplay next to the best songs by AC / DC or Guns'n'Roses, but for every great song they wrote, they did five that were complete rubbish.

Another thing about Lightning Blast was that Sandy was a guitarist truly inspired. When he was in his element, he could blow off the stage any other player on the scene, myself including. It wasn't really his technical skill or speed, but his original, completely unique phrasing, where the rest of the band would play

40

a progression of a few simple chords, and Sandy would come up with a solo you'd never expect to emerge from such a basic harmony, taking the melody beyond the song's original meaning, expanding and developing it as he went, showing who he really was in the most serious and sincere display of emotion. The guy had imagination and he had the courage to be honest. Those were his two main advantages that let him win over all other young guitarists hands down. If he spent more time writing music than drinking and partying, he'd be famous, I knew that. I just didn't know if Sandy knew that himself.

The second reason why Lightning Blast weren't getting signed was their manager Tony. Tony was the biggest idiot rock world has ever known. I've heard that Tony's once been married to a millionaire's daughter, but screwed up in a major way, blowing a lot of his wife's money on cocaine and gambling, so she left him after three years of marriage, taking two small kids with her. I've been told Tony didn't have access to his kids.

Tony could never do anything right. He didn't know how to approach a label, he didn't know how to talk to the journalists, he didn't know how to promote a concert, he was completely incompetent. And he instantly made enemies wherever he went by saying, 'My name is Tony Brown, I'm in charge of the greatest rock band in the world,' as a way of introducing himself to people.

Despite all that, he still managed to have a couple of major rock magazines interview Lightning Blast, but because he understood nothing about PR, he simply told the band to memorise slogans like "We are the most exciting band in the UK right now because we're unique", or "No other band on the underground scene can compete with us because we're real and they are all fake" to be repeated a few times throughout each interview, which they did, to the greatest annoyance of the journalists who interviewed them, who obviously would have preferred to hear something more spontaneous and less pretentious. So Lightning Blast's interviews with Global Rock and The New Rock Zone were practically identical, and both irritated the hell out of all other bands and managers on the scene.

It was hilarious to see how Sandy would always say in his interviews how he hated the Storm Angels because "they are just fake", and how he'd always apologise to me later, saying, 'Tony tells us we should say this, but you know that I have nothing against you, mate.' I used to get pissed at Sandy for badmouthing my band in the press, but then I figured that I'd better stay on good terms with him, because he was one of the very few guys I knew who had a real chance of succeeding in this business, and being on friendly terms with someone like him could later on prove helpful.

'I just can't understand why Lightning Blast are still unsigned,' I mumbled to Zara.

'It's Tony's fault,' she replied. 'Ninety per cent of bands get signed through personal contacts. And Tony doesn't have any contacts because his arrogance alienates people. But it could also be that he's doing this on purpose.'

'What purpose?'

'Sometimes it seems to me that he knows that once they get singed, he'll be out of the picture. Instantly. So he does everything he can *not* to get them signed.'

'But that's absurd,' I said. 'What's the point of managing a band then?'

'Status,' replied Zara. 'They boost his status. He can continue going around saying he manages the best unsigned band in the world.'

I stood there contemplating this grim theory, which seemed bizarrely true, when Zara suddenly said, 'There she is, let's go talk to her.'

Before I could say or do anything, I found myself standing in front of Theodora, being introduced to her as "Joey, one of the best new guitarists in London", my mind blank and my palms sweating. I was then introduced to a short man with black curly hair who wore a suit, and who turned out to be an A&R man from Paris. He was in his mid-thirties and as far as I could tell, wasn't Theodora's boyfriend. I didn't catch the name of the label he worked for, and neither did I catch his name, but still decided to be as nice to him as I could.

'And what kind of music do you play?' Theodora asked me in a slightly patronising tone, but smiling very sweetly.

'Classic rock,' I said. 'With a hint of blues.'

'Oh, like Lightning Blast,' she said.

'Ah, nah, not really, Lightning Blast don't really have any blues influences...'

'What's your band called?' she interrupted me.

'Ah, well, you see...' I laughed nervously.

Zara came to my rescue, saying, 'Joey's between bands right now. His old band is begging him to come back and he's unsure if he should.'

'Really?' Theodora asked me.

'Yeah,' I said. 'They are about to sign a deal with Global Union and they want me to come back.'

The A&R man suddenly looked at me with interest. 'Who are you negotiating with at GU?' he asked.

'I can't remember the name,' I lied.

The A&R man looked surprised, but didn't say anything.

'So what is there to think about?' asked Theodora, looking me straight in the face. 'Don't you like what your band does? Or do you hate your bandmates?'

'You could say that,' Zara said under her breath.

'Nah, it's just that I'd like more control over the creative process,' I said. 'People play too much politics in this band.'

'It's like that everywhere,' Theodora said. 'There's internal politics in every band.'

The A&R man nodded.

'I guess I just need to really think about it,' I said. 'I left them over a month ago and now all of a sudden they want me back.'

'Are you the principal songwriter?' asked the A&R man. He had just a very slight hint of an accent.

'I'm not, even though I write. I play all the leads though.'

'Oh,' he said.

'What's the band called?' asked Theodora.

'The Storm Angels,' I replied.

This time she laughed, throwing her head back in a magnificent spontaneous motion, and I couldn't help but stare again, fascinated by her face, her laughter, the lustrous mane of her hair, and her hand with a ruby ring which sparkled like a small firework when it caught light as she swept her hair away from her face.

'I am sorry,' she then said. 'It's just that these kind of names are unusual these days.'

I decided to be nice and to go for the traditional English self-depreciation, saying, 'Well, the name is actually the main reason why I don't want to go back.'

Everyone laughed and I thanked god for finally being able to think of something more or less witty to say.

I could have stood there talking to Theodora all evening, but Lightning Blast have already begun to play, so the A&R man said, 'Shall we go have a listen?', and we all moved to the dancefloor to watch Sandy's band.

After the first song, Lightning Blast's best tune, Theodora leaned over to me and said, 'The guitarist is very cute. Do you know him?'

'I do,' I said, bringing my face as near to hers as I could, my excuse being that we could hardly hear each other. 'He's talented, but he's got issues. He's a manic depressive. He's been on medication since he was sixteen.'

This was, of course, a preposterous lie, and once I uttered it, I suddenly felt terrible, like I've just spat in someone's drink while they weren't looking, but at the same time if I had the chance to go a few seconds back in time and take back what I just said, I wouldn't.

'Really?' Theodora sounded disappointed.

I nodded.

'Poor thing,' she said.

Lightning Blast did an inspired show that evening, the best I've ever heard them play. They looked, moved, and played like rock stars – with confidence and aplomb, hair flying, guitar necks pointing to the ceiling, their newly done tattoos, cowboy boots, and neck scarves adding to the swagger of the show. Singer Rob's voice sounded exceptional on the night – direct and immediate, opening up to its full range, hitting high notes like it was the easiest thing in the word. Sandy played a lot of impressive leads, but saved his best solo for the last song, which he played standing on the monitors, staring vacantly into the space just above the heads in the crowd. Within just a few moments he went from a loud and abrasive, dense intro into fluid improvisation, mixing skill and intuition to a mind-blowing result. He didn't play too many notes, but the notes that he did play were all beautifully crafted. The tone of his guitar, his pace, and his phrasing showed the truth of feeling that no other guitarist on the scene I knew was capable of. And as I stood there listening to him, I understood that Doug has been right about this band all along. It suddenly began to seem to me that the solo Sandy was playing was nothing else but an open threat directed personally at me. I did recognise though that there was a paradox in Sandy's assault on my status. Sandy was beating me in the way only he could, by expressing himself openly and without inhibition, doing the exact things I couldn't quite do when I played music. Sandy was winning because he knew how to lay his soul bare and wasn't afraid of doing it. It was as if his vulnerability was giving him an advantage.

By the time Sandy's finished, the teenage fans in the audience were going absolutely nuts – screaming, jumping, trying to climb on the stage and taking endless pictures with their phones. The band was getting a huge kick out of all this mayhem, and by the end of the show I felt rotten, not so much from watching all the thirteen year-old girls screaming and shouting "Sandy!" or "Rob, Rob, over here!" but seeing Theodora smile. While Sandy was playing his final solo, she took a small digital camera out of her bag and took a few snaps. I wanted to ask her if she wanted to have a drink with me at the bar, but as I had no money, I just stood next to her like a mute moron, trying hard to think of something funny or intelligent to say. I couldn't, and felt useless.

The A&R man finally came to my rescue.

'I'm going to the bar,' he said to Theodora. 'What can I get you?'

'I'm going with you,' she said, and then, turning to me, 'Would you like to join us?'

I was a bit thrown by the formality of the question, but was extremely happy to follow them, wondering why on Earth someone like her wanted to talk to someone like me, never mind ask for my company. I saw that Zara was standing a few feet away from us, watching the show, and wanted to tell her that we were going to get drinks, but then figured that Theodora might have wanted to talk to me without Zara being there, so I followed her and the A&R man to the bar, telling myself that Zara would always find us.

Once the A&R man got an orange juice for himself (he said he was driving) and a JD and coke for Theodora (I lied that I had an early start the next morning and for that reason wasn't drinking) I asked him what he thought of Lightning Blast.

'They don't have enough good tunes,' he said.

'Bingo!' I thought. 'And there was I thinking that A&R people can't tell shit from gold.'

'But if they had a manager who'd make them work harder, they'd have a good chance of getting signed,' he added.

'You don't need a manager to tell you to work harder,' said Theodora. 'The band should know that.'

The A&R man gave us a Gallic shrug and didn't reply.

'I don't see any future for them,' I said. 'They have too many personal problems to concentrate on serious work.'

I had no idea why I said that. Sure, the boys in Sandy's band partied a lot, but so did all other musicians I knew. It was nothing a good manager couldn't deal with. Again, I felt like a right bastard when I said it, but I wouldn't have taken it back given the chance.

Once Lightning Blast's set was over, Zara joined us, poking me hard in the ribs and saying, 'Oh, *there* you are! Left me on my own!'

'It's my fault,' smiled Theodora. 'I stole him. I thought you wouldn't mind.'

'I knew you'd find us,' I said to Zara sheepishly.

'Ah, I don't mind,' said Zara. 'I really enjoyed that show though!'

'It was good,' nodded the A&R man. 'I wish they had more good songs.'

The guys from Lightning Blast soon appeared too, surrounded by a group of teenagers, all wanting to have their pictures taken with the band. Sandy and Paul were everyone's favourite choice. Drummer Jim, short, with an aquiline nose and a pair of small, sad eyes on his large, heavy face, the only one in the band who even the fans were ignoring, hung around for a bit, but obviously didn't feel comfortable and finally disappeared after a few minutes of watching the rest of the band being fawned over by a crowd of kids.

'Look how the fans are ignoring the poor ugly guy,' half-whispered Theodora, leaning over to my ear. 'Aren't rock fans shallow?'

I was shocked by how plainly she put into words what everyone else saw but didn't dare to express. And I didn't know what would have been the appropriate response. What I thought was, 'Yeah, it sucks to be ugly, on this scene especially,' but I didn't want to say it out loud, nor could I think of anything funny or sharp to say either, so I just made a face that I hoped expressed compassion for poor old Jim, as well as disapproval for the fans' "shallowness".

Lightning Blast were now everyone's centre of attention. Ed Sunders was in the thick of it, having shoved his way though the crowd, and now talking to Sandy, most likely trying to arrange for an interview.

Theodora had her back turned to them now and was talking

to Zara about the exhibition she was putting up in Mayfair. As far as I could understand, the idea behind the show was that there were no art objects on display, but instead sheets of paper in glass cases with descriptions of everyday items, each singed by an artist. It had something to do with a guy named Duchamp and the idea of ready-made art. Theodora was saying that her exhibition was taking the concept of ready-made a step further, like you didn't need an object at all any more. All that was now enough was a description of an object.

'The crucial element is still, of course, the artist's signature,' she was saying. 'Without it, it wouldn't be a work of art but a lot description from an auctioneer's catalogue.'

The A&R man was listening attentively, and finally said, 'But you have to ask who qualifies to be called an artist these days. Will the general public recognise those signatures?'

'Yes, of course,' Theodora said impatiently, 'All those artists have internationally recognised names.'

'Well, in that case, the line between an artist and an auctioneer becomes blurred,' said the A&R man. 'Which is obviously great,' he added hastily, after Theodora gave him a rather unkind look.

'The whole point is that in the field of ready-made we don't need objects at all anymore,' said Theodora. 'A verbal description is enough, simply an idea of an object, a notion. Duchamp's idea was that an artist can create an *object d'art* simply by signing an everyday object. What I am saying with this show is that we don't even need physical objects at all anymore. An idea, a verbal representation of an object is enough.'

Distracted, I began to scan the room. Dirty Lick stood at the far end of the room talking to Tracy Huggins because nobody else was interested in them at that point. Pete, their balding bass player, looked uneasy, clearly embarrassed about being seen talking to Tracy. Our eyes met, and I had to nod before he thought I was too arrogant to acknowledge him. He interpreted this as an invitation to join us, which I obviously didn't want, but he already began walking in our direction. Reluctantly I introduced him to Theodora, who he instantly became fascinated by, starting to babble about his band and their new EP, I guess just out of sheer nervousness.

'I was impressed by Lightning Blast,' Theodora said suddenly, interrupting his outpour of information and unwelcome emotion.

'Oh, well, Lightning Blast are actors more than musicians,' said Pete. 'They should really have chosen acting as their career. They are putting on a good show, but their music is lame, that's what all critics agree on.'

'Sure, critics like Tracy Huggins,' I thought. 'Who say that Sandy can't play to save his life, whereas you are the hottest bass player on the planet since Jacko Pastorius.'

'I like bands that have good things to say about other musicians,' said Theodora and smiled, looking Pete straight in the eye.

He was taken aback by this, saying, 'Well, I just think a lot of other bands deserve more attention than Lightning Blast. I think they play what they play just because this kind of music is becoming trendy.'

'Look who's talking,' I thought.

'It's a shame that promoters can't tell a fake from a real thing,' said Theodora.

She was clearly referring to the fact that Dirty Lick were at the bottom of tonight's bill. I knew that Pete in his stupidity assumed that he was talking to another silly girl who knew nothing about music. He had no clue who Theodora was and he couldn't pick on the signs, he was that thick. Thankfully, by that time Silver Cats began to play, so we had an excuse to walk away.

The five hundred capacity club was now packed. A lot of people have now arrived who weren't interested in the support bands and who bought tickets to see the headliners only. These were all people in their late thirties and early forties who had nothing to do with the underground scene and who were simply fans of Silver Cats from the days they were in the charts and on MTV. Those punters knew nothing about the new trends and the new acts, but remained faithful to the bands they listened to when they were young. Most music fans are like this. Once they hit thirty, they start buying less and less albums, and by the time they are forty, their music collection stops growing completely because they don't want to know about the new trends. New music makes them uncomfortable because it shows how dated the bands that were trendy in their youth have become, and, ultimately, how they themselves have aged.

Silver Cats opened their set with an old hit, the title track of their platinum debut that came out eighteen years ago. The crowd went absolutely berserk after hearing the first chords of the song which most of them remembered topping the charts for months back in 1989. The band was as tight as humanly possible, running through their practiced chops with precision that sounded almost frightening, their focused, dense fire showing years and years of experience. The guys on the stage looked just the way I remembered them from last year's tour – lean, tanned, self-assured, smiling, and on the ball. I've never once seen them do an average show in all the time I've toured with them. These dudes have been playing rock'n'roll for over two decades, and each of their notes was a convincing statement of what it means to be a pro. They haven't made a single mistake during the entire show. I stood there thinking that if I've been playing for as long as they had, I'd probably be just as good, if not better. And while I admired the sleek execution of their expertly written tunes, I still thought they didn't really touch you the way some other bands did. Silver Cats were solid, practiced musicians, clever old cocks, but they couldn't fly.

Towards the middle of the show they made a short break, Paul, the singer, chatting to the crowd, saying the usual stuff about how good it feels to be back in London, and introducing the next song: 'This is for a very special friend who is here tonight. Theodora, this one is for you.'

I looked at Theodora and saw her smile and raise her glass to Paul, just before the band launched into a slow, gentle intro to a weepy ballad.

The women in the room began exchanging worried glances, faces puzzled and anxious, leaning over to speak to each other, wanting to know who Theodora was.

To close their set, the band played two new songs from the album which came out earlier this year and which managed not only to avoid stirring any chart action, but also being reviewed by any of the big mags. The fans, of course, clapped, but still preferred the old songs from the Eighties, which for a lot of them was the soundtrack to the best days of their lives.

The show was finally over after the two-song old hit encore, after which everyone rushed to the bar to get their last drinks. A lot of people were talking about the aftershow party, but practically no one knew where it was going to be, and those who did, didn't share the information. Theodora and Zara knew it was going to be in Soho, and both, as well Jean-Pierre (I finally memorised the A&R man's name) were going. I obviously wanted to go too, mainly because of Theodora, but I was now in an idiotic situation having said less than an hour before that I had an early start the next morning. Jean-Pierre resolved everything by saying to Zara and to me that he could give us a lift to Soho in his car. So we all decided to head to Charing Cross Road instead of waiting to be served in the bar where dozens of people were trying to grab their last drinks before closure.

Jean-Pierre's car was parked on a tiny street just off Camden High a couple of hundred yards up the road. It was an immaculately clean, shiny dark-blue BMW which he said he was hiring while in London. He was leaving for New York the next day and was then going back to Paris where he worked in an office on Champs-Elysees. I still didn't know which label he worked for and was embarrassed to ask.

Theodora took the passenger's seat next to Jean-Pierre, and Zara and I sat in the back. I could now smell Theodora's perfume, which was a very faint, complex, layered scent I've never smelled before.

'What's her perfume called?' I whispered into Zara's ear.

Zara laughed softly. 'It's been mixed for her by a celebrity perfume maker in Paris. It's unique.'

I never knew you could have your own scent designed for you. Not knowing what to reply, I started looking out of the window, watching raindrops stick to the car's window. It was almost midnight.

We finally arrived in a shabby watering hole on one of Soho's miniature streets, famous among professional rock musicians the world over. Most people who drink there are signed to independent labels, but touring American rock stars appear there once in a while too, mostly because the place is unknown to tourists and gives them a degree of privacy. Groupies love this place too, of course. Some of them go there like other people go to work, and there's never been a single one who hasn't entertained a secret hope, no matter how ephemeral, to find a rock star boyfriend or even a husband there.

I have once been told about a woman who used to show up there every day for two years solid, straight after work (she was a receptionist in the City), arriving at six p.m. and leaving at two a.m. After two years of religiously doing that, she ended up meeting a Swedish drummer who was on a UK tour at the time. According to the people who knew her, she was at first ecstatic when he suggested she moved with him to Sweden, but very soon life in a small town in Lapland got the better of her. The guy was on tour most of the time, and it later turned out he didn't have as much money as she had hoped, given his relative fame. I was told she was now back in London, back in the same bar every evening, looking for her next boyfriend.

Silver Cats weren't there yet when we arrived, so we had a few drinks (Zara lent me a tenner) standing on the pavement outside, because both of the tiny rooms were so crowded the lack of oxygen made it impossible to stay inside.

Talking to Theodora was easy, but I still felt self-conscious, guarding myself against saying something stupid, something naïve, or simply talking too much. It's not that I didn't have anything to say, I did, but I didn't want to come through as too eager, too inexperienced, or too simple.

Often when I feel nervous, I pretend that I am someone else – usually a rock star like Slash or Joe Perry. So far this mind trick had always worked for me – I'd instantly feel relaxed, confident, and even generous. I'd imagine myself a rich, successful musician with millions of fans, a beautiful house, half a dozen sports cars, and a Hollywood actress for a wife. Standing now in front of Theodora I realised that my method wasn't working anymore. I was very aware that she was the one with the money, the big house, and all the toys she could ever wish for, and felt like a fraud trying to pretend to know what it's like to have wealth and power – something she was born into and I knew very little about. All this made me extremely nervous. It didn't mean though that I didn't want to be there. Just the opposite, being with her and talking to her, although in a lot of ways torturous, at the same time gave me a buzz, and not only because she was beautiful. I admired the way she spoke her mind, not being afraid to seem mean or callous, something that almost all other girls I knew were always guarding against, at least when they first met you, careful not to show their real feelings behind an exterior of someone sensitive and caring. I always thought this was because an average girl would always try to make an impression of a perfect potential girlfriend when you first met her. Not Theodora. She wasn't eager to please and didn't try to come through as compassionate or particularly helpful. I suppose she was unafraid to show who she really was because she had enough confidence given to her either by her either by the fact that her father was an important record label executive or simply by her beauty. She probably never had to prove anything to anyone. I would have guessed that people were always trying to impress her, not the other way around. I wondered if it was just the money that was behind all this, or if it was something else, some esoteric knowledge the rich and the famous pass on to their children ordinary people know nothing about.

As we stood outside talking, a back cab pulled up, Silver Cats singer Paul jumping out of it a few seconds later. He looked great in his off-stage clothes – casual jeans and a back t-shirt – but you would never have guessed from looking at him that he was a rock star. You could tell that he had a lot of confidence and that he probably had a creative job that paid well, but if you run into him in the street, you'd never think that this was a guy who toured the world four times over, gathering arenas and stadiums full of fans in every city his band went through. Or that his face was once on the front covers of all major rock magazines dozens of times a year.

Paul smiled when he saw me talking to Theodora, and shouted to me jokingly as he approached us, 'What are *you* doing here?' as a form of greeting, before kissing Theodora on the cheek and asking her how she was, and how her dad and mom were, to all of which she answered 'Great, thanks.'

'Where is the rest of your band?' Zara asked Paul.

'They'll be here!' he said. 'I left them at the hotel, but they know the address of this pace, so they'll come down. Or at least I hope they will. I don't want to deal with everything on my own.' He laughed.

'We loved your show,' said Theodora.

'Did you?' Paul smiled, looking pleased. 'The album's doing really well. We're thinking of taking it on tour to Japan and South America, you know, all the places we used to go to before.'

'Just like the old days!' said Theodora. 'You could go paragliding in Mexico like you used to!'

'Oh, yeah,' said Paul. 'I forgot about that! But only if you join me!'

He laughed, and so did Theodora, placing her immaculate hand with long, elegant fingers on his shoulder for a fraction of a second.

'Is it possible to get a drink there?' asked Paul, looking into the brightly lit room through the glass doors.

'You could try,' said Zara.

'I guess I will,' he said, looking in again.

He then smiled at us and went inside.

'He should have taken one of his roadies with him to get him drinks and protect him,' said Jean-Pierre. 'He's going to get mobbed by the groupies.'

'Maybe that's what he's hoping for,' said Theodora with a laugh.

'By the way,' said Jean-Pierre, 'Their last album sold two thousand copies so far. I checked last week.'

Zara and I looked at each other.

'He just said it was doing well,' said Zara.

Theodora laughed. 'He knows that the album's bombed,' she said. 'It was an awful record, their worst ever. I couldn't listen to it, the songs were absolutely dreadful. He knows people have been panning it on Blab. I know for a fact that he checks the comments about the band there every day. You know that guy there who keeps posting saying that Silver Cats are the best band in the world? I think it's him.'

She laughed again and although I suddenly felt queasy about her saying this about a man whose show she just praised to his face, I couldn't help laughing, imagining Paul sitting in front of his computer screen, leaving messages on an internet forum, pretending to be a fan of his own band.

Zara went 'Hmm' and was about to say something, but was interrupted by Theodora.

'Hel-lo,' she said loudly, looking over my shoulder. The greeting was addressed to Rich and Scott, Paul's bandmates, the guitarist and the bass player, who I too now saw walking in our direction. Rich came up to Zara first, kissed her on both cheeks and held her hand for a few brief moments. He then turned to Theodora who introduced him to Jean-Pierre.

Meanwhile Scott shook my hand, saying, 'It's good to see

you, man. Wanna get a drink with us inside?'

I looked around me helplessly, not knowing what to do. Any other time I would have loved to have a drink with these guys, but now I didn't want to leave Theodora, so I turned to her, saying, 'Do you guys want to have a drink inside?'

'No, you go,' she replied.

Inside it was hell. I saw Paul at the far end of the room pinned against the jukebox by five women who were all simultaneously talking, laughing, and touching him while making sure about fifteen other females who stood behind their backs weren't getting access to the guy. As for Paul, he wasn't even trying to hide that he was over the moon, enjoying every second of this mayhem.

Once Rich, Scott, and I came in, there was confusion for about five seconds, and then the women who were until then unsuccessfully trying to get hold of Paul, began to elbow their way through the crowd to get to us. I felt anxious.

Once the chicks grabbed hold of Scott and Rich, one of them dug her fingernails into my forearm and whispered hotly in my ear, 'Are you their friend? What's your name?'

She was well over thirty, wore black tights, a white miniskirt and a low-cut red lace top. Her face was so close to mine I could see every wrinkle accentuated by her foundation. Her small blue eyes underlined with black kohl were staring straight at my face.

'Sorry, baby, I just want to get a drink,' I said.

She didn't seem to hear me.

'Which hotel are they staying at?' she asked.

'I think it's the King's Cross Holiday Inn,' I lied.

'Thanks, babes,' she said, let go of my arm and began making her way to the door. I bet she was heading straight to King's Cross Holiday Inn.

'So,' Scott spoke into my ear, while three women were trying to drag him away from me, 'How long have you been dating Dolly for?'

56

'Who?' I said before realising he was talking about Theodora. 'Oh, you mean Theodora? Dude, we just met! I don't even know her!'

'Well, she likes you, man,' said Scott.

'Why, do you think so?' I asked, trying to figure out if he was serous or taking the piss.

'Sure,' he said. 'If she didn't, she wouldn't have you here with her. I'd say be careful though. Don't know if she's anything like her daddy, but if she is, she's got to be pretty ruthless.'

'Do you know him?' I asked.

Scott laughed. 'He was the man who signed us back in 1989.'

'Did you get a good deal?' I asked stupidly.

'Yeah, we got a good deal. I hope you will too,' he said, laughing.

After that it became impossible to talk to Scott and Rich. Both became completely mobbed by groupies and fans. I hung around for a bit and even took a few pictures for people who wanted to be photographed with the band, before going back outside.

Theodora and Jean-Pierre were getting ready to leave and were offering Zara a lift.

'You know what,' said Zara, 'I think I'll stay. There is something I need to speak to Scott and Rich about. A business proposal to discuss. Thanks for offering me a lift. I'll be OK, I'll get a taxi home once this is over.'

Theodora asked me how I was getting home, and I said I was going to catch a night bus, but she insisted they gave me a lift, even though my place was miles away from where we were. Theodora said she loved driving in London at night, and that Jean-Pierre wouldn't mind driving us both home. I don't know if he did really mind or not, but he nodded curtly in agreement. Theodora said that they would go to Ealing to drop me off first, and then Jean-Pierre would take her home. I couldn't believe Jean-Pierre was going to spend the next hour driving home some guy he just met, in the middle of the night, in a city he didn't know that well.

As we were about to get into the car, Paul came out, a bunch of women filing into the street after him, all trying to hold on to his arms and laughing at each of his slurred words.

Taking a few shaky steps towards me, he suddenly uttered, 'Joe, we're off to a titty bar, wanna come with us?'

'Dude, I wish I could, but I can't! I'm about to take off! I've got an audition tomorrow morning!' I said.

I lied mainly because I didn't have any money and couldn't afford to go, but also because I wanted to ask Theodora for her phone number later on, and I obviously couldn't say to her, 'Theodora, it was great meeting you, I'm off to a strip club, but before I go, could I have your number?'

'An audition?' said Paul. 'Have you left your band?'

'I have,' I said.

'Good move,' said Paul suddenly, moving closer. I could smell JD on his breath. 'A lot of things were wrong with that band.'

I pulled a face which was supposed to express regret over having wasted so much time in a shit band, as well as the fact that we both knew its dirty secret but didn't want to talk about it, even though I had no clue if Paul actually knew anything about our songwriting or not.

'OK, guys,' Paul said, turning to Theodora, Zara and Jean-Pierre, 'We're off! Dolly, thank you for coming down to see us! Say hi to your daddy from me!'

'Will do,' said Theodora.

'Have fun,' said Jean-Pierre.

Paul and the women began walking towards Charing Cross Road to get a taxi. One of the women was wearing hotpants, a denim jacket and high heels, the other – a mini-dress and riding boots, and the third – a knee-length leather skirt and a see-through top underneath a biker jacket.

Zara and Theodora gave each other a peck on the cheek before Zara went through the doors to join Scott and Rich inside. I thought she was going to have a hard time trying to have a conversation with either of them, but then I remembered that she and Rich looked like they knew each other well, and he seemed to like her.

This time Theodora and I sat in the back.

'I'm hearing Paul has split up with his girlfriend,' she said, smiling.

'Really?' said Jean-Pierre 'The San Diego woman?'

'Aha,' said Theodora.

We carried on in silence.

Sitting next to Theodora was torture. She was so close to me, I could now smell the warm, spicy overtones of her perfume. I wanted to touch her, but realised that I had no excuse whatsoever to do that. So I sat there in silence, trying to think of a reason to ask her for her phone number, failing to come up with any ideas.

When I was in a band, I could always say to a girl I liked, 'Our next show is next week, fancy coming along?' That put the ball right in their court, and I didn't have to do anything more. I knew exactly where I stood if they turned up or if they didn't. Here, however, I didn't know what the hell to say. Finally, as we were already approaching my house, I managed to say to her, 'Well, it was nice meeting you, hopefully we'll see each other soon, maybe when I start gigging again.'

'Sure,' she said. 'Take care.'

I was so taken aback by this brief answer that I realised that I still didn't have her number only when I was already out of the car and walking towards my door. The only hope I had now was to try to find her on MySpace. And I didn't even know her surname. Or her e-mail address. Or who her friends were. I knew nothing about her.

III

DO WHAT THOU WILT

I spent the next morning trying to find Theodora on MySpace. I sat on the living room floor with Dave's laptop in front of me, drinking one cup of instant coffee after another, trying to see if anyone called Theodora belonged to any of the music or art groups. There were hundreds of them, and I had no luck. I then checked fan clubs and band pages, painstakingly going through friends lists of each chart rock band, even though the likelihood of someone like Theodora being a "friend" of Coldplay or Black Stone Cherry was next to none. I was anxious to find her on MySpace because contacting her that way would have been the easiest thing for me to do. It would have looked casual, spontaneous, and non-obsessive.

When I was in the Storm Angels, hundreds of girls were getting in touch with me through MySpace every week, leaving comments on my page, sending messages and pictures – either of themselves or of women at various stages of undress they'd pick from one of the ten million cheesy graphics sites that have sprung up in the last few years to serve MySpace. Whenever I saw those anonymous trashy pictures, I instantly knew there was something wrong either with the sender's age or appearance. Otherwise why wouldn't they send their own picture?

A typical girl who would get in touch would be between eighteen and twenty-three, although there were also some disturbingly old women. I remember one who was over sixty and who kept sending me eight-paragraph messages telling me how she saw Hendrix at Albert Hall in 1969 and Led Zeppelin at the Roundhouse that same year. I had no idea if it was all true or not, and I had no clue what the fuck to answer her, but then Doug told us to reply "Thank you for your support" to all freaks who wrote to us.

The majority of girls who sent me add requests were young and naive, but always wanted to come through as experienced and sophisticated. Ninety per cent named Nikki Sixx as their hero, ninety-nine per cent wrote that the people they wanted to meet were Aerosmith and Motley Crue, and about half of them spelled their MySpace names with multiple Xs.

Some girls in their late twenties were a bit sassier and more cynical. There were some who were saying that their ambition in life was to marry a rock star, but none of them said anything about their jobs. Whenever I saw a profile showing an average-looking pasty-faced girl wearing nothing but a mini-skirt and a tiny top exposing her flabby bits, and with a MySpace name like Lexxy Sixxss, or Sexxssy Lixx, or Mrs. Axxxel Sixx, describing herself as a "wild rock chick", I instantly imagined a bored single girl living with her parents in a small town in Essex with posters of Bon Jovi and Motley Crue on her bedroom walls, who had to get up every morning at half seven to catch a bus to some office where she was fitting some typing and answering the phone between endless MySpace sessions, circulating dozens of questionnaires a day with questions like "What did you have for breakfast today?" and "Is there anyone you like?" Having seen hundreds of these sort of profiles, I now know one thing for sure – when I do become rich and famous, I ain't gonna to marry a pasty-faced receptionist from Essex who says her ambition in life is to become a rock star's wife. I'd rather marry Yoko Ono.

Doug forbade us to delete any of those characters from our MySpace "friends" lists. He was saying that the more "friends" we had, the more exposure it gave us. He was also telling us to reply to each person who wrote to us with "Thank you for your support". When I quit the band, the first thing I did was delete all wannabe groupies from my "friends" list and set my profile to private so that only the people I knew could have access to it.

There was a time, about a year ago, when I really cared how many messages and add requests I was receiving each day. Now I couldn't have cared less. I now know that the more MySpace "friends" a person has, the less friends they have in real life. I am especially suspicious of people who get dozens of comments a day. If you get that many comments, you must return just as many. Would anyone with a serious job have time to do that? It seems to me that the only people who do have time for leaving MySpace comments for each other are office workers bound to their computers for the entire day without any real work to do.

At four in the afternoon I finally gave up. I was sitting with my guitar in my room trying to distract myself with playing scales, thinking that this was probably god's way of telling me to stop having ridiculous thoughts about Theodora. I tried to be rational, telling myself that I stood no chance with her. She could choose to go out with any guy in the universe, so why would she want me in her life?

As I sat looking out of my bedroom window thinking about my lousy luck, my mobile rang. It was Zara. I suddenly felt embarrassed about forgetting to call her in the morning.

'Hi, Joey,' she said. 'How are you?'

'I'm good,' I said, sounding utterly miserable. 'How are you?'

'Theodora has spoken to her father,' said Zara, ignoring my question.

'Jesus,' I thought. 'He probably told her never to go near seedy places like the club we met at and never to speak again to losers like me.'

'She found out what the situation is with the Storm Angels for you,' continued Zara. 'Global Union wants you in the band. They don't want the new guy. Doug's been told to get you back if he wants to sign the deal.'

All I could manage in response was 'Wow!' I honestly couldn't come up with anything more appropriate to say. Then I thought for a few seconds and said, 'Why do they want me?'

'Because you look hot,' Zara said matter-of-factly. 'They say you look like a rock star. The new guy doesn't.'

'Wow!' I said again.

'She is also asking if you'd like to come to her exhibition opening at seven.'

'This evening?' I asked, thinking that if it was, I hardly had enough time to wash and style my hair.

'Yes, this evening.'

'Christ!' I said. 'Where is it?'

'It's on New Bond Street. I'll text you the address.'

'Jesus!.. What should I wear?'

'Jeans and a t-shirt. Don't wear a band t-shirt though.'

When I put the phone down, I had two major problems to deal with – what to wear and what to do with my hair.

Gallery Stone was a small showroom on New Bond Street, hidden between two large fashion boutiques displaying obscenely expensive ladies' bags and shoes in their windows. A lime green patent leather bag with a chain handle which was going to go out of fashion in a few months' time had a price tag of just over two grand, making it cost twice as much as my guitar. People with expensive hair cuts wearing cashmere coats and designer shoes were passing by. No one was looking at me. I found this odd because in all other parts of London people always looked at me more than once, mostly women, of course, but guys would stare at me quite a bit too. I always thought that this was because of my hair and my clothes, but recently I began suspecting that maybe there was more to it. Maybe women stared at me a lot because they thought I was genuinely good-looking? I could never decide if I really looked good or not. I knew that my hair and my clothes made me look kind of dangerous and intriguing to a lot of young girls, maybe to some older women too, and even to quite a few blokes, but I always doubted if I would draw as much attention to myself if I got a haircut, dressed casually and didn't have an image that screamed "rock musician". Sure, I've been told millions of times before by dozens of girls that I "look like a rock star" and that I'm "the best looking guy in the band", and that I'm "beautiful" and "look awesome", but I always thought it was because I was in a band. I thought all musicians were hearing the same stuff as often as I did. Rock'n'roll can turn anyone from a kid who everyone bullied at school into a superstud. That's why I never knew for sure how much of my attractiveness was down to my style and the fact that I was a rocker, and how much of it was down to what nature's given me.

I now knew though that here, in the middle of Mayfair, one of the richest areas of London, I was virtually non-existent. Passers-by weren't even acknowledging my presence. It felt strange. Here I was, wearing my two hundred quid jeans that always attracted attention everywhere else, a three hundred quid leather jacket I bought online from Saks Fifth Avenue when I was still in the Storm Angels, Ray Bans I borrowed once from Sandy and forgot to give back, with a new sixty-quid haircut, and no one was even looking at me. It really did feel strange.

Inside everything was flooded by bright electric light. A dozen or so women in their late twenties and early thirties, wearing cashmere shawls, long dresses and heels, were talking to each other, champagne flutes in hand. A few men who looked slightly older than the women were there too – some in cardigans, some in flannel suits. The men had longish hair and most of them looked like they haven't had a shower that morning.

When I came in through the glass door, everyone turned in my direction. This was a change from what it was like outside, and I immediately felt uncomfortable and on the spot. I tried to pretend I was a millionaire rock star passing through London while on tour, looking for art to hang in my newly bought mansion in Malibu, but my usual mind trick didn't help much. I still felt awkward. I took my shades off not to look like a complete prat among these people, even though I wasn't sure if this made any real difference one way or another. Everyone in the room probably thought that I was a degenerate musician lost on his way home from an AA meeting. There were no paintings, drawings, or sculptures anywhere. Instead, exactly as described by Theodora the day before, there were sheets of paper with short passages of text placed inside square plexiglass cases mounted on narrow pillars.

I then spotted Theodora standing next to one of the displays, talking to a balding guy in a grey corduroy suit. She looked stunning. I realised that she looked nothing like I've been remembering her this morning. Her face was so beautiful I felt unsteady looking at her. Her eyes radiated the same confidence I was so stricken by when I first saw her, and her lips were fuller than I remembered them, touched with barely-there pale pink lipstick. Her hair looked immaculate, and her long back cotton dress sat perfectly on her flawless figure with curves in all the right places. She wasn't wearing any jewellery apart from a sparkling ring on the little finger of her right hand which looked like it cost more than my parents' house in Colchester.

The guy she was talking to clearly wasn't paying much attention to what she was saying, but was staring at her face instead. I was surprised he wasn't openly salivating. She then noticed me and waved. I walked up to her with everyone's eyes following me, and managed to say, 'Hi, congratulations, it's a cool show,' my voice slightly coarse.

'It's good to see you!' she said, lightly touching both of my arms with her hands and leaning towards my face. I kissed her on both cheeks, trying not to faint out of excitement. The guy she was talking to was now looking at me with what I interpreted as a mixture of jealousy, curiosity, and dislike. I was used to it though – this is how most guys look at me anyway, wherever I go.

Theodora was glad I stopped by, and I wondered for the

second time today why on Earth she wanted to ever see me again after last night. She then introduced me to her companion, whose name turned out to be Maxwell. I nodded and said hi.

Maxwell has obviously never been in a same room with a rock musician before.

'Are you an artist?' he asked me.

'Dude, do I look like an artist?' I thought, but instead just said, 'No, I'm not.'

'Joey is a musician,' said Theodora.

'Oh, and what kind of music do you play?' he asked.

'I'm a fucking opera singer,' I felt like replying, but 'Rock'n'roll' came out instead.

'Oh,' said Maxwell, obviously not knowing what to say next. He was looking at me like I've just snorted a line of cocaine right in front of him. My response was to blank him, and I was relieved when he finally had sense to leave us alone after I thanked Theodora for giving me a lift the night before.

'And thank you for finding out about my band's deal with Global,' I added. 'I really appreciate your help.'

'Oh, that!' she said. 'Isn't that funny? They said to Daddy they wanted you and nobody else because you looked like a rock star!'

I felt so embarrassed I couldn't even come up with anything appropriately humours to respond with, so I said, 'Yeah, that's mad.'

'So what are you going to do now?' asked Theodora. 'You have negotiating leverage now. Are you going to ask them for more money or an overall better deal?'

'I don't know what to do, to be honest,' I said. 'This deal isn't really ideal for me...'

'If you want total control over your band, you won't get it,' she interrupted. 'Especially not with a major.'

'It's not just that,' I said. 'It's mainly our manager who I really don't want anything to do with.'

'Your manager will play a lesser role once you're signed,' she said, looking at me with what seemed like a lot of sympathy.

I felt that I was coming through as unreasonable, and wished I could tell her the truth about Doug, the band, and how I felt about being a marketable puppet whose only value was in his looks.

I must have looked really confused and desperate, because she suddenly said, 'If you can't deal with this rationally, you have to try to come to a decision by irrational means.'

'What do you mean?' I asked.

'You should hand over this decision to an impartial third party. A party that is not only impartial, but also irrational.'

'What do you mean?' I asked again, feeling even more confused.

'If you have tried to use common sense to deal with this, and still can't make a decision one way or another, maybe it's time to consult an oracle,' she said.

'An oracle?! What kind of oracle?'

She shrugged her shoulders. 'I don't know,' she said. 'But whatever oracle you choose, choose it irrationally.'

I was amazed and I guess I looked it too, because a tall, thin woman aged about forty, wearing a long green wool dress who approached us to speak to Theodora, instead turned to me and said, 'Aren't Theodora's ideas exceptional? This exhibition is the most avant-garde show we've had in years!'

'Oh, yeah,' I muttered, 'It's pretty cool. I've never seen anything like it.'

Theodora introduced us. The woman's name was Anita, and she was the owner of the gallery. Despite my obvious clumsiness and the fact that I looked totally out of place in her gallery, she seemed to like me.

She smiled at me and said, 'I love ideas that go a few steps beyond what people expect. It makes the world a more enchanting place, don't you think?'

'Totally,' I said like a moron, but she pretended she didn't hear the idiotic word and smiled at me again. God knows why she liked me. I began to wonder if I really did look like a rock star. At least people at Global Union seemed to think so.

'Darling,' said Anita to Theodora, 'John from ArtLine is here, are you ready for your interview?'

'Of course,' said Theodora and then, turning to me, 'Joey, don't go anywhere, I'll be right back,' before following Anita to speak to a guy in jeans and a denim jacket waiting for her at the far end of the room, some kind of a journo, from what I could gather.

I picked up a flute of champagne from the window sill and began looking at sheets of paper inside the glass cases. The first one I looked at had the following printed on it: "A round object with a metal hub in the center part, wire tension spokes and a metal rim. 700 mm in diameter. Threads are cut into a hole in the axle. A metal cartridge, shaped like a hollow cylinder, contains the bearings. The bearings are pressed into the hub shell with the axle resting against the inner surface of the cartridge. Spokes are attached to the hub shell, passing through holes in a flange which extends from the axle. The rim is made of aluminum alloy and is an extrusion butted into itself forming a circle. The rim is connected to the hub by 99 spokes under tension. 99 spoke holes on the rim match 99 spoke holes in the hub. Spokes are round in cross-section. Signed: A. Newman."

'Jesus,' I thought, 'They call this art? Is anyone going to buy this? And if so, then for how much?'

Meanwhile I was hearing Theodora say to the journo: '…and because of this, successful functioning of art institutions has historically depended on attribution of artistic value to objects of art. Since Duchamp's *Fountain* we are no longer concerned if an artist has actually made the object himself. What matters is that he chose it and bestowed an artistic value on it by signing it. Duchamp's readymade objects changed the emphasis from what is being depicted to what is being said, from appearances to concepts. This was the beginning of modernism. This exhibition takes the modernist notion further and proclaims that we don't need the object anymore. We can now deal with pure concepts, because we have now transcended the need for the object of art. So you don't see any art objects here, all you see are concepts, verbal descriptions of objects. The object itself is made redundant. If any item, no matter how mundane, can become an art object, so can any concept.'

A few minutes later, as I stopped in front of the next plexiglass case, I suddenly sensed someone standing next to me. I looked and saw Theodora.

'I'm done with the interview,' she said.

'Was it fun?' I asked, glad it didn't take long.

'Yes,' she said smiling, 'Listen, once this is finished I have to go, but why don't you come over to my Thanksgiving party tomorrow? I'll text you my address.'

I couldn't believe she was inviting me to her home, and I felt like saying, 'Thanks, that's awesome!', but instead tried to look as indifferent as I could and simply said, 'That's cool, thanks. Let me give you my number.'

Once I got home, all I could think about was Theodora. In fact, I didn't sleep that night. Instead, I immersed myself in a twelve-hour daydream. I don't know if it was love, lust or infatuation. My rational mind has completely shut off. I wasn't thinking about who she was and who I was, I didn't think about her father, the high-flying record label executive in LA, I didn't think of my father, a chef at a mid-priced Italian restaurant in Colchester, or about the degrading deal with Global Union I was being offered, which was my only chance to ever become anybody. I didn't think of her exhibition at a gallery in Mayfair which I didn't understand anything about even after I've seen it, and I didn't think of the fact that I didn't have enough money to invite her for a decent meal in the foreseeable future. All I could see in front of me was her face, her hair, her eyes, and the way her lips glistened in the darkness of my room as I was running my fingers through her hair.

Theodora lived in a detached four-story house on a quiet planetree-lined street ten minutes walk from Hampstead tube station. When I finally stopped in front of what I thought was the right house, I was faced with a massive gate and an intercom system. I pressed the button and a few seconds later heard Theodora's voice say, 'Joey, I'm buzzing you in.' I pushed the gate which didn't make a single sound, and walked to the front door along a stone path that ran across the lawn. I then saw her appear on the doorstep, wearing a silk knee-length burgundy dress, tight, and so seductive I nearly tripped over.

'Hi,' I said. 'How did you know it was me?'

'There's a camera,' she said smiling. 'You look nice, thank you for coming.'

'Well, look at you,' I ventured. 'You look stunning in this dress.'

She laughed and said, 'Thank you. Come in.'

The back front door led into an enormous hall, where a crystal chandelier shone on the polished pink marble floor and abstract paintings on the walls. I smelled incense and heard some seriously cool music emerging from the door to the left, something that sounded like a mixture of Fifties rhythm-and-blues and Sixties indie, almost like the early Stones, but I didn't recognise the song.

'That's cool music,' I said. 'Who is it?'

'It's my friend Mark's band,' she said. 'You'll meet him in a minute.'

'Oh great, I thought,' as my heart sank. 'She's got a boyfriend. She is playing his music at her party. I bet his dad is in the Rolling Stones... Who else would she go out with...'

It all made sense now. I felt like a total impostor, a retard with ridiculous ideas, who, because of an incomprehensible twist of fate, had just walked into someone else's life that had nothing to do with his, into a set populated with much happier, saner, luckier, wealthier people who could get anything they wanted in life by just being who they were – confident and laidback sons and daughters of people who had talent and power – without having to struggle, prostitute themselves or strike deals with the devil. To this day I don't know why I haven't turned around at that very moment and haven't gone straight back to my shared flat in Ealing. But I didn't. Maybe I just don't let go that easily.

I walked into the drawing room on autopilot, feeling shy, vulnerable, and hurt, and suddenly saw a bunch of teenagers sitting on a huge lilac velvet sofa which semi-circled around an Art Deco coffee table, with glasses and a bottle of Jack on top of it, as well as half a dozen of miniature Diet Coke bottles. Their backs to the tallest sash window I've ever seen, and they were chatting, laughing, and smoking. I began wondering where Theodora's boyfriend was. Upstairs in the bedroom? Having a shower? Shooting up in the bathroom? Was he running late from the recording studio?

'Guys, this is Joey,' said Theodora. 'He's a guitarist in an amazing band.'

'Hey, man,' a guy with chin-length dirty-blond hair instantly responded, raising his glass to me. I knew right away he was a musician.

'Hey,' I said cooly.

'Hello,' a couple of teenage girls smiled at me with undisguised curiosity.

'Come and sit with us,' said the boldest and the least attractive of them, a plump creature with braids in her brown hair and thin lips pained scarlet red.

I ignored her and went up to the long-haired dude who's just said hi to me and who was getting up to talk to me too.

'This is Mark,' said Theodora, introducing us. 'Joey's just been saying that your new track sounds fab.'

'Thanks, man,' said Mark, as I stared at him. There was no way he could have been Theodora's boyfriend. To start with, he was no older than eighteen. Secondly, I couldn't believe that at his age someone could have written a tune as cool as the one I was hearing now. One thing that I acknowledged though was that he was good-looking – large grey eyes, a straight narrow nose, full lips (maybe even too full for an English guy), high cheekbones.

72

'So,' I said, feeling suddenly a lot more confident, 'is this your band's track?'

'Oh, yeah,' he said, sounding casual, but sincere. 'We recorded it last month. I play the guitar.'

'Lead?'

'Yeah,' he smiled. 'Here comes the solo.'

The guitar part that came on at that moment was one of the best solos I've heard in a long, long time. My jaw nearly dropped and it became hard for me to look composed and unaffected. But the fact was that as I was listening to it, my insides were turning upside down. I couldn't believe that this skinny kid standing in front of me, casually leaning on a window sill with a JD in one hand and a cigarette in another was responsible for this impeccably balanced, cleverly structured, sassy, sexy piece of guitar work. It sounded like it was played by some American session man on five grand an hour.

'Hey, cool stuff,' I muttered, trying my best not to turn green from jealousy.

'Isn't it fab?' squeaked one of the girls, approaching us and beaming at Mark.

'Yeah, yeah, way to go,' I said quietly.

'You man from the Storm Angels?' Mark asked me.

'Yeah,' I said. 'I kinda left a few weeks ago but they want me back now...'

I didn't finish, because Theodora came up to us, saying, 'Joey, could you help me bring in the champagne?'

'Sure,' I said, following her out of the room, into the hall and down the corridor into an enormous kitchen, the kind that you see on covers of interior design magazines – a mixture of granite worktops, mahogany, and chrome.

As Theodora began taking one champagne bottle after another from a huge General Electric fridge, I asked her with a forced laugh, 'What's the deal with Mark? Is he a rising star?'

She turned around and looked me in the eye with an earnest expression, in fact, almost too earnest. I felt slightly taken aback.

'I don't know,' she said slowly. 'Nobody knows. Time will tell. They are not signed yet.'

The way she said it made me panic. I wanted to ask her if she found him attractive. If she would go to bed with him if he became a star. If she would go to bed with him the way things were now. If she thought he was a better guitarist than me. If she thought he was a better man.

But instead I said, 'Who are the girls?'

Theodora laughed.

'They are friends of Mark's band. Hangers-on, you know. They are harmless little girls.'

Suddenly I heard a very loud, very drunk voice shouting, 'Daahlin'!!' behind my back, and as I turned around, I saw a tall, dark guy appear in the kitchen door, his arms flung open, beaming at Theodora, the stench of booze all around him, his eyes glinting. He must have been in his late teens, and to be completely honest, I've never seen such a good-looking dude before. (And I'm not even remotely gay, so that you know). The guy's only flaw was that he was too thin, but his features were perfect – a Roman nose, a round and perfectly proportioned chin that was neither too macho, nor too feminine, and a boho haircut that must have cost a fortune – moppy top, long fringe, and even longer layered sides falling just below his chin, emphasising the perfect cheekbones.

He went up to Theodora, squeezed her hard and kissed her on both cheeks, then turned to me and said, 'Hey, dude!!' beaming at me like I was his best friend.

'Hey,' I said, feeling a little disoriented.

I didn't know if I was supposed to hate this guy or accept him as my long-lost twin brother. I went with my gut feeling and smiled at him.

'Come back to the drawing room!' yelled the bloke before disappearing and leaving me staring at Theodora.

She laughed.

'It's Chris,' she said. 'He's the bass player in Mark's band. Half-Spanish, half-Scottish. Grew up in Hampstead.'

'How do you know all these people?' I asked. 'I thought I knew all the rockers, but I've never heard of these guys.'

'I go to a lot of gigs,' Theodora said evasively.

'Are you a big rock fan?' I asked.

'Yes,' she said. 'You could call me a rock fan. Plus I'm doing a bit of work for Daddy...'

She hesitated, as if about to add something, but that was it.

'What kind of work?'

'Scouting for cool bands now and then...' She smiled shyly.

'Wow,' I said.

'Can you help me take these champagne bottles back there?' she asked, changing the subject.

Back in the drawing room Chris was surrounded by the girls tugging at his sleeves, touching his hair, and looking into his mouth, giggling and hanging on to his every word as he was talking about something incomprehensible.

Mark sat on the floor next to a fireplace rolling a spliff. I sat down on the floor next to him.

'Dig your band, man,' I said to him.

He smiled at me and I suddenly thought that I haven't seen such a sincere, cool smile in a long time. Maybe since I left Colchester a year ago.

'Your band is amazing,' he said to me. 'Seen you support Silver Cats last year, you guys have blown me away.'

I suddenly felt an urge to tell him all about Doug, and our songwriting, and Global Union, and my dilemma, but I bit my tongue, and said, 'Thanks, man. It ain't always that easy.'

Mark lit the spliff, had one drag and passed it on to me. I appreciated the gesture, had one drag myself and passed it back. The guy may have been in his teens, but he behaved like a gentleman. I suddenly didn't know what to say to him. I had two options – to be straight and honest, and warn him against all the manipulating money-grabbing managers, and all the assholes and leeches he was bound to come across on his way to the top, or I could simply have had one of those shallow, meaningless conversations I was always having with other musicians.

He stunned me by suddenly asking, 'Dig the new Jeff Beck album?'

Wow, that I didn't expect. I've forgotten how to have normal conversations with people about things that really mattered – like great music, great work by people who've inspired me to pick up the guitar in the first place, real creativity, things more important than the usual shallow gossip about who is shagging who, and who paid how much to go on tour supporting a chart band. So we sat there on the floor talking about Jeff Beck, and Jimmy Page, and Stevie Ray Vaughan, and Al Dimeola, and John MacLaughlin, and I kept wondering how come this kid knew how to have a normal human conversation, and I, being older, have forgotten all about being myself, about being spontaneous? Again, I felt an urge to warn him about all the hangers-on, whores, and show biz turds who made you paranoid, turned you into a liar and a freak, but for some reason I didn't.

'So how do you know Theodora?' I asked him.

'My mother designed jewellery for her mother,' he said simply, sending a puff of smoke up to the ceiling.

'Wow,' I said. 'Cool.'

I didn't know what to say next. I suddenly realised what I knew all along but chose not to acknowledge – Mark was an upper middle class kid, just like Theodora. What kind of jewellery could his mother design for someone like Theodora's mom? Surely not a silver peace sign pendant.

Suddenly I heard a new voice behind my back, and as I turned, I saw Arthur Molsey, the editor of Global Rock, enter the room – his bald head shining, his jeans ripped in all the right places, his t-shirt saying "Aerosmith 1989 World Tour". I got to my feet, god knows why, and so did Mark, even though he certainly had no idea who Arthur was. Chris tore himself away from the girls and made a few shaky steps towards Arthur, beaming, while the girls stared at Arthur with a mixture of fear and interest on their faces. Arthur came up straight to me, put his arm around my shoulder, and I couldn't help shuddering, not from knowing that Arthur was openly gay, which I have no bias against, or knowing what a slimy media whore he was, which didn't matter to me either after working with people like Doug, but mainly from knowing that this guy had connections that gave him access to the people Mark and I could only dream of ever shaking hands with.

'Joey, good to see you,' Arthur began saying to me, 'What's this whole confusion between you and Global?'

He never said "Between you and Doug", mind you, he said "Between you and Global". What a slimeball.

I made an incoherent noise, partly because I was stoned, partly because I really didn't want to talk to him.

He saw that perfectly, and said, 'Stop by my office sometime tomorrow. We'll talk. I'd like to help you, give you a bit of advice.'

At that moment I suddenly felt physically sick, covered my mouth a rushed out of the room.

Looking for the bathroom, I instinctively climbed up the stairs and then saw right door in front of me. I knelt by the toilet pan, threw up once, then again, both times remembering to hold my hair back, flushed the water, cleaned up the toilet seat with some toilet paper, flushed it too, then got up and looked at myself in the mirror above the sink. My hair looked OK, I was pale but that was OK too. What was unacceptable about my appearance were my eyes that looked completely wild – pupils dilated, staring back at me from the mirror with a helpless, nutty, confused expression.

'Shit,' I thought, 'I look like a homeless drug addict on the run.'

I splashed my face with cold water, then sat on the edge of the bath, staring in front of me. My vision was a bit blurred, but I could see shelves and shelves of vials, spray cans, boxes, and bottles with words *Chanel*, *YSL*, *Shu Uemura*, *Sisley*, *Dior*, and *Versace* on them.

'What am I doing here?' I suddenly had a stoned thought before getting up.

I forgot to turn the light off as I was leaving the bathroom, and it startled me when I saw two figures illuminated on the staircase once I opened the door. They were Theodora and Mark. Theodora's back was against the wall, and Mark was leaning over her as if about to kiss her neck, whispering something in her ear.

'Do you realise that I am six years older than you are?' I heard her whisper back to him with a laugh.

I rushed past them, and headed straight to the front door. All I wanted was get back home, get under my duvet and forget about it all. Forget about Theodora, forget about Mark and his über-cool band and the conversation we've just had, forget about this house and this evening, forget that I was a musician and thus a commodity, forget about Arthur fucking Molsey, his magazine and his incredible connections, forget about Doug, forget about rock'n'roll for a while. Because it was ultimately rock'n'roll that got me into this mess. Or maybe it wasn't rock'n'roll, maybe it was the fact that I was too fragile and thin-skinned to be in this business.

'Maybe I should go to the uni, something my dad has been insisting on for so long, get a degree, get a normal job, and forget about my dream,' I thought. Because it was my delusional dream that led me to meet this woman, led me into this house, and now made me feel embarrassed and worthless. I knew that no one's promised me anything that evening, no commitments were made, but I still felt used. I felt that I was provoked and then discarded and humiliated. Why did she invite me? To show me off to all those teenagers? Why was Arthur Molsey here? Was it all a part of a plot to sell me to Global?

With all those thoughts running through my head, I didn't notice how I bumped into a fat balding guy in the hall blocking my way out of the house.

'Wow, what's the rush?' the man shouted in a low, authoritative voice. 'Is your house on fire?'

I looked up and recognised Don Blackman, the photographer to all the stars, from the Seventies legends to the newest chart-toppers. I didn't know what to say to him or what to do.

'Sorry, dude,' I murmured.

'It's OK,' he said. 'Am I taking pictures of you too this evening?'

I opened my mouth to tell him to go fuck himself, but suddenly felt someone grab my hand. It was Theodora. She didn't say anything, just took me firmly by the hand and led me back into the house, through the hall and through the kitchen where Chris was snogging some girl, and into the garden.

Man, that garden was huge. There were flowers and a smell of what I thought was jasmine everywhere. She sat me down on a wooden bench near a rippling water feature, and without letting go of my hand looked me straight in the face, and when I tried to look away, took my face in both of her hands, and made me look at her. I suddenly felt my heart beat faster and had a thought that she was going to say something profound, so intense was the expression on her face. I suddenly felt like something was about to happen. Maybe, after all, I wasn't such a fool for coming here.

'Joey,' said Theodora. 'You are in no fit state to go anywhere. If there is one thing my parents have taught me, it's that you are responsible for your guests. I don't confiscate my intoxicated guests' car keys like my father does, but I can tell you that you are not going anywhere tonight. Let me take you to a guest bedroom. You'll sleep there and will go home tomorrow morning once you've sobered.'

'Is this what you were saying to Mark too?' I asked, trying to sound sarcastic.

'Mark is an infatuated kid,' she said. 'I phoned his mother, she's coming to pick him up.'

I felt like a right idiot.

'I am sorry, Theodra,' I said. 'I need to get home just because I'd be too embarrassed to face you in the morning. Let me go, I'll be fine.'

'You are not going anywhere,' she said. She then took me by the hand again and led me into the kitchen. Chris was there with his top off, the girl bending down to kiss his belly button.

'Chris,' said Theodora. 'Chris, you're going home with

Mark's mother, she'll be here in a minute, and she'll take you home. Emily, I called your mother, she too is coming over to pick you up.' She then opened the fridge door, took a small bottle of orange liquid out, and, without letting go of my hand, took me into the drawing room.

I didn't realise that while I was throwing up and talking to Theodora in the garden, a whole bunch of new people have arrived. Mark and Arthur Molsey were sharing a spliff as fat as a cigar, the girls were drunk, talking loudly to each other, Anita, the owner of the gallery where Theodora had her opening last night, was talking to the journo from ArtLine, and Don Blackman was taking pictures of a tall woman with a blond crew cut who I've never seen before, posing in front of a fireplace that was now lit. I recognised Sammy, the singer from Moondog Superstars, a band which had recently signed a deal with a major, standing alone in the middle of the room staring enviously at the spliff Mark and Arthur were sharing. The Beatles' *And Your Bird Can Sing* was coming out of the speakers.

'Don,' Theodora shouted, 'One shot of Joey, then *one* shot of Joey and me.'

Don appeared right in front of us, flash, flash, and the next thing I knew Theodora was leading me out of the room. She was still holding my hand. She led me up the stairs and opened the door to what turned out to be a guest bedroom. She then gave me the little bottle she had in her hand.

'Drink this,' she said. 'This is what all intoxicated rock stars drink before interviews or before going on stage. There's an en-suite bathroom, feel free use the tooth brush, it's new. You can take a shower if you want. Don't do a Hendrix on me.'

She smiled, and I smiled back. She suddenly seemed so cool and so beautiful.

'Don't go,' I said. 'I don't need a shower. I'll be a stinking rock star. Sit with me.' I smiled at her again and put my hand on her shoulder.

'Joey, I have a party to take care of,' she said. 'They need a hostess.'

80

I tried to put my arm around her waist, but she escaped.

'Good night,' she said, and kissed me on the forehead.

I saw her close the door behind her, and then fell on the bed in my clothes. I looked around me and saw a thick volume on the night stand with golden lettering across the scarlet jacket: *Aleister Crowley. MAGICK.* I opened it randomly and read the following at the top of the page: "Do what thou wilt shall be the whole of the law." The next thing I knew I was fast asleep.

IV

LOVE SONG

I woke up in the guest room of Theodora's house at half ten the next morning, still in my clothes, with Aleister Crowley's book on my chest. I left Theodora a note (I always carry with me a small notebook and a pen in case I think of cool lyrics) saying, "Dolly, thank you for looking after me last night. I've got a splitting headache, I'd better get home. I'll call you soon. Sorry for being such a pain. Love, J." Then I quietly slipped out of the house, went home and went to bed again, waking up only the next day.

Dave and Ben didn't know where I've been or what's been going on with me, but I was grateful they didn't ask any questions. Neither of them knocked on my bedroom door once the whole day. I don't know if it was tact or indifference, but I'd rather have an indifferent cunt leave me alone than a well-meaning friend get on my nerves and ask me questions, especially the ones I don't know the answers to. The first question any well-meaning friend would, of course, ask, would be, 'Where the hell have you been last night?' And my answer? 'At a friend's place?' That would, obviously, have been a lie because Theodora wasn't my friend, not by a long stretch. And if the person asking the question was my best friend in the world (and I don't even have a best friend, I don't think I've had one since I was eight), I'd say, 'I was at the house of a woman I'm falling in love with.' But was I falling in love with Theodora? To be honest, at the time I didn't even know what love was. I knew what lust was, sure, I knew what infatuation was, I was even

familiar with obsession, but love? No, I had no clue. Was I
thinking love was what my parents had? Sticking together after
twenty-five years, still enjoying each other's company? Or was it
an irrational feeling that made you do ridiculous things, such as
throwing an enormous wedding reception like in some Eighties
music video? Did I think it was in poetry, like Auden's? But at the
time Auden to me was just another guy they told you about at
school, who'd send you to sleep after the first page or two. Did I
think it was in music, like Hendrix's or Stevie Ray Vaughan's? To
me they have always been geniuses, but I had a suspicion that their
music wasn't about love for a woman, but about being in love with
god or with the universe, or whatever you feel in love with when
high on your own creativity. I sometimes wondered if knowing
what love was made Sandy a better guitarist than me. But there
was no way of knowing that, at least for me.

From time to time I was still able to step back and think
rationally about the situation, just for a few moments, and then it
would occur to me that Theodora probably did find me attractive.
Or maybe she thought that I had a potential as a musician. I
wondered if she ever heard any of the Storm Angels demos. On the
other hand, it could have been that she wasn't attracted to me at all
and was simply feeling sorry for me.

The truth was, I didn't know what I felt for Theodora at the
time. I was fascinated by her, and wanted to spend more time
getting to know her, but the party at her house really intimidated
me. It was strange how we both belonged to the same world
defined by music, but the difference between us couldn't have been
greater. She belonged to the very top of the hierarchy (was it really
Don Blackman at her party? I still couldn't quite believe it), while I
was struggling at the very bottom.

From time to time I was still able to step back and think
rationally about the situation, just for a few moments, and then it
would occur to me that Theodora probably did find me attractive.
Or maybe she thought that I had a potential as a musician. I
wondered if she ever heard any of the Storm Angels demos. On the
other hand, it could have been that she wasn't attracted to me at all
and was simply feeling sorry for me.

Even though I had her number, I couldn't bring myself to
ring Theodora for a week after the party. At the same time I
couldn't stop thinking about her. I would think back to that

evening and remember her looking magically beautiful. I also realised that a lot of things intimidated me about her, not least her confidence and her wealth, to the point where I wished she had less of both, so that I could feel better in my own skin being around her. Sometimes I wondered if I was really meant to become a rock star if all it took to overawe me was a rich, beautiful, confident woman.

I thought about Theodora most nights. She was in my fantasies and my daydreams even when it made me tired and at times nauseous. And sometimes I would suddenly see a perfect image in my mind of her and me as a couple – me an international rock star, a millionaire, and her – my girlfriend, someone who added to the definition of who I was, the woman who inspired admiration for what I've achieved, even in those who knew nothing about rockn'n'roll or thought it to be losers' music. Did I think I stood a real chance with her? I didn't know. But in the end I figured that I'd never find out unless I asked.

I called Theodora a ten days after the party to ask if she wanted to meet me for a coffee. When I dialled her number, it rang out, no one picked up, and I was left with an option to leave a voice message, which I didn't. I tried again the next day, but her phone was switched off, so it went straight to her voicemail, and I finally left a message, my voice as blasé and unconcerned as I could make it sound, saying, 'Hi, Dolly, I just wanted to see how you are. Hope everything's cool.'

After that all I had to do was wait for her to call me back. She ever did. After another week had passed, I began to panic. At that point I didn't know what to do. I felt like I've blown it. I felt like a complete idiot who tried to play games with one woman no one in their right mind would play games with. I rang her again a few times, left messages, but she still wouldn't return my calls. Now that she became inaccessible, all I wanted was to see her. I suddenly felt completely sick. Lovesick. *Now* I knew I was falling in love. I couldn't think of anything else but her.

Doug kept calling and I wasn't taking his calls. I felt that if I accepted his deal, people would lose the little respect they had for me, and Theodora would be the first one to do so. Even more importantly, I knew I'd lose all respect I had for myself if I accepted. And with that – what I had left of my confidence. I knew that I'd never be able to approach someone like her if I was in on this contract.

Three weeks after the party at Theodora's house I went out with Dave and Ben, got completely wasted, started hitting on some minging girls (they all seemed minging compared to Theodora), then got disgusted with myself, went home, got stoned and even more drunk, and went to bed. That night I had an ugly dream. It was about being at a wedding ceremony which for some reason was taking place on the stage of Albert Hall, with five thousand people in the audience watching the proceedings lit by nothing else but an enormous chandelier hung from the ceiling above the stage, spotlighting the bride and the groom. I was in the front row trying to make out the bride's face. Suddenly she turned to me and I recognised Theodora. Her face and her veil were covered in blood. I then saw that the groom was Jim Morrison, and immediately realised that he was dead, a corpse, and that he had strings attached to his arms and legs, and that Doug Scrivener was the guy pulling at them, sitting on the chandelier. Theodora was marrying a dead rock god. Then I heard the music. A brass band on the left side of the stage began playing *Five to One* by the Doors. I woke up petrified.

My nightmares continued since that night. I'd dream about dead rock stars walking around like zombies, witches who made them shoot their fans from the stage with machine guns, demons offering me trunks of gold in exchange for my notebook with lyrics, and naked blind nymphs who looked like Shawna, with green scabby skin and hands covered in blood trying to steal my guitar. I'd wake up sweating and cramping in the middle of the night, turn the light on and try to read, but would soon fall back into sleep, no matter how hard I tried to stay awake, and the nightmare would continue from where it ended.

I knew this had to stop. I knew I was going to pieces because I couldn't resolve the situation with Theodora, and I hated myself for not being able to do anything about it. Sometimes, after waking up from a particularly nasty dream, I'd wonder if I really deserved to be a rock star. A lot of times I felt like a good-for-nothing useless geek, the same nerd everyone picked on at school all those years ago. I felt I didn't deserve fuck. I felt like I've lost this woman because I doubted myself. And the silliest part of it was that all this time I've been secretly hoping she would get in touch with me first. I hoped she'd be the one chasing me. Which began to seem completely irrational by the end of the third week. On the one hand I wasn't sure I was good enough for her, and on the other – I was waiting for her to pursue me.

While I was despairing and trying to think of what I could do, I still practiced every day, maybe even more than I ever did before. Four weeks after I've last seen Theodora, just before Christmas, I suddenly wrote a really good song. It was a ballad and it was the first time in my life I've written an entire song, complete with verses, a chorus, a guitar solo and the lyrics. It wasn't a rip-off of any other song, it was completely original, and both Dave and Ben were telling me it sounded great. Only after I've written it did I realise that this ballad was about Theodora. For the first time in a month I finally felt good. I was even proud of myself. At least something worthwhile has come of this mess. Dave by that time had gotten a job with a recording studio in Primrose Hill, and offered me to come over one Sunday when no one was there to record the song. He didn't have to offer twice, so three days later I was there, ringing the bell of an inconspicuous narrow door in a cul-de-sac just a few minutes walk from Primrose Hill tube. You would never have guessed this was the place where all the rock stars I adored have recorded at one time or another. Dave opened the door telling me he was there alone, taking me into a small reception. There was nothing there apart form a worn-out leather sofa and a flat TV screen, but what really grabbed your attention once you entered were dozens of framed album covers on the walls – from those by the early Sixties psychedelia pioneers who went on to become huge stars in the Seventies, to major American Eighties stadium acts. Those were the people who have recorded here over the years. There was an eerie feel to the contrast between the unassuming, almost shabby interior and the evidence on the walls of unimaginable power and glory this place was capable of generating. I, of course, realised, that it wasn't the place itself that was responsible for the genius music that came out of it, and it wasn't even the equipment, or the engineers, or the producers who worked there, but musicians who chose this place to record. Still, to me it was akin to a shrine, somewhere where real magic could happen at any moment. A place where you went to work once you became successful. Somewhere where gods went to create the world as we know it. Or at least my world the way I knew it then.

It didn't take us long to make the CD. We first recorded the acoustic guitar track, then I did the vocals and finally some electric guitar overdubs, and three hours later I had a CD in my hand that had a simple, no-frills but, I hoped, still compelling version of my song. I posted it off to Theodora straight after we came out of the studio, putting in a note that said, "Dolly, I couldn't get in touch properly until I had something meaningful to say. This song is for you. Please answer your phone the next time I ring." Dave thought I was sending it to a record label and I didn't want to tell him otherwise.

I bought Dave a pint in a pub across the road from the studio, and he told me how in the Seventies it used to be one of the best in London, and even remained that for the most part of the Eighties, but A-list acts stopped recording there almost fifteen years ago.

'How come you don't get any big names anymore?' I asked him.

'Our desks are out of date,' Dave said, 'and we can't afford new equipment. Really big bands on corporate budgets don't record with us anymore, so these days we get mostly indie bands on modest money or heavy metal acts. We can't compete with the new technology anymore.'

Has there ever been a girl who didn't respond to a rocker writing a love song for her? It turned out that if there ever have been any, Theodora was one of them. A week after I posted the CD to her, I still haven't heard back. Christmas came and went, and I spent it in London alone, having told my parents that I couldn't get away from work. The truth is that I just couldn't face going home, sitting down with my family for Christmas dinner and having to lie about still having a job and being in a band. Spending New Year's Day on my own in the flat (both Ben and Dave went home for holidays), drinking cheap vodka and watching children's movies on TV was my lowest point. I guess after that I just didn't care any more. I called Theodora on the second of January. This time she picked up the phone.

'Hey, Joey,' she said. 'How are you?'

'I'm good, thanks,' I said, trying hard to suppress the bitter overtones in my voice. 'How've you been? Haven't heard from you in a while.'

'I've been busy with coursework...' she started saying, but I interrupted her, unable to contain my annoyance anymore, her casual voice and her indifferent tone making me want to tell her how miserable she's been making me feel all those weeks.

'Did you get my CD?' I blurted out, looking for an excuse to lash out.

'I did,' she said. 'Thank you. I liked that tune.'

That's all she had to say about the song I've written for her. There was a pause.

'So...' I said, still somehow able to control myself, thinking of what to say next, and trying really hard not to yell at her, call her a name, or say something I'd later regret. 'Will I be able to see you sometime soon?'

'Let me see,' she said slowly. 'I don't know.'

All I wanted now was to strangle her. There was nothing I felt for her now but pure hatred. I even hated her West Coast American accent.

But I still somehow managed not to let it show, saying, 'Look, Theodora, I really need to talk to you. I'm sorry it looks like I'm pestering you, but I really need to speak to you.'

There was silence on the other end of the line, and then I heard her breathe in deeply.

'I am going to a gig at 100 Club on Oxford Street next Wednesday,' she finally said. 'You could come along too.'

When I hung up, I was seething, but I least I knew I managed to get something out of this conversation. I just didn't know why she was making it so hard for me. What have I done? Written a song for her? And at that moment I realised that I now wanted to see her more than ever before.

When I finally saw Theodora at 100 Club the next week, it turned out I have almost forgotten how she looked. All those weeks I've been constantly brining up an image of her in my mind that became more and more blurred with each day that passed. When I finally saw her again after such a long break, I realised that she was more beautiful than I could ever remember in my daydreams. For the first few moments it was difficult for me to even look her in the face, so dazzled I was by her all over again. She was with a friend, a plump Japanese girl who didn't say much but kept smiling at me. I came up to Theodora and tried to kiss her, but she had to lean over to her friend at that very moment to tell her something, so my attempt was suspended half-motion, and, not knowing what to do, I just ended up staring helplessly at the

Japanese girl.

'Listen, Theodora,' I said, 'I am sorry for disappearing for a few days after that party. I just felt... You, know, I didn't feel well, I was ill for some time...'

'I'm sorry to hear that,' she replied, looking completely indifferent. 'Are you feeling better now?'

'Well, you know, about that song I sent you... I wrote it for you...'

I stopped, waiting for her to say something, but she didn't. I decided that I wasn't going to continue either.

'It's a beautiful piece of music,' she finally said casually. 'By the way, how is it going with your record deal?'

'I haven't been thinking about that really,' I said. 'All I was thinking about for the last couple of weeks was that song.'

Her face suddenly looked serious and she nodded.

'Joey, I have to go now,' she said. 'Let's talk later.'

The next thing I knew I was on my own, watching some lame indie band on stage, wondering what I had done to deserve all this. I now knew that she agreed to meet me out of pity. I only wondered why she didn't just say to me, 'Joey, you're a nice enough guy, but I don't feel the way you do.'

As I walked home, I felt shattered, but at the same time relieved. I knew that Theodora never cared about me and that I could stop worrying about it all now. I could start forgetting her. I could heal my wounds and move on. I could focus on my own life now. I could start thinking about my career again. I could start thinking about getting a job. I could stop living in a daydream.

When I got home, I sat on the living room sofa for a while, had a few beers, and tried to think of what to do next. I was going to call Doug the next day and tell him on what terms I was going to sign. I wanted one third of his publishing. I knew I wasn't going to feel good about myself with this deal, but I least I would get some money. Enough money to live like a human being, not like a tramp.

Enough money to buy some decent art to hang in a decent flat in a decent area of London. Enough money for a decent car. I wanted a... Ferrari. I didn't want a Lamborghini or something ridiculous to draw attention to myself with. But I wanted a Ferrari so that any son of a bitch would know that I wasn't just another nobody anyone could take advantage of.

I woke up at quarter to ten the next morning feeling calm and almost happy. The next thing I knew, my phone was going off. It was Theodora. At first I decided not to answer, but then did take it just before it was supposed to stop ringing.

'Morning, Joey,' I heard her voice that suddenly sounded beautifully soft. 'How are you?'

'Good, thanks,' I replied. 'How are *you*?'

'I'm great, thanks. What are your plans for this weekend?'

'This weekend?' I repeated, like a moron.

'Yea, this weekend. I was planning to paint my drawing room this weekend and was wondering if you could help me...'

'Sure, no problem!' I exclaimed without thinking.

'I want to paint it white. It was cream before.'

'Sure, I'd love to help! Have you got the paint already or do you want me to get some?'

'No-no, it's OK,' she said. 'I've got paint. All you have to do is show up.'

'Consider me there,' I said.

'That's great, I really appreciate it,' she said. 'Come over Saturday morning. We'll have breakfast together.'

As I was putting the phone back into my pocket, I didn't have a single thought in my head. I just knew that I was wildly happy.

When I arrived on Theodora's doorstep on Saturday morning, she opened the door wearing a lilac kimono, her hair like liquid silk flowing down her shoulders, looking absolutely dazzling. She was smiling at me, almost laughing, her eyes connecting with mine, as if saying, 'Nothing in the whole world makes me happier than seeing you again.' I just had to come up to her and hug her, even though I've decided earlier, while still on my way to Hampstead, that I was going to be cool and reserved, act the way I usually did with Ben or Dave, and try to avoid showing much emotion. That was when the euphoria brought on by her phone call has slightly subsided, but hasn't completely worn off for me to change my mind about going to her house. So as I was leaving home that morning, I knew I was going to be polite, friendly, and helpful, but by no means gushing. Once I saw her, of course, all my planning went out of the window. I suddenly felt totally overwhelmed by her presence. I hugged her, kissed her on both cheeks, and again inhaled the exquisite perfume I first smelled in Jean-Pierre's car almost two months ago. She laughed, and then gently pushed me away. We went into the house, and she offered me breakfast. I said no to pancakes, but we had coffee together, while I was telling her about Doug pestering me about the deal (she laughed when I told her how I've been ignoring his calls making him leave desperate messages), and how I was now writing songs, and how I thought it was because of her. She didn't talk much, but each time she smiled I felt like I was being washed over by a soft, warm wave of affection. I didn't notice how I just kept talking, almost the way I sometimes talk to myself, only this time – out loud, until I realised that she's finished her coffee and was probably just waiting politely for me to stop babbling. I felt awkward.

'Well, look at me talk,' I said. 'Why don't you show me what needs to be done.'

'Ah, I like listening to you,' she replied. 'But yeah, let me show you the paint I've bought. In fact, I didn't go out to the shops to choose it, I bought it online. That's terrible laziness, isn't it?' And when she smiled, I nearly said, 'I love laziness!' a second later feeling glad I didn't. I knew I've said enough stupid things that morning already.

Once I was done painting the room (that room was huge, so it took me almost the entire day), she asked me if I wanted to stay for dinner. Staying for dinner, of course, went against everything I've been planning and telling myself that morning before leaving home, but I simply couldn't say no. I guess if she asked me if I wanted to stay there forever, I would, without even going back to my flat to collect my stuff.

She cooked a stir-fry (I would never have thought someone like her could cook, and so well too), and we had a bottle of Rioja with it, and talked about the musicians we both knew – Dirty Lick, Lightning Blast, Sandy and his manager, and my manager Doug, before she began telling me about all the rock stars she grew up seeing at her parents' house, and all the movie stars that were coming to their dinner parties, and rock stars' children she went to school with.

'Most rock stars' kids can't spell,' she said authoritatively. 'And that's not because any money has been spared on their education.'

'So why can't they spell?' I asked.

'Who needs to know how to spell when your daddy is a rock legend?' Theodora answered, laughing, with just a very slight note of annoyance in her voice.

'So tell me how come you are so good at it all – creative ideas, art, highbrow stuff?'

'Ah, it's a different ethos altogether. My father didn't make his money by displaying his emotions to the whole wide world,' she said. 'He made his money and a name for himself by using his brain.'

At half eleven I didn't want to go, but I knew I had to because the underground stops running stupidly early in London.

On my way home I was missing her already, wondering if

there really was any chance for me ending up going out with someone like her.

Since that day I began seeing a lot of Theodora, and if you asked me then if we were in a relationship, I wouldn't have known what to say. Luckily (or unfortunately) no one asked me that at the time.

Sometimes I'd bring my guitar down to her house and show her the songs I've written. She listened, said she liked them, fed me dinner and kept telling me that those who write their own material end up having it all. Sometimes I'd sit with my guitar in her drawing room, playing a new tune, and she would come up to me, wrap her arms around my shoulders, and kiss me on the forehead. I didn't care about anything anymore apart from spending time with her, and I've told her a million times that I loved her, earnestly to her face and thousands of times in my songs. She never said anything to that, but the way she looked at me sometimes convinced me that my feelings weren't entirely unreciprocated. There was one time I'll never forget when I finished playing another song I've written for her, when she suddenly took my hand in hers and kissed it. It felt almost like an electric shock – so unexpected and so spontaneous that I responded without thinking, cupped her face in my hands, and kissed her on the lips for the first time. It felt amazing. I was so into it that I almost forgot how to breathe and nearly ended up fainting.

She withdrew soon though, saying, 'Wow, Joey, that's too intense for me... '

I didn't say anything, didn't insist on anything. I guess I thought that the time wasn't right for us to go any further. But some irrational part of me was telling me that one day things would change.

Meanwhile Doug was pressuring me to give him an answer. We've had a few strained conversations over the phone where every time I had to finish it first because he was beginning to get impatient and push me just a bit too hard for my liking. I could tell he was desperate and perplexed as to why I was dragging my feet. It gave me a sort of perverted satisfaction to see this guy go from begging to almost threatening me within a space of just a few minutes, and it certainly delighted me to know that I had an upper hand in the game this loser was trying to play with me.

One evening, a few weeks after I've helped Theodora paint her drawing room, when I was down at her place again moaning about Doug chasing me about the GU deal, she offered to do a tarot reading for me. We went into her bedroom, the part of the house I've never been to before – a huge room where an enormous Persian carpet on the floor was the central feature, with a pattern so complex and intricate, you could only follow it if you looked at it from a distance. We sat on the floor, surrounded by candles she lit, and cut flowers that were everywhere – on her dressing table, in large Chinese vases on the floor, by the sides of her king-size bed, on the coffee table, and on window sills. She gave me a pack of cards to shuffle and told me to concentrate on my question. I tried to focus on the deal Doug was offering me, on Doug, on the guys in the band, and on Global Union, or what I've heard of them, which wasn't much. I became so absorbed in this that I almost forgot I was supposed to hand the cards back to her.

'Joey,' I suddenly heard her voice. 'Joey, are you ready?'

'Yes,' I said. 'Here you go.'

She held the cards in her hands for a few moments, and then fanned the entire pack in front of me.

'Pick ten cards,' she said. 'And as you do, hand them back to me one by one.'

'Wow!' she said as I handed her the first card.

'Is this bad?' I asked anxiously.

'No-no, keep going,' she said.

'Ha!' she exclaimed as I passed her the second one.

'Oh please, stop torturing me,' I said. 'Just tell me what it means.'

'I can't until I've seen all the cards,' she said thoughtfully.

She finally had all ten cards I've picked in front of her, arranged in a cross-shaped figure.

'Well,' she began. 'You're destined for greatness.'

I sniggered.

'No,' she said, smiling. 'Look, here is *The World* and *The Wheel of Fortune* – the cards that stand for triumph and success. Both are in your future. And I see a woman represented by *The High Priestess* who is going to help you achieve that.'

She then looked fixedly at me. I stared back pretending I didn't know what she was talking about.

'Don't do that,' she said, knitting her eyebrows. 'Just listen. The cards show some kind of a block in your life right now, an obstruction that really has little to do with the objective reality, more with your frame of mind. There's a man who is a very negative influence, who keeps promising things to you, but who will never deliver. If you follow the path he's offering you, your career will end in a disaster.'

'Is his name Doug?' I asked, smiling.

Theodora pushed the cards away, looked me in the eye and said, 'Joey, one doesn't have to be a tarot reader to tell you that what Doug is offering you is the worst deal in the world.'

'Why?' My voice suddenly began to sound defensive. 'At least I'll get to work with the producers who know what they are doing, never mind the fact that they are *name* producers. I'll get to put out a record that will be sold in actual *stores*. I will get to tour the world. I'll get reviews in the magazines that matter.'

'And what will those reviews say?' Theodora asked me with a wry smile.

I tried to read her face to see if she knew.

'Hopefully they will say that I'm not such a bad guitarist,' I finally said.

'No!' She shouted, throwing the rest of the pack flying across the room. It was the first time I saw her show temper. 'They will say that you are another Milli Vanill! Some shmuck from Global Rock, not even Rolling Stone, because Rolling Stone would never touch you, some shmuck from Global Rock will point his grubby finger at you and call you a Milli Vanilli! No one's gonna notice or care how well you play! Guitar magazines wouldn't want to interview you. People like Satch would go "Who?" when asked what they think of you. Don't you understand?'

'Well, what choice do I have?' I began, now feeling wound up too. 'Tell me, Theodora, what choice do I have? You seem to know everything about this business, so tell me. I'll tell you how it is for me – I can't stay on the dole for much longer. Either I put my foot through the door pretty soon or I would have to either go the university, get trained for some profession that has no relevance to who I am, or go into full-time work. Neither of which I want to do. I am a musician, not a lawyer, or a civil engineer, or a chef. I belong on stage. If I do anything else with my life, I'll end up being so miserable I'll either become an alcoholic or a manic depressive. Or both. Music for me isn't something I want to do out of vanity or because I crave social status. I do it because otherwise my life would be ruined, and I would become an emotional cripple, like some of those miserable losers who run their tiny grimy music venues in Camden. I will become a disillusioned failure who hates all young people with a spark of talent and a chance of success.'

'Oh, the drama,' smiled Theodora cooly, even though I could tell that my little speech did make an impression.

'You know, if I had money, it wouldn't be such a drama,' I said bitterly. 'If I had money, it would buy me the two years I need to get from being a guitarist with a potential to being a brilliant guitarist *and* a real songwriter. I need two more years to become that.'

'Joey, this is very admirable,' began Theodora. 'But...'
'But what?'

'Ah, forget it,' she said.

'No, tell me,' I insisted. 'But what?'

'Listen, it doesn't matter, what I want to tell you is something different. You are so wrapped up in this little world, the London scene, you really need to see what lies beyond all that.'

'What do you mean?'

'I mean that maybe you should come out to LA with me and see what's there. There are zillions of bands there playing in all styles, people get signed there all the time, the whole scene is different. You'll get more experience, you'll have more options, it'll be easier for you to find what you need there.'

'You know, Theodora, I'd love to do that,' I said. 'I'd love to go and live in LA for a bit, I'd love to get out of London, I'd love to play with musicians in the States. But I can't even afford the air fare there. So forget it. Just let me do what I need to do right now. No one's gonna call me a Milli Vanilli. No one calls Ronnie Wood that, right? And he doesn't write that many songs for his band either.'

'Oh, everyone knows who can do what in any given band, trust me,' said Theodora, sounding annoyed. 'Including all the people you are mentioning. At least with Wood you know it's him playing. And it's the people in his band who write the songs. You are missing the point. The point is – why do you feel you need to pay for your ticket? I thought we were a couple.' And she looked at me so innocently as she said it, that I almost began to doubt if I heard her right.

'Are we really?' I asked, staring at her.

'Why, you don't think so?' she asked in an almost offended tone.

'No-no-no, it's just that... we've never...'

She scrutinised my face for a moment and then said, 'Joey, I should have probably told you this before, but I don't believe in sex before marriage. That's all. But I thought that we were still a couple. I thought that you understood.'

Marriage? I nearly flipped. In all those months I've known

Theodora, the thought of marriage had never occurred to me.

I opened my mouth to speak, but she interrupted me.

'I just think we need to get to know each other really, really well before we venture into anything. And going to LA together could make that happen. You could stay in my apartment there. I will let my family know about you. In fact, I'll let all my friends know too.'

And as she said those last words, the weirdest smile I've ever seen appeared on her face – I've never seen her, or anyone else, smile like this before, and it almost scared me. Was it deep-seated viciousness I suddenly saw? Was it a grimace of pain? Or some kind of exquisite pleasure? I just didn't know how to interpret it. But she didn't seem to notice that I've noticed, or maybe she simply didn't care.

'And would you please call Doug and tell him you're out,' she said to me with a mixture of playfulness and irritation, perfectly composed now, as we walked out of her bedroom.

I kept thinking about our conversation on my way home. I was amazed that she considered me her boyfriend and was inviting me to LA. And I was thrilled at the prospect of going there. But at the same time the no-sex-before-marriage thing scared me, and I didn't know what to make out of her being so confident that I was really going to have some kind of career in LA. More opportunities there than in London? But didn't they have more brilliant musicians there per square mile than in any other place in the world? I knew that competition there was ten times fiercer than in London. So her offer didn't make me completely stop thinking about Doug's deal.

V

THE SEER OF ESSEX

The next day Theodora and I were going to a gig in Islington she said she absolutely had to be at. Mark's band was headlining, and Chrome Dew, an outfit from Essex, were supporting. Jean-Pierre was flying in from Paris to check out both acts. I was looking forward to talking to him, feeling that being Theodora's boyfriend gave me a different kind of status altogether. Maybe I could even ask him for an advice about my career. Somehow, amazingly, I thought that I *was* Theodora's boyfriend now, despite her making it clear there was no chance for me to find myself anywhere near her bedroom any time again soon.

I was trying to make myself read a fresh issue of Kerrang seated on Theodora's drawing room sofa waiting for her to get dressed. But all I could really think about was the proposed trip to LA. I've never been to the States and I couldn't even imagine what it was like there. All the tall tales I've read in the Eighties LA rock star autobiographies seemed to me little more than clever marketing ploys devised to sell more records and concert tickets for those who wrote them. Did I believe all the stories of wild sex, near-death experiences, and fantastic twists of fate described in those books? I certainly did believe all that was possible, and most likely did happen in one form or another, but I didn't believe it was all there was to those people's lives. Sometimes what you leave out is just as telling as what you choose to tell about. So in no way did I assume I knew anything about LA, the music scene there, or America in general. And I was very aware that I didn't know a soul there apart from Theodora.

I then noticed that she's been gone for some time, wondering what was taking so long. I knew she usually wouldn't spend more than twenty minutes to get ready to go out. So when she finally entered the room, I almost gasped at how magnificent she looked. She wore a sleeveless pale grey chiffon dress with hem ending just above the knees, and a wide golden corset-like belt. Her hair was falling over the low neckline in a cascade of multi-coloured curls – black, brown, golden, and white, her face shimmering, dusted with snow-white glittery powder, and her eyelashes suddenly sparkling with overtones of blood-red and purple as she turned her head to the window, letting me see her flawless profile, asking in a suddenly changed, husky voice, 'How do I look?'

Kerrang with Slipknot on the front cover dropped out of my hand, and all I could do was stare. She looked like a porcelain doll whose hair and face have been painted by a quirky fairy – ultra-feminine, artificial, over the top, but completely mesmerising. It was one of those looks I always found irresistible, the kind you'd never see in the streets or in crowds at gigs – girliness taken to its utmost point, to the degree of an absurd farce, of being unnatural, but in the end going full circle in its extremity only to start expressing nothing else but maturity. Because it takes confidence of an adult to carry off this look with total disregard for any clichés or conventions. This, I knew, was art in its purest, boldest form. I've never seen Theodora make so much effort with the way she looked, and I was amazed at the audacity of her imagination. This was a side to her I've never known before – brave, daring, and absolutely enigmatic.

'So how do I look?' she asked again, coming closer and now standing in front of me with her feet in golden platforms wide apart. Close enough for me to smell her perfume.

'Ah, you look stunning,' I said, and then paused, not being able to think of anything else to say. 'If you wore a necklace, it would look awesome,' I added, just to say something.

She sat next to me on the sofa and touched my neck.

I was about to turn to kiss her when she said, 'Can I borrow your chain for this evening?'

I was wearing a thick silver link chain that ended with a massive padlock – a staple piece of jewellery for rock musicians all over the world that year, something I bought when still in the Storm Angels.

'Sure,' I said, baffled, and about to take it off, when she moved ahead of me, and I felt her fingers touch the back of my neck, undoing the clasp. I pushed her gently onto the cushions, but before I managed to lean over her, she was already up, standing in front of me again, now wearing my chain which suddenly made a fantastic contrast with her soft flowing dress and her shiny multi-coloured curls.

'Looks cool,' I said, sighing.

'Come on, Joey, let's go,' she said, turning around and walking out of the room, the sound of her heels resonating against the tall sash windows and now echoing in the hall as she walked across the marble floor towards the front door.

The first person we saw once we arrived was Ed Sunders. As usual, he was overexcited, began shouting in my face about Doug going mental because of the Global deal, then stared in amazement at Theodora before trying to engage her in a conversation, but she brushed him off, taking my hand and walking away.

As we sat down at a table in the far end of the room, Mark and Chris came up to say hi. Even though both were excited to play what for them was an important gig, Mark looked like all he really wanted to do was talk to Theodora tête-à-tête. I was actually going to finally let him do that, beginning to feel sorry for the guy, but she then turned her back to him, introducing me to a thin blond guy who looked like he was miles away thinking about something else – a blue-eyed young kid with a scarf around his neck and a faraway look.

'This is Robert,' she said to me, 'He sings in Mark's band.'

Robert didn't stop to talk to us, and I could sense he was politely avoiding Theodora. She, by contrast, was very sweet to him – kissed him on both cheeks and squeezed his arm while wishing him good luck with the show. A moment later I saw her exchanging kisses with Jean-Pierre who's just arrived, dressed in jeans, a blue t-shirt and a black leather jacket. We barely had time to ask each other all the standard questions, when Ed Sunders suddenly sat himself down at our table right next to Jean-Pierre, grinning as he banged his pint of Guinness onto a beer mat. I was about to shoo him off when I realised that he and Jean-Pierre knew each other, and as it later turned out during the conversation, Jean-Pierre was interested in Ed's opinions about the bands that were playing that night. This amazed me because I've never thought of Ed as anything more than a loser and a hanger-on.

Then the music began.

The first band on was Chrome Dew, a hard rock outfit I have heard of but have never seen play live before. They have fired their bass player a few months ago and hired a female bassist instead – Sally, who was hugely popular on the unsigned London scene. She wasn't much of a bass player, but she was beautiful – blond, slender, and graceful. I've heard her family had quite a bit of money – they said her dad owned a courier company. I've even been out with her once, and she was the sweetest girl I've ever been on a date with – she didn't talk incessantly about herself, was a good listener and had lots of genuine compassion, kindness, and a quirky, cheeky sense of humour. I guess I could have fallen in love with her, but we never did have our second date because she joined Chrome Dew a few days later and began going out with their drummer Ron almost immediately.

I never liked Ron, even before he and Sally got together. There was something creepy about him, like the way he would stare at you while you'd be talking to someone else, but the moment you turned to him to make him join the conversation or just to see what on Earth he was doing gawping at you for, he'd immediately stop, pretending he wasn't looking at all. I caught him do that a few times and found it unsettling.

The other guys in this band I didn't know at all. Their singer, a heavy bloke with shoulder-length curly hair, turned out to be a generic wailer imitating Ian Gillan, while being completely unimaginative about it. Their guitarist, however, was something else. I knew pretty soon that the guy was a different kind of musician altogether. To begin with, his style didn't resemble anyone else on the scene, so unique and eccentric he was as a player. He was an exuberant, almost Hendrixian guitarist, playing purely on impulse all the way through the band's thirty-minute set, rather old-fashionly in terms that he didn't have any speed to speak of and didn't use any flashy technique, but what he did have to say was a million times more interesting than all the showy guitarists on the circuit put together. His leads were one hundred per cent pure improvisation delivered in a way that made you forget about comparisons with anyone else's style or about influences.

His appearance matched his playing. He was stick-thin, tall, with greasy blond hair, evidently not giving a toss about how he looked, and every note he played somehow found an expression on his face. I knew that there were musicians who played like that – Hendrix and Paul Gilbert to name just two, but I've never seen anyone do this live, and I thought you had to be American, and either super-successful or simply a genius to really let go like this. And by the end of Chrome Dew's set I still had no clue if this guy was a genius or a freak. I guess he could have been either if only he made his mind up.

Once Chrome Dew came off the stage, Jean-Pierre turned to Ed asking what he thought.

'Absolutely no hope for this band,' Ed said authoritatively as

Jean-Pierre raised an eyebrow. 'I'll tell you why,' he continued, suddenly beginning to sound like he's been rehearsing this. 'The material is too generic. The guitarist is too weird. No one wants to hear this kind of playing these days, it's too freakish. But the main thing really is that in two months' time this band won't be around. The girl is on a downward spiral – another spoilt rich girl. Always out of her head on drugs, spending shit loads of her daddy's money on that and on gambling, driving when high, running her car into pedestrians, getting into fights… And she's the only visual attraction this band has, the only one who can entertain. In two month's time she'll be either dead, in a rehab, or in prison. And without her this act is as good as non-existent.'

'Sally?' I gasped.

'The guitarist is too weird?' snarled Theodora.

Ed gave us a slow patronising nod.

I got up to go to the men's room, mainly because I didn't want to continue listening to Ed slagging off a great band.

As I was waiting in the queue, I suddenly remembered something that explained to me why Ed was talking what at first seemed like utter bollocks. A few months ago, before Sally joined Chrome Dew, Ed was trying to ask her out on a date. I knew that from Sally herself – Ed was trying to get his leg over, and once she told him she wasn't interested, Ed must have made an enemy out of her. So all those lies and venom must have been his revenge on Sally for turning him down.

The queue was moving slowly – there were three cubicles and no one's been coming out of the one at the far end. Suddenly a familiar noise began emerging from it, the kind you'd never mistake for anything else – barely audible gasps and whimpers at first, followed by semi-suppressed groans and grunts. By now everyone knew what was going on in there. Some guys in the queue smiled, some laughed. I grinned, wanting to know who was in there. This was nothing new to me – at rock shows you get slappers giving musicians blow jobs all the time, even full-on sex, no matter how talentless or destitute the musician is. I gave up trying to

106

understand the reasons for this a long time ago, basically concluding that women are incomprehensible and explaining it all with the old truism that rock'n'roll can get anyone laid. Suddenly the door of the cubicle opened and I saw Ron, Chrome Dew's drummer, Sally's boyfriend, coming out of it with his usually flat, sleek hair style now a mess, and sweat patches under the arms of his Motley Crue t-shirt. A couple of blokes in the queue – chavs in baggy jeans and ironed shirts (god only knows how they found their way to this show) greeted him with two or three half-sarcastic, half-admiring claps, a few musicians gave him fleeting glances full of either jealousy or contempt – I couldn't tell which – and I just looked the other way to let him know that I wasn't acknowledging his presence.

When he left, I realised that whoever Ron was shagging, was still remaining in the cubicle.

'That wouldn't have been Sally,' I suddenly thought.

So I decided to stay for as long as it would take me to find out who it was.

Ten minutes later she finally appeared – a dishevelled little trollop, no older than eighteen with her hair bleached white sticking out of her small head, her dull, empty eyes circled with black eyeliner, wearing a denim mini-skirt, a nylon leopard print top, ripped fishnets and plastic boots with worn-out heels. It took me less than a second to categorise this specimen. When I was in the Storm Angels, packs of girls like her were coming to our shows. They weren't even groupies, just silly little things with nothing else to do, no identity of their own, and no way of expressing themselves other than by copying some male Eighties rock star's hair cut, wearing animal print clothes and going to see bands like ours. If bands are defined by who their fans are, then the Storm Angels were the heroes of the lowlife trash pit. I suddenly felt happier than ever before about being out of that band. And then, for just one brief moment, I felt like coming up to the girl, slapping her primitive face and asking if she knew that Ron's girlfriend played bass in his band. But then, horrified and disgusted, more with myself than her or Ron, I turned around and almost ran out of the door.

I got back to our table somewhat shaken, but determined not to let it show. The only person I cared for in the episode I've just witnessed was Sally, but then I figured that it was her choice who she wanted to be with. So a few moments later I forgot almost all about it.

Meanwhile, Ed was prattling on about how he "keeps an eye" on all unsigned bands in London and how Jean-Pierre can ask him for information any time he wants, while writing down addresses of websites he was contributing to on a dirty napkin, presumably for Jean-Pierre to take away with him and keep on his office desk next to his phone at all times.

Theodora sat motionless throughout the conversation without saying a word. She was now looking in the direction of the bar, and I followed her gaze, seeing the guys from Chrome Dew trying to get drinks, which seemed almost impossible, as the bar was now besieged by dozens of punters wanting to talk to them.

'Let's get something to drink,' Theodora finally said, her face looking tense.

'Sure, what do you want?' I asked, getting up.

'I'll go with you,' she said.

Once at the bar, I found myself standing next to the Chrome Dew guitarist, who now looked even thinner than he did on the stage, his hair – greasier, and his clothes – dirtier. He had cheap Celtic tattoos on both shoulders exposed by a soiled denim vest he wore on his bare torso. While I was looking at him trying to remember if I've seen him anywhere before, Theodora hasn't looked in his direction once. So it startled me when she suddenly turned to him, pointed her manicured finger in his face, and said in a voice almost trembling with anger, 'My father would appreciate an answer.'

He finally saw her, his face melting into a grin, and

exclaimed, 'Dolly, mate! Where've you been all this time?'

'I am not your mate,' said Theodora. 'I've been in London all this time.'

'He-e-e-y, baby!' he began, making a step towards her, while ignoring me, and giving her a big, sweaty hug. I watched Theodora's face as he did this, and instead of rage or at least annoyance all it expressed was helplessness, and an emotion I couldn't recognise, and which to me looked like pain more than anything else.

'Hey,' I began saying to him aggressively as he finally released Theodora, but she interrupted me.

'Tom, this is Joey,' she said, wrapping her arm around me.

'Are you guys together?' asked Tom, appearing more amused than annoyed.

'Yes,' said Theodora, looking at him with what seemed like accusation mixed with pride.

Tom laughed as if he's just heard the funniest joke.

'Baby, I'm afraid I can't do it,' he said. 'I can't leave my band, you know! That's all I got, it's my life!'

Theodora stared at him for a second, her lips tight, and her eyes glaring.

'You moron,' she said quietly to him, with so much bitterness it stunned me.

She then turned around, and dragged me back to our table. When we sat down, I realised that we didn't get the drinks.

'You know, I tried to help Tom,' she began, before I could say anything. 'I got my father to listen to his demos, to do him a personal favour and see if he could get him out of this band that's going nowhere, see if he could have a chance in the States. Daddy listened to him and he basically said yes, let him come over to the States, we could place him in an up-and-coming blues-rock band.'

'And what happened?' I asked, fascinated.

'Well, you've just seen what happened,' Theodora said through clenched teeth. 'He doesn't want to leave his fabulous band.'

'Well, he's an idiot,' I mumbled.

We left before Mark's band came on because Theodora wasn't feeling well. In a taxi heading home we didn't talk. I tried to hold her hand, but she withdrew it.

Once back in the house, she opened a bottle of Jack, and we were about to sit down in the kitchen for a drink or two, when her mobile rang. Once she answered, I saw the same pained expression on her face that surprised me so a just few hours ago when Tom was wrapping his arms around her.

'Are you sure you have absolutely nowhere else to stay?' she half-sang, half-moaned.

Then a pause.

'OK, that's fine, you can,' she then said, clicking off a second later.

I looked at her inquiringly, and she told me. 'Tom's stranded in London. The trains have stopped running, and he needs a place to stay. I told him he could come over.'

Tom arrived forty minutes later – tipsy, loud, and seemingly unable to stop talking.

'I am so sorry, baby,' he yelled, hugging Theodora with one hand while letting the other drop his guitar case to the marble floor in the hall.

'You know, Tom, I'm tired,' Theodora said to him, 'I'd better show you your room. Joey and I have had a long day.'

'Thank god,' I thought, 'At least we won't have to put up with him for much longer.'

'Oh, come on, Doll!' yelled Tom. 'You can't call it a night! At least let's have a drink first! A nightcap! C'mon, Doll, why are you being so mean?'

Theodora smiled sourly, saying, 'OK, I'll pour you a drink,' and went into the kitchen. Tom and I followed her, but I soon realised that I might as well have stayed in the hall because suddenly the two of them became entirely absorbed in each other's presence. It was as if I wasn't even there. Before Theodora had a chance to pour the drinks, Tom embarked on an elaborate rendition of his recent magic mushroom trip, and from that moment on it was just him talking and Theodora listening.

'It's like beyond language and beyond all the visual stuff,' he was saying. 'It was pure telepathy. I was imagining this tune in my head, and Sal was playing the bass line to it. But our instruments weren't even with us. We didn't even need them to communicate. You know?'

I stared at him sarcastically as he said this, but he wasn't noticing me, addressing to no one but Theodora, who was listening with real interest.

'It was beyond sound,' Tom was continuing. 'We could communicate without our instruments, and still hear each other's music. So this means I was communicating with Sal in a language that was obviously beyond the normal verbal language, but also beyond sound too, so it was pure telepathy.'

He looked triumphantly at Theodora.

She smiled.

'Well, do you remember this music now?' she asked. 'Can you play it?'

'I'll play it to you now,' he said confidently.

'Go on,' she said. 'Where's your guitar?'

'Do you have an amp?' he asked.

'You don't need an amp, I'll hear you,' she said.

Tom went back to the hall to get his guitar, while I grabbed Theodora's arm and whispered, 'Dolly, get rid of him.'

'No,' she said. 'I want to hear this.'

A moment later Tom was back in the kitchen holding his cheap white Mexican Strat.

'Now shut up and play,' said Theodora with a sweet smile that negated the rudeness of the actual words.

Tom sat down on a black leather bar stool and strummed a

few chords.

'It's out of tune,' said Theodora.

He spent the next five minutes tuning his guitar, while Theodora and I sipped our drinks. When he was ready, we finally got to hear the music, and it instantly confirmed to me things that I have always feared to hear from other musicians. I now knew that Tom's ability went beyond simple talent. It was one of those rare gifts that bordered on genius, and it scared me. Did the tune sound like the Doors, Hendrix, or Led Zeppelin? In a way it did, but it was still Tom's own – simple but unpredictable, nuanced but memorable, confident but reflective. I could almost imagine it being played on the stage of Albert Hall or Wembley Arena, the audience exploding in a thunder of applause for what Tom was now playing for Theodora on his cheap unplugged guitar while slumped on a bar stool in her kitchen. And I could tell she knew what I knew, from the way her gaze was fixed on his right hand, while her eyes looked like she was miles away, the music having taken her to a place no one knew anything about apart from her and, maybe, Tom.

'There,' he said once he finished. 'But that's not what I want to talk to you about. I have an idea about this thing... You know, it really has nothing to do with music as such...'

He was now again talking exclusively to Theodora, ignoring me. Or maybe he was never aware I was there in the first place.

'It's all about a language that we all knew once but have forgotten because our assemblage point became fixed at one spot all those years ago.'

'Oh, no, not the assemblage point,' groaned Theodora in a voice I've never heard from her before, dismissive and sexy at the same time.

'No-no-no,' protested Tom, 'Not in the Castaneda kind of sense. To me it all has to do with the Celtic heritage.'

'Now I know how he ended up with all his cut-price tattoos,' I thought.

By that point we've moved into the drawing room, Tom

seated on the floor, Theodora – on the sofa, and I – next to her, only that Tom still kept ignoring me.

'I think each culture is really about fixing your assemblage point in one particular place, and once enough people have it fixed there, they become a nation,' Tom was saying. 'But I've recently read this book about the Druids, and I realised that the Celts were completely unique, they weren't like anyone else. They could move their assemblage point at will and enter other worlds and other states...'

'If you believe all that, isn't this what people in Mexico were able to do for centuries?' asked Theodora.

'No, I think that the Celts were able to channel it into their art, which makes them unique.'

'Why don't you go to Mexico and see all the Aztec art for yourself?' Theodora said. 'Or simply go to the BM.'

'Where?'

'The British Museum,' she said, sighing.

'I still think that the kind of freedom the Celts had with their parallel world journeys, and then expressing it all in their art was unlike anything else.'

'Right,' said Theodora, smiling. 'Who needs the BM when you already have it all figured out. '

'Anyway,' Tom carried on, 'My cousin can now do rebirthing rituals. And she did it on me, and you wouldn't believe what happened! The next day I was at Ron's house, and his parents have a piano in their living room, you know, so I was there with Ron just having a beer, and suddenly it was like a magnetic pull – the piano was drawing me towards it, and I was completely sober, I've only had half a bottle of Beck's. So I opened the lid and it was as if the piano keys were speaking to me.'

'Christ,' I thought, 'Is this guy for real?'

'And the moment I touched the first key it was as if it already knew what I was going to play. The music has already been written somewhere, in some other dimension, and all I had to do was really press the right keys. Which I did, and which the instrument was showing me how to do. I almost saw the keys I had to touch in different colours. And it was the most important thing I've ever learnt about music. That it's not us writing it. It's given to us, it comes from a place we know very little about. Music is a kind of energy that speaks through us, but it comes not from another place, not from within us. It just chooses certain people to express itself through. Because really, to think that it's us, people, coming up with all this incredible music would be just stupid, wouldn't it, Dolly?'

'Depends what kind of music,' Theodora said.

'Well, I mean real music. Of course, I don't mean the stuff in the pop charts. Even though sometimes I really wonder where those dimwits get some of their melodies from. Surely not from their own heads.'

'Out of the heads of record label staff writers,' Theodora said, smiling wryly.

'I never thought I'd say that,' Tom was going on, ignoring her remarks, 'but I personally have nothing to do with my music. What I do is get in touch with those energies and let them speak through my instrument.'

At that point I've had enough. I've heard it all before. I knew what the twenty-first century hippies were all about. I went to school with some. I jammed with many in London. Yes, I knew that magic mushrooms and peyote could get you to places you wouldn't otherwise be able to explore. But I also knew that you completely lost focus and a sense of direction with that stuff. And, to be frank, I didn't want to sound like a spaced-out hippie on my records. I wanted to sound razor-sharp and confident playing my music. And before anyone starts saying anything about Hendrix, I think he was a genius despite the fact that he occasionally took mind-altering substances, not because of it. And I really despise those who think they can buy their way to achievement with drugs.

So I left Theodora and Tom chatting away (in fact, him chatting away and her just sitting there listening, because that's how it always works with hippies – one of them is embarking on a

114

profound verbal trip, while all others have to succumb to acting as passive receptacles of the speaker's outpourings), and headed upstairs, straight to bed. I didn't even feel guilty about leaving Theodora on her own to endure Tom's verbal diarrhea because she seemed like a willing victim.

Before falling asleep I had a weird thought about all those poor veteran music journalists like Lester Bangs and Al Aronowitz in the Sixties who had to endure all sorts of meaningless crap from "visionary" musicians back in the day. I could guess that for every Jim Morrison they got to interview, there were thousands of wannabes on spaced-out oration trips who'd leave them with hours and hours of senseless babble to transcribe, random streams of consciousness of mummy's boys with what essentially was the Fifties mentality, who suddenly imagined their minds to be liberated from it all by marijuana and magic mushrooms.

'I wouldn't want to be a music journalist if you paid me a fortune,' was my last thought before drifting off to sleep.

I don't know why I suddenly woke up in the middle of the night, but as soon as I did, I realised that it was Tom' tune that was playing in my head, making me dream of guitars set on fire, the sea, and long-haired girls – human above the waist, fish below – stretching their hands to the sky, picking the stars one by one and dropping them into the ocean below where I sat in a boat trying to catch a few. The tune Tom played to us on his cheap Strat in the kitchen that evening has spellbound me in my sleep. Now I knew with even more clarity that this music was pure magic. Nothing I'd expect myself to come up with in a million years. I was so stricken by this thought that I immediately went back to sleep, continuing to dream about underwater kingdoms where stars shone as brightly as they once did up in the sky. I guess the realisation that Tom was in a different creative universe from mine was too much for me to deal with while being awake.

When I got up in the morning and went downstairs, Theodora and Tom were still in the drawing room, sitting exactly where I left them the night before – her on the sofa, him – on the floor facing her. Theodora was wearing the same dress she wore last night, but her face looked tired and sad now. Tom looked tired too, but happier and brighter. She then saw me standing in the doorway staring at them, trying to take in the fact that they have spent the entire night together talking. Theodora got up and came up to me, putting her arms on my shoulders and kissing me on the cheek.

'Morning, baby,' she said.

Tom just grinned and said, 'Yo, man' to me, to which I didn't reply.

I didn't know what to say, or what to think. Staying up all night talking was what I'd sometimes do with Ben and Dave, but Theodora and I have never done that, not because I didn't want to, but because she would always say she was tired by the time it was getting past eleven, so I either had to go home, or go to the guest bedroom while she went to hers. So I had no idea what to think when I saw them.

Theodora asked me if I wanted breakfast, to which I said no, leaving them both in the drawing room, and wondering if I was still asleep and dreaming while staring at the front cover of a free morning paper in the tube carriage on my way home.

The first thing I did when I got home was call Zara. Just because there was no one else I could talk to who knew Theodora, and because there was no one else I could ask for an advice. I haven't spoken to Zara since the day after the Silver Cats show in Camden when she rang to invite me to Theodora's exhibition opening. I knew I'd have to update her on a lot of what's been going on, and was rehearsing the summary of the events that happened since then when she answered the phone. I was so glad to hear her bright, upbeat voice that my problems suddenly seemed less severe, and my situation – less desperate.

'Hi, Zar, how are you?' I began.

'Joey? Is that you?' I could almost see her beam on the other end of the line.

'Yea, that's me, baby,' I said, laughing. 'How've you been?'

'Oh, great!' she exclaimed. 'Rich is in town!'

'Who's Rich?' I asked.

'Rich Mills from Sliver Cats,' she said.

'Oh, I didn't know that. Are they back in the UK? I heard nothing about it.'

'No, silly,' Zara said. 'He's come to see *me*.'

'To see *you*? What, for a photoshoot? Just him?'

'No! We are a couple, don't you know?'

I was completely shocked. I knew nothing about Zara dating Rich.

'I thought everyone knew by now,' Zara said.

'Well, I don't read the Metal Sludge board,' was my clumsy attempt at a joke.

'Ha-ha, very funny,' Zara said.

I knew she was smiling.

'Isn't he married?' I then asked rather stupidly.

'They are separated,' Zara said. 'He's filed for a divorce last month. They've never had kids.'

'Wow!' I was completely amazed. 'How long have you two been going out for?'

'Four years,' she said flatly.

'What?! Four years?! And you didn't tell me?'

'Well, this isn't exactly something you hurry to tell people while the man is still married.'

'I guess not...' I mumbled.

'So, how have *you* been?' Zara asked me.

'All over the place,' I said frankly.

'Oh! So what happened to the Global deal in the end?'

'Nothing happened to the Global deal. I've got people telling me to do all sorts of things – from going along with it to ditching it and moving to LA.'

'Moving to LA? Who tells you to do that?'

'Your friend.'

'My friend?'

'Theodora.'

'Theodora? She's not my friend!' Zara laughed. 'Are you talking to Theodora?'

'Every day,' I said, feeling slightly proud.

'No-o-o-o-o!.. Are you guys?..' She paused coyly.

'What?'

'Going out together?'

'Yeah, we go out. Now and then.' I laughed.

'And she is telling you you should come to LA?'

'Yeah, but it's all weird, you know... I can't really figure her out, and I don't really know what I should do, Zar.'

'I don't really know her that well, Joey. We haven't spoken for ages.'

'I know, but I still have to ask you a few things...'

'Go on.'

'She tells me she doesn't believe in sex before marriage. Is this something...'

But Zara didn't let me finish. She laughed so loudly I had to move the receiver away from my ear.

'She told you she doesn't believe in sex before marriage?'

'Yes. Why? Does she have a sex tape out there I should be aware of?'

'No, but she could have had!' Zara kept chuckling.

'Why? She dated Mr. Lee?'

'Not him, a much bigger name.'

'Really?! Who?'

'Can't tell you.'

'C'mon, Zar, I'm drowning here! Who was it? Or is it?'

'Joe, it doesn't matter who it was. A big LA rock star from back in the Eighties.'

118

'And what happened?'

'He left his wife and three kids for her.'

'And?'

'And they moved in together, and two months later he left her.'

'He left her?'

'It was really weird. Nobody knows what happened.'

'Did he go back to his wife?'

'No.'

'She just told me she doesn't want to jump into anything before we get to know each other really well, which I can understand. Maybe she feels weird about the physical side of things after what happened with that guy, but it's other things that sometimes confuse me...'

'Like what?'

'Listen, have you ever heard of a band called Chrome Dew?'

'Shot their set a few months ago in Camden.'

'Do you know their guitarist Tom?'

'Oh, I see where it's all going,' Zara said.

'What? Why?'

'Is Tom still in the picture?'

'Please elaborate.'

'OK. Dolly wanted to arrange for him to join some über-cool blues-rock band in the States. Her father was ready to do this for him. Or, rather, for her. Not because he thought that Tom was such a genius as Theodora portrayed him, but because he loves his daughter and whatever was going to make her happy after a painful break-up, he was ready to go along with. Theodora thought Tom was the next Hendrix. I don't know how intimate they were, but I think she really fell for him at one point. Or she needed to convince herself that she had and that she had finally found a real genius, not some grubby LA junkie with a pile of money. Money doesn't really interest her, she's got plenty of that herself. She's always wanted a genius. And a real looker. She's always been into good-looking boys. That's why I guess you two have hit it off.' She

119

laughed. 'So when is he moving to the States?'

'Who?'

'Tom.'

'He's not.'

'He is not?'

'He doesn't want to.'

'He doesn't want to?'

'Is repeating things a new trend I'm missing out on?'

'You are welcome, Joey. For all the vital insider information you've just received from me that will help you make an informed decision instead of completely wrecking your love life, your sex life, and your career at a tender age of twenty-three.'

'I'm twenty-two.'

'Oh, that changes everything. I take it all back then.'

She laughed.

'Listen, Zar, Tom doesn't want to go to LA. He doesn't want to leave his band.'

'He's got a point.'

'Why? Because Dolly will chew and spit him out?'

'No, musicians' careers are not all about Dolly. It's just that with the kind of music he plays he stands a better chance of getting singed in England. In the US they slot you into genres – you're either metal, or Southern rock, or classic rock, or this, or that, and Tom is much more versatile than any of this. They wouldn't know how to market him in the States. They'll either try to box him into one genre, or leave him hanging on the fringes as a weird novelty act with a small freak following.'

'Well, it seems that now it's my turn to decide if I want to go with her to LA.'

'Hey, why don't you talk to Rich?' Zara suddenly said. 'He's got loads of experience. Not only did he work with Dolly's father, he knows the scene. Well, sort of. Even though he now lives in New York, he knows all the LA musicians...'

'I don't know. I hardly know the man.'

'He's awesome.'

'Yes, doubtless. It would have been weird if you didn't think that.'

'No, seriously. He's the best human being on the whole scene. It took me a long time to pick the right guy, but I made sure I've picked the best.'

I laughed. 'Well, how about I invite you guys for a drink in Soho next week?'

'No, I've got a better idea,' she said. 'Why don't you join us tomorrow for dinner? We've booked a table at the Other Realm in Mayfair, so why don't you come along?'

'The Other Realm? What's that?'

'It's a place record execs take new bands to before they sign them, to show them the good life,' Zara said with a laugh.

'Zar, I'm skint!' I protested. 'I'm still on the dole! I haven't signed anything yet and haven't seen a penny of Global's money!'

'That's OK, don't worry about it. Rich isn't gonna make you pay. We are inviting you.'

'Man, that's very kind of you,' I said, slightly embarrassed. 'What should I wear?'

'Oh, just wear jeans and a cool shirt,' she said.

VI

RICH

From touring with Rich a year before, I knew that he was born into a working class family in LA "the year the Rolling Stones released their first album". He used to play in cover bands on the LA club circuit since he was seventeen, working at a food processing factory during the day sticking labels onto cans and bottles. He joined Silver Cats in 1986, and three years later they got their big break. Their debut album went platinum, and in 1989 the band went on a headlining world tour that lasted two years.

Their pictures were virtually not coming off the front covers of all major rock magazines. He told me that one monthly mag had their picture on its front cover five times in 1989. I first read about them in Big Roar when I was thirteen. It was a four-page retrospective and had photographs dating back to their first year as a chart-topping band. I remember noticing that Rich had brown hair at the time when everyone in rock was dying their hair either peroxide-white or jet-black, and on the first photograph I ever saw of him he was looking shyly into the camera from under his bushy eyebrows with his head bowed down. He didn't look like a rock star at all, rather like a small-time crack dealer, or so I thought when I first saw that image. I then borrowed their first album from someone at school and really dug it. And if somebody told me then that in eight years time I would go on tour with this band, I'd ask they what they were on.

I still remember feeling something stop for moment inside

me when I first heard his guitar drop airy fragile sounds between the verses of the only ballad of their debut – just a handful of notes that to me sounded like they were coming from a different world, a world where emotions were expressed with clarity and ease, instantly telling me that Rich Mills was a good man. I felt his music was telling the truth about him as a human, and I was overwhelmed by how he could single-handedly bare his heart by playing those fleeting passages in between the vocal lines, his emotions and his vulnerability given away in just a few lucid notes. I listened to that song so many times throughout my teens that it made me think I knew Rich. Not only did I think I knew him, I thought that I knew him intimately, the way one knows a close friend. I thought that he was revealing a deeply private and personal part of himself which could only be exposed to the select few. I didn't realise at the time that so he was to millions of other people all over the world, in fact, to anyone who'd pay twelve bucks to buy the album, but, then again, I was just a teenager at the time. 'Your own music always speaks the truth about you', I used to think then. 'With music you can't hide behind a façade the way you can when you are a writer or a painter. When you play your own music, it is all laid bare, and to try to deceive or to be obscure would not only be meaningless, but impossible.'

I arrived at a smart-looking restaurant near Green Park tube at quarter to seven and realised I was early only when I've already walked in. I had no choice but to wait at the bar trying to make my glass of Perrier last until Zara's and Rich's arrival. Then, twenty minutes later, they came in through the door. He was letting her through first, gently touching her elbow with his hand, and as they approached me, I could hardly recognize the man who I have toured with a year ago, saw briefly again a few months back at his aftershow in Soho, and whose face, on a photograph which looked more like a mugshot, I saw for the first time in a music magazine for teenagers when I was still a kid. Now he looked assured, at ease, and full of quiet, contained energy, not a trace left of the vulnerability his photographs spoke of at the time when his band was just starting to get publicity all those years ago.

These days he was a confident, smiling man of forty-three, not very tall but well-built, lines running from the edges of his nose to the sides of his mouth, and crow's feet just beginning to show around his brown eyes. His face was a peculiar combination of brutality and susceptibility. His thin-lipped mouth curved in an almost feminine way, but his jaw was all about pure unyielding manliness. His brown eyes were fantastically large and would have made him look exposed if not for the heavy brow ridges that gave him an almost fallow look, but, again, softened by an unusually high forehead. He was wearing his brown hair astonishingly long, almost down to his waist, at the time when all other bands, including his own, have cut their hair short. He wasn't good-looking, not even by today's standards, which aren't clear-cut, but there was a presence about him which made his appearance all come together and made his features intriguing rather than ridiculous, which they could have been, had he had less poise. You could tell that he was well-travelled – both geographically and emotionally, but he looked like he's enjoyed the experience.

'There you are,' Zara said, giving me a peck on the cheek which I didn't dare reciprocate in the presence of Rich.

'Hey, man, good to see you again,' Rich said with a broad smile that showed almost all his teeth, slightly uneven and discoloured, which looked strange in an American rock star. Only now I was beginning to notice things about Rich that I've never paid attention to before.

'Last time I was here was like fifteen years ago,' he said, looking around. 'They sure have changed the décor.'

We were shown through to a table by the window that looked out into the back garden where lanky birches stood decorated with garland lights.

'Tell us about how your band got served cocaine for desert at this place,' Zara turned to Rich. 'We've read all about it in your manager's book!'

I heard Rich laugh for the first time, and it was a soft, almost coy kind of laughter.

'I was at the bar trying to get a beer when all this started to happen,' he said. 'Everyone's been drinking cocktails, and I just wanted a beer. So I went to the bar and got talking to a guy there who was some kind of East End historian, who was telling me about the East End mobster clans in the Fifties. So I missed the whole thing. When I got back here, they were all gone. I always miss the best parties. Whenever I leave a room all of a sudden there's a wild party starting to happen. I had to walk back to my hotel because it was too late and there were no taxis. I was wandering around London for hours trying to find my way back to Park Lane Hotel, which is around the corner. It was hilarious. I think I got to my room at five in the morning.'

Zara and I laughed, and he smiled at us, looking first at Zara, then at me. His was a big smile, the one you flash from the stage into a crowd, somewhat larger-than-life, but again, it went with his features, maybe because they were slightly exaggerated too.

'Wow, Park Lane Hotel,' I said.

'Yeah, those were the days,' he replied.

'You must write an autobiography,' Zara said.

'It would be identical to what's already out there,' Rich said. 'Town after town, country after country, all I have are stories of young dudes partying, getting wrenched, and occasionally playing shows.' He laughed. 'I don't think our story is much different from the story of any other Eighties band. Everything that can be told about that time, has already been told by other people in their books. At least *our* story is pretty much the same, only no one died or got killed.'

'I don't know,' said Zara, narrowing her eyes and looking up at one of the chandeliers. 'I'd love to read the story of Silver Cats if it ever comes out.'

'I'll have to remember it all first if I ever write a book,' Rich said, leaning back in this chair. 'I honestly don't remember much of our world tour. It's still a blur. I remember drinking and I remember flying in airplanes. I hardly remember anything else.'

'You just say that,' smiled Zara.

'Maybe I do,' said Rich at her wine glass and for a brief moment looked uneasy.

'I know there are people who should definitely write something, but for some those memories are painful,' I said.

'What I really don't understand,' said Rich, rolling a paper napkin into a ball, 'is how some people just went through their money like it was water. To me it's just baffling. People who spent all their money on blow, cars, and penthouse pets. You know how some guys would spend something like five million in two years and now they are either bankrupt, broke, or up to their ears in debt. Amazing. I toured with people who used to make millions and lived it large back in the day. A lot of them have nothing now.'

'Well, obviously rock stars are different one from another. Some would never do that, ' said Zara and smiled slyly at Rich.

'I guess I'm just cheap,' he laughed without of trace of embarrassment.

After that we didn't talk much about rock stars. I couldn't tell if Rich was simply not interested in this sort of conversation or if he really wanted to talk more about life in London. He did want to know about the jazz gigs at Ronnie Scott's and the recent documentaries that started coming out about the Seventies British heavy metal bands. We then talked about films running at the National Film Theatre, and I mentioned one of Michael Moore's.

At which point Rich turned to me with an intense look I couldn't decipher at first, saying, 'Don't you hate Americans who hate America?'

Zara looked up at him from her plate and smiled as if she knew what was coming next, and there it was: 'At the time when all Americans should unite, people like Moore discredit their own country. It just undermines what the rest of us are trying to do right now. Sometimes I wonder where people like him are getting the money for their movies from. Who funds him. Because he does

127

nothing but attack his own country. I wonder who's behind him.'

I sat there for a few moments wondering if he was having us on or if he was serious. When I realised that it was the latter, my initial reaction was to laugh, but I had enough sense not to.

'Rich, Joey wants to ask you about the deal he's been offered,' Zara said, changing the subject. 'Only now that you are going off on one about politics he feels weird to ask you.'

'Oh, no problem,' said Rich. 'Go ahead and ask. Just remember that you are not asking a megastar here.'

I suddenly felt apprehensive. Not because it would have been awkward to explain to Rich the details of how our songwriting worked, but mainly because he wasn't exactly the right person to talk to, and we both knew it. It wasn't like he's been consistently making all the right decisions in his career for all those years and could now give me the right advice. His own career was now at its lowest point, the band having gone from playing stadiums to playing clubs, so advising me from where he was now would have been difficult for him. But I decided to give it a try anyway.

'You know my old band the Storm Angels,' I began.

Rich nodded.

'Global Union's offered them a deal, and they really want to have me in on it because they reckon it would be good for the band's image.'

'My own band has been offered a deal back then mainly because our singer was a stud,' Rich said plainly. He didn't even smile as he said it.

'I didn't know you were the singer in the beginning,' said Zara, laughing.

Rich smiled. 'I was the guy who found the singer,' he said.

'So they want me back,' I continued. 'But I really don't feel like doing that because they don't write their own songs. Their manager does.'

Rich seemed completely unperturbed by what to me was an incredibly embarrassing revelation to make.

'Does he write *all* the material?' he asked.

'Yeah,' I said, staring at my plate and poking my stuffed tomato with a fork.

'Well, a lot of people end up in bands where they don't write,' Rich said. 'The question is – do you see yourself as a songwriter? Do you write? And if you do, how come your manager is doing it for you?'

'I do write now,' I said. 'But I didn't then. And our manager was hell-bent on making us play in a very particular style, kinda retro classic rock that he is good at imitating, and which he reckons is the business these days.'

'The other thing,' Rich continued, 'is that if the fans find out, it's gonna be the end of your career. This ain't pop music where it doesn't matter who writes the songs. This is rock'n'roll.'

'I know,' I said. 'But I was thinking of joining back, singing the deal, and then leaving after the first album.'

'Sooner or later it will all come out anyway,' Rich said. 'Your best move right now would be to join back and then fire the manager before you sign the record deal. Do it with the help of the record company. And then release the first album with your own songs on it. If nobody else in that band writes apart from you, you could end up looking at a neat pile of money if the album does well. But you have to check your contract with this guy. Have you signed the management deal yet?'

'I know that the other guys have after I've left.'

'There are still ways around that. You need to talk directly to the record company, without your manager. Tell them that he's trouble. That you can't work with him, that he's too difficult. Tell them he's pressuring you into a direction you don't want to go in. Tell them he interferes with the songwriting process to the point where it becomes impossible for you to function.'

'Can this be done?'

'The only thing is that they are probably offering you the deal based on the songs he's written.'

'Right.'

Rich laughed. 'So you'd better come up with something

better than that, and quick. Then talk to the record company and show them what you've written. Tell them the old stuff is irrelevant now. Out of date. Doesn't represent you any more. Too much unwelcome influence from the manager in those songs. Or if you're unsure about your songwriting, tell your manager you won't sign unless he credits you in as a co-writer.'

'Can this be done?' I asked again, wide-eyed and amazed at the deadpan tone in which Rich was spelling all those things that to me sounded utterly incredible.

'It's being done all the time,' Rich said. 'Just ask... Ah, anyway, specific names don't matter. The point is, it's being done all the time.'

'That's great advice,' I said. 'Thanks. I just wish I didn't despise my bandmates so much.'

'Name one band where people are great friends,' he said.

'The Jimi Hendrix Experience?' I ventured, purely out of my innate stupidity.

'Well, are you Hendrix?' Rich asked me, raising an eyebrow.

It wasn't what he said, but the way he said it that made me laugh and finally relax. It was strange, but he was telling me the most difficult things a musician ever gets to hear, while his voice, his tone, and the expression on his face made me completely at ease. I haven't met anyone before who'd make me feel so secure. I guess this was because he knew his own shortcomings only too well to get hung up on other people's faults or slip-ups to preach, or to try to prove some selfish point. And I found it really comforting. I just liked being in his company. I liked his humour and I liked his sincerity. I could now see why Zara had chosen him of all the musicians she could have ended up with.

'I've also been told I should walk away from the deal and go to LA to see if anything pans out for me there,' I said.

'Nothing pans out for anyone in LA just like that,' Rich said. 'Unless you are Hendrix.'

He smiled, and so did I.

'Just like anywhere else,' he said.

130

'The person who's saying that to me kinda knows people.'

'Really? In that case you're lucky. But I still wouldn't throw away the deal Global is offering you. Chances like that are rare. Don't find yourself regretting a stupid decision unless you don't mind busking in the gutter at the age of fifty. I'm not saying it's gonna happen, but you'd better find out what chances you have with Global before you give it up.'

'So what's LA like?' I asked.

'Tough,' Rich said. 'Just like everywhere else. Chopsmen are a penny a dozen. What they need there more than anything are songwriters.'

I didn't admit to Rich it was Theodora who was offering to take me to LA, even though I knew that Zara would later tell him. It just wouldn't have felt right to tell him that a woman was looking after me, no matter how understanding and easygoing Rich was. As the three of us walked through Mayfair to Green Park tube, I looked over at him and Zara, and thought that the last thing they probably talked to each other about when they were alone, were record deals, royalty payments, record sales figures, and the music business in general. They looked so happy, so attuned to each other, I realised people could have all kinds of opinions, experiences, and social backgrounds, but when they found the right person, it was about other things, a connection that went deeper than all the superficial stuff. And I suddenly remembered the things Tom was talking about the other night, as I smiled, wondering if I too was turning into a hippie.

On my way to Theodora's, after saying goodbye to Zara and Rich, I finally realised that the precise nature of the connection the two of them had was going to remain forever unknowable to the rest of the world. It didn't surprise me that she picked him of all other people, but I also knew that her real reasons would never be known to me or anyone else.

The other thing I was now thinking of was Rich's advice about not throwing the Global deal out of the window, which I found hard to absorb once I was alone. I began wondering how seriously I was supposed to take advice given to me by someone who was so out of touch when it came to bigger things in life, like, for example, politics. Which, of course, had nothing to do with music or with show business, but which I still found unsettling. Until a few hours ago I didn't know rock stars could be so reactionary. I've always had a rather old-fashioned idea of a rock musician as maybe not exactly a political activist like John Lennon, but at least liberal enough not to support the establishment propaganda. And here I suddenly came face to face with someone who was so vehemently pro-establishment, it staggered me. But I also thought it was rather amusing.

This was what Theodora and I were talking to about an hour later, me sitting on her goosedown drawing room sofa sipping my Lapsang Souchong.

'Zara's always been the most left-wing person I've known,' I was saying to her. 'Can you just fall in love with someone and not care what they believe in, like, on a larger scale of things?'

'When you fall in love, the scales of things shift,' Theodora said sharply.

'I guess,' I said. 'But, you know, she could have picked anyone. Or maybe not anyone, but someone who'd be more free-thinking, you know.'

'No, she couldn't have,' Theodora snapped. I could tell she was in a rotten mood.

'Why? You don't think she's pretty?'

'Being pretty has nothing to do with it,' she said. 'It's mandatory to be pretty if you want to go out with a rock star. It has to do with who she is, and she is a photographer with little to her name apart from a few front covers. Just a regular working girl.'

'Rock stars have been known to marry photographers.'

'Yes, and those photographers have been known to be

millionaires' daughters.'

'So who do rock stars marry?'

'Millionaires' daughters. Models. Actresses. Other rock stars.'

'So you reckon Zara's done pretty well for herself?'

'She's very lucky.'

'I think they are in love.'

'Oh, we all fall in love, but what good... Anyway, forget it.'

'It was cool seeing them together. They are a good couple.'

'She is lucky to have found someone who isn't that young and who isn't at the peak of his fame. Someone like her would never be able to deal with the madness of being with someone who's young, rich, and famous.'

'Why?'

'Because she's not stupid or cynical enough to feign oblivion to everything what would have been going on behind her back if he was. So someone who's past it is her perfect partner. What is the worst thing Rich Mills can do these days? Get drunk and fall off his porch?'

'Hundreds of girls must still fall for him.'

'Yeah, but not the kind of girls he'd want to risk his relationship for.'

'He still has money.'

'Stashed away for a rainy day. It's not like he's spending any of it. His heyday was twenty years ago. They are just a nostalgia act now. Remember how badly their last album did. He can't even leave his band and start a new project. People will only pay attention to him as long as he stays in his old band. And it's the name and the money that holds them together, not their steaming creativity, or a desire to release hot new material every year. Without this band, each one of them is nothing.'

'I don't think Zara really cares that much about money.'

'Exactly. That's why they are an ideal couple.'

We sat in silence for a while.

'So what did Rich say about the Global deal?' Theodora

suddenly asked. 'You did talk about it, didn't you?'

'We did. He said don't throw it away.'

'Well, he's looking at it from his own perspective. He himself was incredibly lucky to get signed all those years ago. He just knew people who knew people. Pure luck. You don't think he's worth anything as a guitarist, do you?'

'I liked his stuff on their first album.'

'He didn't write any of it.'

'He still played the guitar leads, and that's what I dig on that record.'

'You shouldn't be comparing yourself to him anyway. He's just a bigoted redneck who got lucky. For a few years.'

'He's a good guy. He's got his opinions, but he's a good guy. He was willing to give me good advice.'

'Well, it's just that his advice proves to be quite useless and inapplicable to your situation. You should aim higher than Rich Mills. You write music, he doesn't. That's all there is to it. I can't believe you're still having doubts about going to LA.'

'I'm not,' I said. 'I'll go with you to LA.'

And as I said it, I finally realised that I have finally made my mind up. I decided that trying to outsmart Doug, the record company, and the band would be too great a feat for me. Maybe I had the smarts to play Doug and Global against each other, like Rich has been suggesting, but I knew that dealing with the band would have been a completely different game. The Storm Angels weren't one of those bands where people grew up together, shared one vision, and had a common creative goal. They didn't even like the same kind of music. The only thing they had in common was their desire for fame. Over time we've learnt how to tolerate one another, work not with each other, but around each other, and how to diffuse awkward situations instead of rowing all the time. Everyone in the band thought they deserved to be rock heroes, each constantly thinking about nothing else but stardom, and we all hated to be in a situation where we had to play songs written for us by some dodgy fifty year-old geezer. But at least we knew we were all in the same boat, united in our resentment for Doug and our dependence on him. If I suddenly came in with my own material and asked them to play it, they would probably be even unhappier with that than with playing Doug's songs. Each of them was a difficult bastard, prone to jealousy and constantly entertaining conspiracy theories, just like everyone else on this scene. And I somehow didn't think that all this would inspire me to write my best songs. And writing my own songs was what I knew I had to continue doing, especially since I began making good progress with it.

Zara rang me late in the evening, when I was already in bed in my Ealing flat, asking if Rich's advice was of any help.

'He's a really cool guy,' I said. 'And I really appreciate his advice. But I've made my mind up to go to LA.'

'Rich says you'll be alright whatever you do,' said Zara.

'Really? Why?'

'Maybe because you look right for it all,' Zara laughed.

'OK. That's very flattering,' I said, not sure if I should have really felt flattered or offended by the fact that everyone was always commenting on my looks and never said anything about my playing.

'Looks are everything in this business,' said Zara, 'Trust me. I'm a photographer.'

'Listen,' I said, changing the subject, 'does it bother you that he's a Republican?'

'What do you mean?' she said in a slightly tense voice, and I sensed that it wasn't a comfortable question for her.

'Well, you know, with his ideas about America and all that?'

'Those are just regular sentiments over there right now.'

'How come?'

'What do you mean "how come"? Their country is going through a tough time.'

'Right. Of course.'

'You can't pass judgements unless you live there.'

'Sure. I just asked because I thought you were quite... you know, you were always reading the Guardian and all that.'

'Of course I do. But, you know... Once you fall in love with someone, you begin seeing their point of view. They say you can't really understand somebody unless you love them.'

'Well, I'm envious because you've found this person and you know for sure what it is. It's love, isn't it?'

'Of course. I've known him for four years and I've never loved him more than I do now.'

'That's amazing.'

'It is.'

We then paused.

'So how is it going with Theodora?'

'I just can't understand her sometimes,' I laughed. 'Which sounds funny given what you've just said about understanding people.'

'Have you made any progress with her?' Zara asked.

'Ha-ha. Very funny.'

'So what is it that you're trying to understand but can't?'

'I just don't understand why she keeps me hanging around.'

'You underestimate yourself,' Zara said. 'It's not every day that you meet someone who was born to be a rock star – the looks and all.'

'You're joking, right?'

'No, I'm dead serious. Look in the mirror.'

VII

CLAIRE

Ben was going to do sound at this new place in Bethnal Green that opened a month ago, a tiny pub-come-music-venue that could only fit fifty people in tops. Having nothing else to do, Dave and I decided we'd go too. Ben still didn't have a job and was doing odd gigs here and there, mostly open mic nights in pubs. He tried to ask around and see if he could to do bigger shows at bigger venues, but it turned out that gigs he was welcome to do weren't paid, and to get the ones that did pay one had to belong to a certain clique he had no desire to hang with.

'What the hell do you care, just go out with them for a drink one night,' we'd say to him. 'You've got a LIPA honours degree in sound engineering, the best producer in the world gave you masterclasses, it's not like they gonna think you're some self-taught nerd.'

Ben's usual answer was that the fact alone that he had a LIPA honours degree was enough for the majority of the small-potatoes sound techs on the London scene hate him without even knowing anything else about him. Which told me that Ben didn't know the first thing about networking.

'So who's playing tonight?' I asked him a few moments before the three of us were supposed to leave the house.

'Oh, some chick doing acoustic guitar songs, some old-school hippie stuff, like Fairport Convention or something,' he said.

'Dude, I bloody hate this hippie crap!' I said, feeling

disappointed and almost regretting having agreed to come along.

'I love it,' said Dave. 'I love Sandy Denny.'

'Yeah, you'd love any chick with a guitar...' I mumbled under my breath, putting my biker jacket on and running my fingers through my hair one last time in front of our full-length mirror in the living room.

It took Ben forty minutes to set up the pub's small eight-track portable desk, tune all the mics, and put pop shields on them. There was no drum kit and even if there was, there would have been no point in miking it up – the place was tiny. The show wasn't supposed to start until eight, so Dave and I left Ben to finish off and headed to a cheap shabby boozer across the road for a quick drink.

'So when are you off to LA?' asked Dave while we were waiting for the first pour of our Guinness to settle.

'Oh, man, I don't know,' I said vaguely.

I didn't feel like telling him about my insecurities, my doubts, and especially about how I felt about my relationship with Theodora.

'This chick Theodora must be really into you,' said Dave.

'Oh, there we go,' I thought with a silent moan. 'Why does everyone want to know about me and her?'

'Yeah, she's desperate to marry me,' I said and smiled.

'Really?' Dave's eyes widened.

'Yeah, really,' I thought. 'So desperate she doesn't let me touch her.'

But instead I just sniggered into my pint and shook my head.

'Wouldn't it be ace to go to LA?' continued Dave, oblivious to my realities. 'You'll get to hang at the Rainbow, get to meet all the rock stars.'

'Aha,' I said.

'And then, who knows, maybe there'll be a record deal for you there?'

138

'Listen, Dave,' I said, 'what do you think of all those new Cubase applications that have just come out?'

Dave instantly forgot about Theodora, my trip to LA, and my career prospects, launching into a half an hour long monologue about pitch shifting, filters, "the perfect waveform", and god knows what else, always remembering to give his opinion on every aspect of the new version of his favourite music production programme.

It was quarter past eight when he finally remembered that the gig across the road must have already started.

'Come over to the studio and I'll show you how it all works,' he said. 'Let's go see now how Ben is getting along.'

'And his fabulous Sandy Denny impersonator,' I added sarcastically.

'Come on, man,' said Dave. 'Gotta love Sandy Denny.'

As we came in through the doors, the first thing that hit me was the vibrating, high-pitched voice which I first thought was a CD. I turned my head towards the stage and saw a thin, pale, blue-eyed face with miniature doll-like nose and a soft, curvy mouth that made the girl look like one of those Botticelli faces Theodora loved and had prints of in her house. I then saw cascades of long blond hair running down the girl's shoulders, reaching her waist, and only then I noticed that she had a Spanish acoustic guitar, finally realising that it was *her* singing and playing. The chords she strummed were really basic, something you learn in the first couple of days of picking up the guitar. But her playing didn't matter. What mattered was her completely otherworldly voice – strong, pure, and lucid, touching on the barrier that separates the cute from the sublime, conveying something that to me which sounded like a message from my childhood, a distant, sweet, and unsettling memory of things I've forgotten a long time ago. And then the chorus started, in stark contrast to the verse, sounding like she was revealing something entirely different, something I had no idea about before, but what she knew, something that almost scared me,

139

but fascinated me at the same time. Things that were completely unknown to me. Until now.

'Good god, Sandy Denny has nothing on her,' I whispered to myself.

I watched her until the song was over, and while my hands clapped, my mind was at different place – I wasn't even sure where. Then my eyes wandered across the room and I saw Ben at his mixing desk, his mouth half-open, staring at the girl, waiting for her to begin the next song. I made my way through the tiny crowd to his desk, leaned over to him, and asked, 'What's her name?'

Ben made a small jumpy movement, turned to me, stared, and finally said, 'What?' sounding disoriented and almost frightened.

I repeated the question.

'It's Claire,' he said. 'Claire something.'

I nodded and went to the back of the room.

'Thank you, this is really overwhelming,' Claire was now saying into the mic. 'This next one is called *Raglan*. I wrote it on holiday in Wales when I was sixteen.'

She smiled coyly to herself and strummed her guitar. And when she began singing, I realised that she could shift between moods and tones of her voice like no other singer I've ever heard. The next song was nothing like the one she's just played. It had a solid, dense rhythm, strong staccato passages, and even a solo – clumsy and rudimentary, but still a solo she wasn't afraid to play unaccompanied. I suddenly imagined a completely different lead running over the harmony, and realised that I could really make this song sparkle. An electric guitar overdub would have sounded awesome for this song if she ever wanted to record it.

Claire's entire set was a mix and match of different styles – folk, old-school rhythm-and-blues, Fifties rock'n'roll, and even reggae, and when the show was over, I still had no idea which of those suited her best – she sounded amazing playing them all.

A couple of people wanted to talk to her once she came off

the stage, and she spoke a few words with everyone who approached her, while at the same time trying to make her way to Ben's desk. That was where I was heading too.

'Ben, is it?' she asked him once she reached him.

'Yeah, Ben,' he said, beaming, not knowing what to say next.

'Thank you for all you help,' she said. 'And for putting those pop shields on the mic.'

'No problem,' Ben said, blushing, before an uncomfortable silence ensued.

I stood there waiting for Ben to introduce to me, but he just kept staring at Claire, the effort of finding something to say reflecting glaringly on his face. Realising that neither Ben, nor Dave were going to act as my publicists that evening, I had to introduce myself.

'Hi, I'm Joe,' I said to Claire, 'I'm a friend of these two maniacs. I play guitar in the Storm Angels.'

It turned out Claire's never heard of the Strom Angels, but still wanted to know what kind of music we played.

'Well, a bit like yours, actually,' I said, which was, of course, an absurd lie.

'Really?' She looked genuinely surprised.

'Well, at least we try to take the best from bands like Led Zeppelin and Fairport Convention, which you do so well that I'm now beginning to doubt how well we actually manage it.'

I have now completely forgotten that a few hours ago I was about to change my mind about coming to see this gig, so repulsed I was by the thought of hearing someone even remotely resembling Fairport Convention.

'I'm sure your band is fab,' she said. 'Anyone who's into Led Zeppelin...'

'Yeah, well, at least we try to be versatile,' I interrupted her, overjoyed that she was actually responding to me. 'But you've just given a new meaning to "versatile" with your set, I've gotta admit I'm utterly stunned by your music. How come I've never heard about you before?'

'Thank you, that's kind of you,' she said, smiling.

'Do you have a CD or a demo?'

'No,' she said. 'I know I need to make one, but...'

Here I grabbed Dave by the shoulder, turned him towards Claire, and said, radiantly, 'Here's your man!'

'Actually...' began Dave, but I've given him such a hard poke in the back that he stopped and stared at me, bewildered.

'Our mate Dave here works at one of the best recording studios in London,' I continued, addressing Claire. 'And he'd be more than happy to help you make a demo. And so would I, if you need anyone to do electric guitar overdubs or just tune your guitar... Or make tea... Or run errands...'

I knew I was babbling but I couldn't stop. I felt that if I did stop talking, Claire would walk away, disappear, and I would never see her again. But instead she beamed.

'Really?' she said. 'That's amazing!'

'Is the studio free this weekend?' I asked Dave.

'Actually, we have Beck in this weekend,' he said, still unsure what to make out of my uncontrolled enthusiasm.

'Beck who? The American Beck? Jeff Beck? Tell him to come back later!' I yelled.

Ben was now looking pleadingly at me, and I realised that I had to calm down if I wanted to keep my chances with Claire and have my flatmates continuing to think of me as a sane human being.

'OK, what about next weekend?'

'I really don't want to...' began Claire, but Dave finally was able to suggest she came over in two weeks' time when he'd be able to record a few tracks with her.

When we finally went out into the street, I offered to carry Claire's guitar case, which she let me do, to my delight. Then my phone rang. It was Theodora, but instead of answering it, I switched it off. Claire was going to catch a tube to Victoria and then to Croydon where she lived, and I said I'd go with her on Victoria line. Ben and Dave looked at me like I was completely mad but, thankfully, let me go without saying anything. Though not before I made Dave promise again that he would definitely let Claire record at his studio.

The tube carriage was almost empty apart from a small group of teenage girls travelling back home after a night out – open-toed high heel shoes, the kind of footwear I could never stand, mini-skirts, décolleté tops, cheap jewellery, awful haircuts, and tons of badly applied makeup. Any other day they'd irritate the hell out of me, but this time I couldn't have cared less. All I wanted was talk to Claire. I didn't feel self-conscious, or shy, or hesitant, I was simply genuinely interested in talking to another musician, especially the one who played the kind of music I knew so little about and which completely stunned me just a few minutes ago. It turned out Claire knew nothing about the London rock scene. She's never heard of Lightning Blast, or Mark's band, or Chrome Dew, or any other bands I knew so well and used to be on the same bill with a million times. I found this fascinating, and suggested she came out with me one night to hear Sandy play. I suddenly really wanted to know what she would think of him.

'He's pretty unique, that bloke,' I was telling her. 'You can hear him reference a lot of people, but as a whole his style is really original. We should go see him play one night.'

'I'd love to,' she said.

'Really? Why don't I find out when his next gig is and then text you?'

She gave me her number and I was so overjoyed at the prospect of going out to see a show with another musician, who also happened to be a very pretty girl, that I almost made us miss our stop – I just couldn't stop talking.

I kissed Claire on the cheek after saying goodbye to her on the train platform at Victoria, and she didn't seem to mind, smiling beautifully and waving before disappearing through the doors of her carriage.

On my way home I realised that she didn't talk much but still seemingly enjoyed listening to me. Or at least I hoped so. Once she was gone, I couldn't wait to see her again. I was cursing Beck (if it was the American post-modernist whose music I detested, or Jeff Beck who I adored – I still didn't know) who was scheduled to record at Dave's studio that weekend, and then began thinking of an excuse to ask Claire out before we were supposed to see each other in two weeks' time. I then thought that I probably could try and add some electric guitar leads to her songs. I texted her there and then, telling her I had some ideas for her tunes if she wanted to try them out before her recording session. She replied right way.

'Would love to try your ideas', she wrote, 'when do you want to meet?'

She must have still been on a train when she texted this. I was prepared to rehearse anytime, anywhere.

'What do you think you are doing?' was the question Ben asked me in what seemed like an almost offended voice, as I walked into our flat at quarter to midnight.

He and Dave were sitting on the floor smoking hash.

'Meaning?' I asked, trying to sound unperturbed.

'Meaning why are you trying to get off with another girl when you already have a rich fit girlfriend?'

'Get off? Is that how you call it?' I asked, slightly raising the pitch of my voice in a half-hearted attempt at indignation.

'Did you tell Claire you are going to LA?' Dave asked.

'Give me that,' I said, taking the spliff out of his hand.

I then sat down on the sofa, took a long sparkly drag, held it in my lungs for a good half a minute, and then, as I exhaled, finally said, 'Nothing has been decided about LA yet.'

Then I got up and headed towards my room.

'Theodora called,' Ben yelled down the corridor. 'While you were out womanising. Wanted to know why you cut her off when she called.'

'Next time she calls, tell her she can't keep tabs on a musician,' I replied before closing the door to my room.

I spoke to Theodora the next day while waiting by the entrance to Ealing Broadway tube station, expecting Claire to turn up at any moment, so that I could take her to our flat to rehearse. Claire lived with her parents and her younger sister somewhere in Norbury, and as it was going to be awkward for me to go down to her place, we've agreed she'd come to Ealing. I promised Ben and Dave a tenner each to clear out of the flat and leave us alone for a day. Ideas for Claire's songs were all I could think of while Theodora wanted to know if I was going to come over that weekend and help her host a party she was throwing for the students on her course.

'Dolly, I've got a project I'm working on this weekend,' I said to her. 'I don't think I'll be able to make it this time.'

She became slightly annoyed telling me about how she was counting one me, but I had to cut her short.

'I'll call you this evening,' I said, before clicking off.

Claire turned up looking pretty in her black wool coat, her hair hidden underneath, and her face touched pink by the chilly early spring wind. I took the guitar case out of her hand and kissed her on the cheek, telling her our place was quarter of an hour walk from the station.

While I was making tea, Claire sat on one of our wooden kitchen bar stools, her hair loose, streaming down her shoulders, while telling me what she wanted to do with the four tracks she

145

had chosen to record at Dave's studio next week.

'It's really, I think, about the balance between expanding the melody,' she was saying, 'and at the same time not cluttering it with embellishments.'

I was all ears at that point.

'If you think of... oh, I don't know, if you think of stuff like the first Jefferson Airplane album, you'll get an idea of how the electric guitar isn't really trespassing onto the harmony...'

'Sure,' I said, trying not to mention the fact that I've never heard the first Jefferson Airplane album, or any of their albums for that matter. The only song by them that I knew was *White Rabbit* which I heard a few times on the radio.

I was secretly admiring her as she sipped her tea – she looked so relaxed, but at the same time so engaged in the conversation, and so clear and articulate about her ideas. I knew that all she was thinking about at that moment was her music, and that to her I was no more than someone who could help her with that.

She looked very pretty, and it wasn't just her long bond hair. Her eyes were sharp, but at the same time feminine, with a kind of forlorn expression which intrigued me but which I didn't know how to read. Her nose and her mouth were small, maybe even too small, but her entire face was elfin, and that, instead of making it seem disproportionate, just made her eyes look larger. She was wearing a black long-sleeved top and a pair of bootcut jeans – nothing fancy, something she probably got from New Look or Topshop. I doubted she even noticed that I was wearing my best pair of jeans and that I've spent over two hours styling my hair that morning. If she hasn't been around rockers much before, then she must have assumed that hair that was spiky at the ends but had lots of movement at the roots was a completely natural thing. I smiled at her and put my tea cup down on the worktop, leaning against the wall where we had all the flyers from clubs I played at with the Storm Angels.

I was about to ask about her plans for that evening, when

she said, 'Ready?'

'Yeah, sure,' I said, moving my half-finished cup of tea into the sink and following her into the living room.

It took me a few minutes to tune my fifty Watt Marshall combo, and once I did, we were all set to go. Claire sat on a chair across from me and played the harmony for her first song.

'Now do the guide vocals,' I said, and once she sang, felt gradually transported to a place so remote from our surroundings I stopped noticing where I was any more. Her singing was so open, but at the same time so focused and resolute, and had such disconcerting vulnerability to it that I suddenly felt a heart-wrenchingly unsettling sensation rise up inside me. And I had no idea what to do about.

'This is beautiful stuff,' I said, once she finished. 'So, you want to do an electric guitar solo somewhere after the third verse, right?' I tried to sound as together as I could, but it wasn't easy.

'Right,' she said and nodded.

My throat suddenly became dry and my hands went cold, but I asked her to play the harmony again, and then heard an extension to her vocal melody in my mind that sounded simple and modest, something I would never have thought of before, given that all I ever wanted to sound like in my life until then was either Edward van Halen or Randy Rhoades. I don't know how it came to me, but when I began playing, I somehow managed to tap into a place within myself that responded not only to the melody, but to the timbre of her voice, some parts of my lead replying to her vocal tone, others – posing subtle questions to the melody, and at privileged moments uniting with them both.

By quarter to seven we had a rough demo of two of Claire's songs taped on Dave's portable recorder, and I knew what my job was going to be for the rest of the next two weeks – my solos needed more work, and some of the middle eight sections needed rethinking, but I was glad that Claire seemed to be pleased with what I've managed to come up with so far.

'Thank you,' she said, as we both went into the kitchen for more tea. 'I love your ideas. This is all very new to me. I've never worked with another guitarist before.'

'Neither have I,' I replied. 'Even though I thought I have before I met you.'

'You're very kind,' she said, smiling. 'I don't even know how to thank you.'

'Why don't you stay for dinner?' I asked. 'I can cook a mean spag bol. My father is a chef, you know. He's Italian.'

'Really?' she asked, smiling and looking at me somewhat differently now.

'Yeah,' I said.

I suddenly wondered why I felt so at ease talking to her and telling her about my working class background. I suddenly remembered that I've never told Theodora what my parents did for a living. And she never asked.

'I wish I could stay, but I can't,' she said. 'I'm on a night shift today.'

'A night shift? I didn't know you worked.'

'I'm a receptionist at an A&E,' she said.

'Wow, you must see lots of gross stuff,' I blurted out without thinking.

'You can say that,' she laughed. 'I'm thinking of training to be a nurse. I wanted to be a doctor when I was at school, but now I know I won't be able to study and keep playing music. To be honest, I don't even know if I should do the Common Foundation Programme. They say it's hard work.'

'Well, that's why I'm on the dole,' I said. 'I had a job before I joined the Angels, but then I had to quit because we started touring.'

'Do you still tour a lot?' she asked. 'It's funny I've never heard of your band before. I guess I should have.'

'Well, to be honest, I'm between bands now,' I said. 'I've left, but now they want me back because Global Union's offered them a record deal, and they reckon my rock star looks are going to improve their chances of succeeding in this biz. Don't laugh, I'm not making this up. As ridiculous as it sounds, that's what Global told our manager.'

'I'm not laughing!' she said. 'And you do look like a rock star. Like that guy from Motley Crue, but cuter.'

'Like the guy from Motley Crue, but cuter! That's the best compliment I've ever received in my entire life!' I exclaimed. 'Apart from when people tell me I don't play guitar too badly, of course, ha-ha! I won't be able to sleep tonight! You just told me I'm cuter than Tommy Lee! Or who did you mean? Surely not Mick Mars?'

'No, not Tommy Lee!' she laughed.

'Oh, shit, you did mean Mick Mars, didn't you?'

'No, the bass player. The moody guy.'

'Oh, it gets better and better! Am I dreaming?' I laughed, feeling genuinely pleased. In fact, I was on cloud nine.

'But you do look the part,' she said. 'How many girlfriends do you have, Mr. Rockstar?'

'Wow!' I yelled, laughing. 'Hold it! Girlfriends? None!'

'I don't believe it,' she said, smiling.

'Trust me on this,' I said. 'Trust me. I don't want the girls who want me, and those who I do want, aren't interested in what I have to offer.'

I then burst out laughing to hide my embarrassment.

'So you're looking for a Hollywood actress to go out with,' she said. Not in a vicious way though.

'A Hollywood actress? I've never thought of that!'

'Sure you haven't,' said Claire, continuing to smile.

'I honestly haven't. I don't even go to the cinema these days. And I don't watch TV. I would just like to go out with someone who's pretty, intelligent, and nice. And if she then turns out to be creative, I'd be over the moon!' I then paused. 'Wow, haven't I just described you to a tee?'

'Hopefully it will all improve once you sign with Global

Union,' Claire said, ignoring my question.

'Well, see, I don't want to sign with them,' I said, 'That band doesn't write its own tunes.'

'What?' Claire looked at me half-amused, half-horrified.

'I know,' I said. 'That's why I don't really feel like signing the deal. Their manager Doug writes all the material. It's dismal, isn't it?'

'Sounds like it...' she said quietly.

'Anyway,' I said, 'This American girl I know has been telling me I should go to LA and see if anything pans out for me over there.'

'Does she live there?' asked Claire.

'She's originally from LA, but she lives in London now. Her university course is about to finish, so she thinks of going back and says I could go with her to check it out.'

'Knowing people there would help,' said Claire. 'I have a cousin in Los Angeles who's trying to get his screenplay seen by someone in Hollywood. I don't know how it's working out for him, but I could give you his number, if that would help.'

I felt touched and thought how awkward it was going to be to tell her who Theodora's father really was.

'Thanks, that would be great,' I said. 'Theodora says she knows some people too. Or, rather, her parents do...'

'Her name is Theodora?'

'Yes. She's American. An impressive name, isn't it? She really knows how to impress people with... you know, with wealth really. And the way she acts... She's just very different from anyone I usually hang with... I think I'm sort of scared of her.' I had to laugh again to make myself sound less pathetic. 'She dated this mega-famous rock star back home before she came to England.'

'Really? Maybe you should think of getting to know her better,' Claire smiled.

'Ha, she reckons we are in a some sort of relationship, which is really hilarious if you think of it.'

'Why?'

150

'Just because we are not, it's not like we are even very close, we've never been close in any way... We've never even shared a single creative idea. She's into high-brow modern art. That's what she's studying here in London.'

'Creative people can be very different from one another,' said Claire. 'You and I are very different but we can still work together. I think what you did with my songs was amazing. I'm really grateful. And I can't wait to show you the remaining songs.'

'Well, sometimes people just click,' I said.

I walked Claire back to the tube station, and as I was returning home, I suddenly found myself utterly amazed at how I've behaved around her that day. I've told her everything about Doug and the deal, I told her all about Theodora, and I found myself not regretting a single word I said to her. In fact, for once I felt really good about being able to talk openly to someone who could just listen without judging me.

Claire left her guitar at our flat, meaning to return the next day to work on the remaining two songs she picked for the demo. I was sitting down with some chord charts trying to see what I could do for the middle eight section of one of the songs we've rehearsed that day, when my phone rang, and once I looked at the screen I saw it was Theodora who I forgot to call earlier, even though I've promised.

She didn't sound annoyed anymore though, just tired.

'If you can't make it to the party, Joey, that's fine,' she said. 'But I would really have appreciated you letting me know.'

I told her I was working on a music project, but she didn't ask me what it was.

'Save up your ideas for the time you're in LA,' she said, before hanging up.

'Joey, don't sign that deal with Global,' was the first thing Claire said to me when she walked into our flat the next morning, before taking off her coat. 'Go to LA with that American girl, I think things will turn out that way much better for you. You know, with the kind of music you play maybe you stand a better chance of getting a proper record deal there.'

I really didn't expect her to worry or care about me or about my career. I was really touched, in fact, even moved.

'I have intuition for those things,' Claire was saying to me later over a cup of tea in the kitchen. 'I think you'll do rather well in America. And I really mean this because, see, I really don't have to tell you this. I'd, obviously, rather prefer for you to stay here and continue working on songs with me... Who's gonna help me with all this stuff once you're gone?'

She then smiled, and I wondered if she meant it. But she must have because by lunch time we've come up with arrangements for her songs that to me sounded stunning, one solo in particular, which I thought was the best solo I've ever played – short, sharp, and entirely to the point, and which flowed so naturally I sounded almost like I haven't made any effort with it at all and was playing on pure inspiration.

We finished just in time because a few minutes later Ben and Dave returned home after a morning out shopping for a new shower head for our bathroom. The four of us had buttered toast in the living room while my flatmates where having their best go at a normal conversation without their usual bad taste innuendos and crass observations. For once I wasn't embarrassed to be with someone else in their company. And for the first time as long as I could remember I was having a serious discussion about music with them, suddenly realising that both actually did have some taste and could form their own opinions as to who was worth what on today's rock scene.

Claire, as I have now discovered, could talk for Britain. She told us about other songs she had written and how it worried her that they were all so different stylistically. She had an idea of bringing them together in an album which she hoped would have artwork that would explain some of the ambiguities, and dreamed of a producer who would do something to unify the material. The surprising thing was that the more she talked, the more I wanted to hear, because I've never met anyone before who could describe so vividly and so passionately the kind of music they had in mind and the kind of things they wanted to do.

She then told us how in the summer she would sleep in her parents' back garden and how the most amazing songs would come to her in her sleep, so that she ended up having her guitar and a tape machine next to her so that she could record her ideas when she woke up.

'Looking at the stars at night is the most amazing thing ever,' she was saying. 'I can look at the night sky for hours, it takes you in completely. Just to think that you are looking out into the worlds we know nothing about. I think that when in the Sixties they used to say "far out" they actually meant this sort of thing, seeing something that lies beyond our universe. And the night sky is so beautiful. I once went to an art gallery after looking at the stars the night before, and none of the paintings really came close to what you see and feel when you look at the cosmos.'

I haven't been seeing Theodora during the time between meeting Claire and finally going into the studio two weeks later to record her demo. We spoke a few times on the phone and she told me that her party for the Courtauld girls went well with Mark and Chris making quite an impression on the Courtauld crowd, as well as the other way around. At any other time I would have felt uneasy hearing about Mark hanging at Theodora's house without me there, but I was so absorbed in working on Claire's material that I let it go without giving it much thought.

Theodora finally asked me what kind of project I was

working on. I told her it was somebody Dave was moonlighting with, a singer songwriter, but I didn't tell her it was a girl. Women musicians are so few and far between in this business that I was sure it didn't occur to Theodora that I was working with one. She then asked me if I wanted to go with her to an opening at a photography gallery in Camden, but that was the day of our recording session with Claire, so I told her I couldn't make it. She then suddenly asked me if I have told Doug to count me out of the Global deal. I told her I was still unsure about it, and the last thing she said to me before hanging up was that I had to do it as soon as possible, "before Doug's visualisations of you returning to the band finally materialise".

I was really fired up on the morning of our recording session. Ben, Dave, and I left home at ten, even though Claire wasn't supposed to turn up until lunch time. She was doing some weirdly scheduled shifts that week and was only going to make it to the studio by one. While we sat in the control room waiting for her, I suddenly felt I wasn't going to be able to play shit if I didn't calm my nerves with something stronger than Stella that we were drinking. (Despite drinks being strictly prohibited anywhere near the mixing desk.)

As I was walking out of the front door heading to the off-license to buy a couple of JD miniatures, I suddenly came face to face with Claire who was just coming in. Her guitar case bashed me on the knee, and I laughed out of pain, nervousness, and surprise at seeing her turn up early.

'I'm gonna nip to the off license,' I said, 'Do you want anything?'

'I'll come with you,' she said. 'I feel really nervous. I need something strong.'

We ended up buying a 35ml bottle of JD, two cans of Coke, and downing them all in ten minutes outside of the studio before going back in. I began feeling much better and could now think and talk like a normal person, not like a kid before his first big exam. I suddenly noticed that Claire looked really pretty that day – she wore skinny blue jeans, an oversized long-sleeved white shirt, and a chunky necklace that looked like something from a history museum. I asked her what it was and she said it was a replica of Aztec jewellery.

I then gave her a guided tour of the reception area, which consisted of me pointing at framed cover art on the walls, saying, 'Look at this,' and her instantly naming the artist, the album, and the year of release. It then occurred to me that this was the same place I felt so miserable visiting just a few months ago when I was here to record my song for Theodora. It all seemed like a different era now.

It didn't take Dave long to set Claire up. She did her acoustic guitar parts first, which took less than an hour for all four songs. She worked fast and, surprisingly, needed no more than three takes to get it right – something that amazed Dave who was used to big names sometimes taking up to a week to lay down a simple acoustic guitar track. She then sang guide vocals for me to do my solos with, and it was now my turn to come up with stuff. Dave sat me in the live room with the mic five feet away from the back on the amp. He said this was the way to go about it if we wanted "the authentic Sixties psychedelic sound". Which neither Claire, not I were sure we particularly wanted, but still went along with simply because of Dave's LIPA credentials and the fact that he worked in a legendary studio. And, surprisingly enough, it worked. My guitar suddenly began to speak in a deep, sonorous voice that enveloped Claire's acoustic parts in layers of resonance, giving them balance and authority I never thought such simple harmonic structures could have. It was the first time in my life when I began to appreciate what sound techs could do for musicians.

We finished at nine p.m., and left the studio an hour later after listening to the finished tracks a few times over. During the first listen I didn't recognise myself playing. I sounded meditative, brooding, and completely different from the way I did on my demos with the Storm Angels, where I was always trying to imitate the sharp, edgy style of the Eighties glam metal guitarists. Here I suddenly found myself going with the flow of the songs, not trying to impose my chops onto them and letting the vocals take the front seat.

Excited, the four of us filed into the street, each clutching a copy of the demo, no one wanting to say goodbye. So, all of us being skint, we wound up back at our flat with a bottle of JD and a one and a half litre bottle of Diet Coke. We had such a great time talking about the demo, the ideas Claire had for songs that weren't recorded yet, and what we could do with them, that we realised what time it was only when Claire's parents rang telling her it was quarter to midnight, wondering where she was. It was too late to think about going back to Croydon for her, so I offered her my bed and said I'd sleep on the living room sofa. But it never came to that because our small party continued until five in the morning, at which point we all decided it was a good idea to watch Led Zeppelin's *The Song Remains the Same* DVD, which we did, Claire finally falling asleep with her head on my shoulder to the sounds of *No Quarter*.

'Dude, you'd better carry her to your room,' said Ben half-jokingly, but I brought my finger to my lips not wanting to disturb her, enjoying every moment of us being close.

She eventually woke up as the band launched into *Whole Lotta Love*, not realising at first where she was, but then smiling at me with the sweetest, warmest smile, before getting up, saying it was time for her to go home. I couldn't persuade her to take my bed while I made breakfast, and soon we were both walking to the tube station in the morning cold, me carrying her guitar case and her holding on to my arm.

156

Dave was asleep in his room when I got back, but Ben was in the kitchen making breakfast. He offered me a piece of toast, but I refused.

'Trying to keep fit before LA?' he asked teasingly with his mouth full.

'LA?' I repeated absent-mindedly.

'Theodora called while you were out,' he said, smiling, trying to read my face. 'Said your mobile was switched off.'

'Oh, no,' I moaned, leaning against the door frame and rolling my eyes.

'Oh, yes,' Ben said, smirking.

'You've never met her, have you?' I asked.

'No. But I'm hearing she's fit.'

'Yeah, here,' I said, taking my phone out of my pocket, turning it on, and showing him a picture of Theodora I took the last time I was out with her in Islington.

Ben whistled and then shook his head.

'What?' I asked, my voice suddenly sounding nervous.

'You can't mess around with people like that,' he said. 'They only appear in your life like once and then it's up to you what you do with it. How you deal with the opportunity. And it seems you've been messing around for far too long with all the opportunities that have come your way lately.'

'It's not all about opportunities,' I said. 'I mean, it is, but a business opportunity is often poles apart from a creative opportunity.'

'You're right,' said Ben. 'The two birds might as well have been from two different galaxies.'

VIII

COMBINATION OF THE TWO

I thought a lot about what Ben said to me that morning. And I thought about Doug's Global deal too for the next few days, until nature put a stop to that.

The call came from Johnny, the Storm Angels drummer, five days after we recorded Claire's demo at the studio.

'Doug has died,' he told me in an emotionless voice I knew so well.

'Doug Scrivener?' I asked, shocked.

'Yeah, Doug. The funeral is tomorrow.'

'How did he die?'

'Heart attack.'

'No.'

'Sad, but true,' Johnny replied, making me wonder if he was trying to stay respectfully sombre or was, in fact, showing some kind of macabre sense of humour.

'Are you going to the funeral?' I asked.

'Yes, all of us in the band are going. We wanted to let you know.'

'I'll be there,' I said, without thinking.

The first person I rang was Claire. I was so shocked and disoriented that I simply blurted out the news pretty much straight after she answered the phone. She asked if I was going to the funeral, and before I could reply, offered to go with me. I felt so grateful I could hardly keep myself from beginning to bawl my eyes out. Which was exactly what I did right after I hung up. It wasn't because I was sad that Doug was gone, or because I felt guilty for thinking so badly of him and telling everyone else during all those months what a dreadful human being he was. It was mainly because I suddenly realised that his death brought my childhood to an end. I was now completely independent. I was on my own and was going to start making my own decisions.

There was, of course, no denying that Doug was a father figure to me. Not a kind of father anyone in their right mind would wish for, but who still did take over my real father once I moved to London from my parents' house. My real father never had time for me, not because he was indifferent, but because he worked fourteen hours a day, coming home from work at half past midnight every night, making it impossible for us to spend any time together in the evenings, or in the mornings, for that matter, because he'd be still asleep, exhausted, at the time when I would be leaving home for school. All my father did in his life was work. And being a chef is one of the hardest jobs there is. Something I'd never want to do myself.

I guess I was also crying out of relief, realising that I wasn't going to have to think about the Global deal anymore. And in a way it felt like I've just received my freedom back. I was also crying out of the sheer shock of encountering death at such a close range for the first time in my life. I've never known anyone who's died, and I've never been to a funeral before. And that was when I realised that I had to think about what I was going to wear. Ripped jeans and a band t-shirt certainly weren't going to do. So I spent the rest of the day planning my outfit.

I only understood what a tough gig this was going to be once Claire and I actually got there. Johnny and the rest of the band stood in the background, but the first person I recognised in their group was Shawna, who in her unusual display of bad taste wore a full-length black leather coat that made her nylon hair extensions stand out even starker, their limp uneven yellow strands hanging lifelessly from under her own thinning hair. She and Johnny must have gotten back together – he had his arm around her. Claire, in her black wool coat, and I, wearing black jeans I haven't worn since Colchester and a black military-style jacket I borrowed from Dave, came up to say hi, and were pointed in the direction of a sullen woman who looked like she wore shoulder pads to prevent her brown coat from hanging off her frame like a shapeless rag, standing a few yards away from us with a thin long-haired blond boy who couldn't have been older than twelve.

'That's Doug's ex-wife,' Johnny told me. 'With their son.'

'Oh my god,' I couldn't help whispering. 'I didn't know Doug had a son. Or that he's ever been married.'

Claire held my hand as we approached Doug's ex-wife and two other men in their forties wearing black suits, who turned out to be Doug's cousins. My condolences sounded as if some other person was saying the words, while the real me was hiding at the bottom of my stomach, curled up in a tight, tense ball of nerves. I couldn't bring myself to look at the boy, who I knew was staring at my face all those excruciating moments I spent offering sympathy to his mother. She acknowledged my words with no more than a nod and then turned to speak to the other men. She, her son, and Doug's cousins were the only people who were there from Doug's family. I didn't know if his parents where still alive, and I didn't want to ask anyone in case I heard the answer I was fearing. There were seven of us altogether at the cemetery, including the band, Clair, and Shawna. I winced at the thought of Claire and Shawna having anything in common, even such a trivial thing as their boyfriends playing in the same band at one time or another. I then caught myself thinking of Claire as my girlfriend, which surprised and exhilarated me at the same time, and I squeezed her hand thinking of how sometimes things just came about without you noticing or trying to make anything happen.

'Well done talking to his wife,' Claire said to me, as we returned back to join Johnny and the band.

None of the guys in the Storm Angels have changed much since I last saw them four months ago. Johnny had his shoulder-length brown hair permed now, and it sort of suited him, while the others looked fashionably gaunt, although a bit too aloof, the reason for which I couldn't work out at first until I realised that all three were completely stoned. Johnny was the only one who could still talk. I wondered why the kid who got hired in my place wasn't there, but then decided against asking, fearing that the question would open a whole can of worms.

'Thinking of worms at a graveyard,' I thought to myself, and nearly smiled.

I felt grateful all of us could be civil and grown-up with each other, apart from Shawna that is, whose resentment towards me and Claire she wasn't bothering to disguise, or probably decided to amplify just to piss me off. Surprisingly, now that I had Claire with me, I felt no hostility towards Shawna, who kept drilling us both with her bulging pale eyes. I felt pity and slight contempt, but even that went away soon despite the hateful ritual she was continuing to play out on me. Her antagonism stopped bothering me as soon as I realised that it wasn't real arrogance on her part, or genuine hatred, or envy, but simply self-loathing, pure and simple she was projecting onto me, because we all need someone to blame for our bad luck at one time or another. One thing that Shawna always wanted – the glamorous lifestyle – was now further away from her grasp than ever, and she must have felt rotten. With Doug dead there was no chance for the Storm Angels getting signed. They didn't have enough tunes for an album, and none of them could write to the level Global expected from their acts. I suddenly wanted to tell Shawna to try to set other goals for herself and redefine what constituted achievement in her book, and almost laughed a second later imagining the barrage of abuse this well-meaning suggestion would provoke.

Johnny asked me if I had a band going.

'Not a band per se, but I've just finished working on a demo with Claire,' I said, addressing him, but looking at her, to which he replied with a polite nod and a "hi" addressed to her.

'What about you?' I asked.

'Well, until last week we were waiting to hear from you,' he said dryly, 'but now, obviously, it's time to disband.'

I nodded, feeling uncomfortable, as if there was something I owed Johnny and his band or as if there was some kind of agreement between us, my part of which I didn't fulfil.

I then heard voices coming from behind, and as I turned, I saw four young guys talking to Doug's wife, one carrying a bouquet of white roses. I realised that I too should have brought something with me, but it was obviously too late now.

'Did you bring any flowers?' I asked Johnny.

'No,' he said curtly. 'But do you realise who those guys are?'

'Who are they?'

'The Space Truckers Incorporated.'

'Who?!' Both Claire and I stared at him as if he's just told us they were the actual Teletubbies.

'A band. Always strutting around Camden pretending to be signed.'

I suddenly realised that I haven't been to Camden in months.

'And what are they doing here?' I asked.

'I have no clue.'

Meanwhile, the new arrivals, all wearing pretentious boho outfits – scarves, expensive-looking tailored jackets, and high heel boots – approached our group, nodding to us.

'Alright, Johnny,' said one of them.

'Hey, Dan,' Johnny replied.

Dan, a smartly dressed plumpish bloke with dirty blond

curly hair, then asked if smoking was allowed, a question no one knew the answer to.

'So you knew Doug quite well,' said Johnny to Dan after a pause.

'Just as well as you guys did,' replied Dan, sounding slightly surprised.

'We were managed by him, you know,' I said.

'And so were we,' Dan said, now looking even more surprised.

We stared at the Truckers.

'Are you serious?' asked Johnny.

Dan smiled. 'We signed our management deal two weeks before he died.'

'I knew nothing about it,' said Johnny, and then, addressing to his bandmates, 'Did you know about this?'

I'm not sure if the rest of them actually understood what the question was, or what the conversation was about, but all three shook their heads.

'Fucking prick,' said Shawna under her breath.

She probably didn't expect anyone to hear her, but we all did, and it became painfully embarrassing. Not as much for her though, as for Johnny.

'What?' she asked suddenly, fixing each of us in turn with a hard stare. 'Don't you know he was a complete prick?'

'No,' said Dan.

'Well, at least now you know!' she shouted. 'Isn't it obvious he signed you without telling the other band?!'

'It's his business who he signs,' Dan said patronisingly.

'Yeah, but it was our band that got him in touch with Global,' screamed Shawna.

Now everyone was looking at us. If the Earth could swallow me whole at that moment and never let me back out again, I would have been grateful. Johnny tried to calm Shawna down, while Dan walked off to join his band, who were now all looking at us.

'Come on, Johnny, we're going home,' Shawna said, grabbing his arm.

'We can't go now,' he said weakly, but she was hell-bent on leaving.

'Why are we even here?!' she began screaming again. 'Why are we here?! He was just a miserable old wanker who tried to make a quick buck at our expense!'

One of Doug's cousins was now approaching us in quick broad steps, his fists clenched, ready, so I could guess, to kick the living shit out of us all. I instinctively stepped in front of Claire.

'Listen, mate, just go,' I said to Johnny just when he finally gave in, letting Shawna drag him away.

It became eerie by the graveside when it came to the actual burial. The vicar was out of his depth, talking about Doug's "passion for music" and "helping young talent", ending his speech with a string of platitudes. Doug's son was hiding behind his mother's back, who stood there looking tired and drained. The cousins both wore expressions of grim fury, and all of us musicians stole awkward glances at each other from time to time, each wishing the whole ordeal to be over with before one of us had a hysterical fit, or made a joke, or stumbled over and fell into the grave, so stoned everyone was apart from Claire and me.

Claire and I didn't go back to the house. I didn't think any of us from the Storm Angels were welcome there after Shawna's scene, and even if we were, I wouldn't have been able to cope with it. Being at the burial was difficult enough, so I asked Claire if she wanted to have a drink in a pub nearby once it was all over.

'It must have been hard for Doug to manage this band,' she said, as we sat down in the far corner with our pints.

'He found it rather easy,' I said grimly. 'He knew how to run a tight shift.'

'That girl looked very upset,' said Claire. 'It must be her way of dealing with grief.'

I choked when she said it, nearly spitting my beer back into my glass.

'Shawna is the most cynical, calculating, cold-hearted individual you'll ever meet,' I said, finally being able to swallow. 'She doesn't understand the concept of grief. Or death. Or life. Or anything that has to do with anything normal or human.'

'How do you know?' asked Claire.

'Trust me, I've spent enough time around her. She's a damaged individual.'

'Well, we all are in one way or another, aren't we?'

I stared at Claire. I've never thought of it that way.

'I suppose we are,' I said. 'But we have different ways of dealing with it. Or expressing it.'

'Think about bands like Metallica,' she said. 'If they weren't damaged, we'd never hear the most beautiful music of our time. Stuff like *Master of Puppets*.'

'That's what Doug was,' I said, smiling.

Claire smiled back and had a sip of her pint.

'His death must have quite a meaning for you,' she said.

'I'm sure it does, but I'm still trying to figure out what it means to me,' I said.

We then sat in silence for a while before I said, 'Sorry, Claire, I really didn't realise how hard this whole thing would be. If not for you, I'd probably have left with Johnny. I'm really glad you came along.'

She smiled and patted my hand. I moved to sit next to her and put my arm around her shoulders. As we continued sitting there in silence, I suddenly realised that I have never felt so good in months. In fact, in years. I've never felt so good ever before, I finally realised. I could have sat next to Claire for the rest of the day, without worrying about having anything to say or feeling it was necessary to talk at all. Or to communicate in any other way than by simple touch. I suddenly felt confident, calm, and completely at peace with myself and everything around me. And I felt like I never really wanted anything to be different. I realised that I haven't known her for long and probably didn't know her at all, but having written music with her I felt I knew her better than anyone else in my life. I realised that there was still a lot to find out about her, but it excited me. Going away to LA now seemed like madness. I could have searched the world over and would never have found someone like her. And then, as I thought about it, my tranquillity suddenly lifted as quickly as it descended on me. I started worrying that I could somehow still lose her. I couldn't tell how or why, but the thought made me squeeze her shoulders tighter, without noticing it, until she turned to me with a smile and asked how I was feeling.

'I'm fine, fine,' I said in an anxious-sounding voice, turning my face to hers and moving a strand of blond hair away from her face.

Explaining to another person how you feel about them while in a pub with a pint in your hand, is the corniest thing anyone can do, and being fully aware of that, I asked if she wanted to go for a walk.

I had no idea which direction we were heading in when we left the pub, until I decided that it didn't matter. We were somewhere in Northwest London, a leafy, quiet area, which should have reminded me of Theodora's house, but somehow didn't. I had my arm around Claire as we walked up a narrow, almost country-like road, with trees growing on both sides, telling her that the last thing I wanted to do was go to LA.

'It would be good for you to go,' she said, 'but I think it really doesn't matter where you are – London, LA, or New York. I think that someone like you can get signed anywhere.'

'Why?' I asked.

'Because you're very talented,' she said.

'People say that's not why I'll get signed, if I ever will.'

'Who says that? And what other reason could there be?'

'A lot of people seem to think that I'll get signed because of my looks,' I said, letting out a short burst of nervous laughter.

'That's nonsense,' she said. 'It takes a musician to know what another musician is capable of.'

'I never thought of it this way. So what do you say we get to know each other better?' I said, stopping, and kissing her for the first time. And once I kissed her I didn't want to let go no matter what happened. For the first time in my life being with a girl felt exactly right – there was no anxiety, no lingering resentment, no doubts.

When I woke up the next morning on what I now thought was my side of the bed, Claire was gone, and the realisation made me panic. I had no idea why she had to leave so early. Was she now regretting the whole thing? Have I done anything to upset her? The only way to find out was to call her, which I did as soon as it was noon.

'I'm sorry, Joey,' I heard her voice. 'I just didn't feel comfortable being around your flatmates in the morning. They are really nice, it's just that...'

'You should have stayed,' I said. 'I would have made you breakfast in bed.'

'That's sweet,' she said. 'How are you feeling?'

'I'm OK, but I wish you were here,' I said.

'I miss you too.'

'When will I see you next?'

'Joey,' she said quietly. 'Are you going to LA?'

'Oh my god, Claire!' I nearly screamed. 'Of course not! And I want to move out of this flat as soon as I can so that I could spend more time with you.'

'Are you sure you don't want to go to America?' she asked.

'Positive,' I said, feeling suddenly proud of myself. 'Absolutely positive. I want to stay with you in London.'

As soon as I finished talking to Claire, I went straight out and bought a paper to see if I could a) find a job, and b) find a flat I could rent on my own. I knew it wasn't going to be anywhere near the first four travel zones, but I didn't care. I felt it was time to move out of a flatshare and find a place where I could have some privacy. I then took a shower, put my best pair of jeans and a John 5 t-shirt on, ready to head out to Charing Cross Road to see my old boss at the guitar shop. I wanted to know if I could have my job back and if anyone he knew needed guitar lessons. Or bass lessons. Or lessons on surviving on the unsigned London rock scene.

Before I could leave the house though, my phone rang. It was Theodora.

'Haven't heard from you in a while,' she said. 'How are you?'

'I'm fine,' I said. 'I was just about to go out.'

'Really? Are you going to be anywhere near Hampstead?'

'No,' I said. 'I'm off to Charing Cross Road to see if I my old boss would give me my job back.'

'What job, Joey?'

'I need a job to move out of this flat and get my own place.'

'Really? Why can't you wait for a few weeks before we go to LA?'

'I don't think I'll be able to go to LA,' I said, feeling as if a weight has been lifted once I uttered the actual words.

'You. Are. Not. Going. To. LA?' I heard an ice-cold voice on the other end of the line.

'I know. I'm sorry, Theodora, but I got involved in this project here in London that I'd like to continue working on.'

'Project? What project?'

'There is this songwriter I'm working with and it works out amazingly well,' I said.

'Well, let me hear it!' Theodora suddenly sounded enthusiastic. 'What kind of music is it?'

'It's pretty old-fashioned,' I began saying, not really wanting to tell her much more.

'Like what?'

'Well, a bit like acoustic Led Zeppelin, I guess,' I said.

'Yeah, right!' She laughed.

'Seriously though, it's awesome. Listen, I have to go now...'

'No, wait. Do you have a demo?'

'Not as such...'

'Whatever you have, bring it over, I'll have a listen, and I'll let my father hear it too maybe?'

'We are not really ready to send out any demos,' I began, but she interrupted me.

'Or I have a better idea,' she said. Meet me in Belsize Park for lunch, I know an awesome Italian place there. You'll love it.'

And she hung up while I was still trying to think of an excuse not to see her that day.

'Listen, Theodora, I can't really stay for long, I still have to make it to Charing Cross Road before they close today,' I said, sitting down in front of her at a table of some "rustic" Italian place a few minutes walk from Belsize Park tube.

'Don't be silly,' she said. 'If your project is any good, we'll get all of you guys over to LA.'

'No, I don't think Claire wants to go to LA,' I replied without thinking.

'Who's Claire?' asked Theodora.

'Sod it,' I thought. 'What do I care if Theodora knows about my relationship with Claire? She'd have to find out sooner or later.'

Theodora was now looking at me intently from across the table.

'Claire is the girl who writes the songs,' I said.

'She writes those amazing songs you're working on?'

'Yeah.'

'So she is the female Jimmy Page of your new band?'

I smiled. I knew what Theodora was thinking. Just like the majority of people in the music business she would never believe that a female could write good songs. At that moment she probably thought that I got involved with some girl who wasn't even a proper musician simply because I was bored and had nothing else to do.

'Look, Joey, I don't think you quite understand,' she began speaking slowly, as if explaining a simple equation to an imbecile child. 'I will make sure you meet all the right people in LA. I'll network for you. I am positive you'll find musicians to work with there and the kind of musicians who really do have a future.'

'That's very kind of you,' I replied sincerely. 'I really do appreciate that. It's just that me and Claire work very well together, and I'd like to stay in London for now to work with her.'

'And what about us?' she suddenly asked.

'What about us?'

'You know I will be finishing my course in three weeks' time and going back to the States. All this time I thought you were coming with me.'

'So did I...' I began.

Her face changed. 'Please don't continue,' she said. 'It's all very clear now. Every time you told me you loved me you didn't mean a word of it, did you?'

'Theodora, you never did let me love you,' I said. 'You know I was crazy about you. I could have loved you. But you never let me.'

'Because I never actually slept with you, is that what you are trying to say? Is that your definition of love?'

'Theodora, can you honestly say you ever had feelings for me?' I asked, and was myself surprised at how bitter my voice suddenly sounded.

'I could have loved you,' she said, looking away. 'If you gave me more time.'

'But life isn't like that. It never lets us pause and wait when we need to. Like with Doug...'

'Oh, please!' she exclaimed. 'What does Doug have to do with all this?'

'He's just died. We buried him yesterday.'

'He died?'

'Heart attack.'

'Oh, well,' she sighed. 'I never knew him.'

She glanced quickly at the menu and then pushed it aside.

'Funny, I'm not hungry anymore,' she said.

'Neither am I.'

'Are you sleeping with her?' she asked, looking me straight in the face.

I didn't reply.

'Anyway, Joey,' she said, getting up and picking her python leather bag from the chair next to her. 'I'll see you around. You don't have to walk with me.'

I never did make it to Charing Cross Road that day. I was so pissed off with myself, with Theodora and with just about everyone else apart from Claire that I simply went back home and spent the rest of the day sulking and getting stoned. I wondered how things would have turned out if Theodora really cared for me and we did end up as a couple. I knew it was pointless to think about it now, as I have realised a long time ago it wasn't going to work out between us, even though I chose not to admit it to myself for ages. Theodora and I could never have a future together. And it wasn't that we were different. Zara and Rich were different. Theodora and I were incompatible. And now I was actually glad that it never worked out. If it did, I would never have met Claire. And I was so happy I found her I knew that nothing could ever drag me away from her.

I never thought I'd hear from Theodora again after our conversation in Belsize Park, and, frankly, I didn't care. Claire and I were looking for a flat to rent together, and although my old boss couldn't take me back, he told me to check another shop where they said I could start within a week. Claire and I were spending most of our time together, making good progress on re-writing her old songs and writing new stuff. We went to see Sandy's band play in Shoreditch one night, and she though he was a great guitarist, but the band wasn't good enough for him.

'Wait until you meet his manager,' I said to her, laughing. 'If you think the band is not good enough for him, that guy will be the one who'll end up ruining his career.'

We had a drink with Sandy once he came off the stage, and I found him looking drained and sounding crabby. He said he was sorry to hear about Doug, but I could tell his death had left him totally indifferent. He was telling me how his band was falling apart because their drummer had quit and their rhythm guitarist was about to, all because of their manager who's been consistently fucking up every opportunity that came their way. He told me they did go to Japan, and the Japanese labels were put off by Tony's attitude.

'The mentality is different in Japan, isn't it?' I asked him diplomatically.

'The mentality is the same everywhere,' Sandy replied gruffly. 'If they think they can make money with your band and you are all reasonably sane – not too mad or horribly addicted, or dangerously delusional – they'll sign you.'

'I don't see what the problem is then.'

'I spoke to a journo from Global Rock the other day, asked him if they would do another interview with us, and he said he didn't mind, but the editor, apparently, hates us. Which surprised me, and then it turns out he doesn't hate *us*, he hates Tony, and so do a couple of other editors. They think he's an arrogant twat. And you know how it always filters back to the labels. I bet the jouros don't tell the labels that our manager is an arrogant dickhead, they tell them that he's a complete and utter nutcase, and that everyone in his band is either a hopeless drug addict, or a closet nazi, or that we are about to break up anyway because we hate each other and squabble constantly over songwriting credits.'

'Right,' I said. 'Well, why don't you get rid of Tony then?'

'We've signed a management deal with him,' Sandy said. 'And he says he's busting his ass for us because he keeps arranging all those industry showcases and constantly introduces us to all the "important" people. He just doesn't realise that once he finds an opportunity, he, and no one else, ends up blowing it. And it happens every time. Our only option now is to disband and regroup again under a different name. But I'm really fucking tired of changing bands and having to deal with personnel issues, and egos, and band politics. I've been doing this for over ten years now.'

I didn't realise Sandy was that old. I always thought he was slightly older than me, but I never knew he was over thirty.

'I thought you guys were getting along pretty well in your band,' I said.

'We were. But not until our bass player began muscling in on my songwriting.'

'So you *are* at each other's throats over songwriting credits,' I thought. 'I wonder who's doing more damage to this band – the manager or the musicians.'

Claire wouldn't stop smiling at Sandy while he was talking, and at this point suddenly cut in and told him she thought his band didn't do his playing justice and that he could do really well in another outfit.

He smiled at her patronisingly, as if only now noticing her presence, in the usual arrogant response most women on this scene receive from musicians. Even reasonably intelligent, talented people like Sandy see women either as groupies or simply silly little things with no understanding of music – its language, it's principles, its technology, and its meaning. Which is a much talked about fact anyway, something women on this circuit know

174

and talk about a lot these days. What really baffles me though is the fact that they don't help each other either. When a woman on the London scene suddenly finds herself in any kind of position of influence or power, she'll more often than not deny opportunities to other women, putting much more effort in undermining a female colleague or a woman below her in the food chain than a man ever would. What exactly goes on in their heads is a mystery to me because I don't see what harm one woman in this business can do to another. And it felt strange how Claire was completely oblivious to one of the biggest prejudices on this scene, looking at Sandy with an open smile, bright-eyed, the way you'd look at a silly but cute little child. She clearly wasn't offended by his arrogance, but I knew it was because she knew little of the twisted ideas he and all others like him have been having about women ever since they began playing guitar all those years ago.

Given Sandy's reaction to Claire, I didn't feel like spending much longer talking to him. I knew he thought that Claire was some naïve girl I hung out with to gratify my vanity, and that I could probably have done better with someone more glamorous if I wasn't so much in love with myself. A projection of his own attitudes, no doubt.

Sandy had a few girls approach him a couple of times while we were talking, who I knew would later join him once Claire and I have left – chicks Sandy certainly knew, and who epitomised his idea of a perfect female companion – cocky little things wearing skimpy shiny clothes, elaborately cut and dyed hair, lots of foundation and eye makeup, and who I could instantly tell understood fuck all about Sandy's band or what he was trying to communicate as a musician. The chicks looked like they were first-year students on some pointless university course, the first generation in their families to go to the uni, or, probably, simply worked in shops, the kind of girls to whom anyone who's in a band is a deity by default. It's difficult to see why someone like Sandy was so irresistibly attractive to this contingent. After all, he isn't even signed and can hardly afford to buy his own booze after coming off the stage. But then I knew that these young girls have never been near any musicians or artists while growing up, coming from backgrounds where any kind of creative activity is regarded with a mixture of adulation and fear. So hanging with a wannabe rock star for them was akin to being introduced into a Masonic order – elevating, glamorous, and dangerous in the eyes of the crowd they ran with at the uni or at work. I could bet my Strat though that none of the girls who now hung around Sandy cared if he got signed or not. To them he was enough as he was – a man to be worshipped simply for the fact that he had long hair and played guitar in a band. And the more arrogant his attitude was towards them, the more rock star cred they were prepared to give him. From the condescending but at the same time overprotective way Sandy talked to those girls I knew he found their ignorant adoration flattering. He probably needed them as much as they needed him – their hero worship added to his confidence. He wasn't interested in their opinions, or their friendship, or what they thought, or what they had to say, but simply needed them as hangers-on. If Sandy wanted to talk to anyone about music, he could do that with the guys in his own band, or plenty of other people on the London scene. Ed Sunders, for one, was always willing to talk to anyone about music who'd care to listen. He'd even go as far as actually record, transcribe, and put online everything someone like Sandy had to say. So whatever Sandy was looking for in a female companion, it wasn't emotional closeness, intellectual exchange, or even understanding. It was the opposite. He hoped those girls would continue being silly and delusional, helping him to uphold an artificial image of himself he was trying to create for the outside world, using them as mirrors he hoped would continue showing him what he wanted to see.

Leaving Sandy to his groupies, Claire and I went to the Ealing flat to write. Claire had some new ideas about taking a traditional blues song and turning it into something heavy and austere, almost an industrial number, and I couldn't wait to see how it was going to work out. In the weeks that we have spent writing together, I have discovered things about myself and about the guitar I never thought I'd tap into. One of the things I could never imagine until then was getting so much pleasure from taking the back seat to another musician and being content with playing no more than miniature electric guitar adornments to what were fundamentally no-frills acoustic songs written by Claire. My terms of reference and the nature of my ambitions suddenly changed, and I was surprised I could now begin thinking not in terms of a solo, the glorified focal point of any piece of rock music, but as a composer, able to work on a song as a whole, instead of being concerned with isolated parts of it. I could finally take the point of reference outside of myself and put a song in its entirety above my personal ambitions. And at other times it would surprise me how I could take a very basic folk or blues harmony and use it as a platform for diving into electric guitar experimentation with complete abandon, unconcerned about overplaying or overindulging in my instrument. At those times the entire piece would be about the electric guitar and nothing else, about my instrument creating, unifying and cohering the entire track, responsible for everything from start to finish, allowing me to approach composition from a completely different angle – not as a balance of different instruments, but a creation of one single voice. I guess I was finally learning to work as a composer, not as a band member who knows little else apart from his own narrow function.

Every time Claire and I sat down to write, the outside world would virtually stop existing. It then became just her, me, our instruments, and our music that took us into a dimension that had nothing to do with our surroundings, our everyday lives, or who we appeared to be to anyone else. Not only this gave me another view on the world, it gave me a different view on myself, and a confidence of a kind that is unknown to most people. It gave me freedom to be who I ultimately wanted to be, all pretences and affectations dropped, and that was a high nothing else I have known before could compare to.   At least not at the time.

Thinking back to those hours when we worked together, I realised that I became very selfish about our writing. All I thought about and looked forward to in my waking hours was writing with Claire. It wasn't exactly an addiction, but there was certainly a great degree of compulsion to it.   After some time I began noticing that my other attitudes were changing too. I more or less stopped caring what sort of impression I made on people I knew or didn't know, or about my clothes, or what sort of image I was supposed to project in social situations. I had no time to spend hours styling my hair, and I had no time to plan my outfits days before going out. The only thing I could now think about was our music.

The other thing that was changing was my changing view on a lot of music I thought I knew so well. A lot of it was now beginning to sound completely different to me – fresh, new, and almost unfamiliar, showing layers of meaning I used to miss out on before. It was as if I was only now starting to discover other people's music in earnest. The nuances and possible implications of a lot of classic and modern rock began emerging only after I started writing with Claire. Even the lyrics that were so familiar to me before, to the point of becoming meaningless, suddenly stood out again in a different light, as if I was hearing them for the first time. Metallica's *Nothing Else Matters* suddenly sounded like a description of what was going on when Claire and I wrote together. Or maybe an account of one of the many things that went on between us when we wrote.

Trusting someone completely in the most intimate of all situations – in the creative process – brought out things in me that I never thought were possible. It gave me the self-belief I needed to start exploring wider and deeper than I've ever been able to before with my old band, and finally let me stop doubting my musical ability for the first time in my life. I was now so certain about our material that I stopped asking other people's opinion about it.   It wasn't even confidence per se, it was a feeling beyond confidence, beyond a desire for recognition, beyond interest in the status music gave me. All I wanted was to find expression to what I was now finding out through my music, nothing interested me apart from that, and consequently, nothing else mattered.

I had no clue what Claire's and mine prospects were in terms of getting a record deal, but it was the last thing I cared about at the time. All I wanted was continue spending as much time as possible with her and to continue writing. But it soon transpired that the direction I chose for my life all those years ago wasn't going to change simply because I have now fallen in love in earnest for the first time, and the girl happened to be who she was.

I have once read about the egregore, an esoteric concept used by some occultists to explain almost all events. It is a name given to collective thoughts, attitudes, and aspirations of people making up any group – be it religious, cultural, educational, criminal, occupational, artistic, or any other. All professions, organisations, and belief systems allegedly have their own egregore, each fuelled by thoughts and emotions of the people who belong to it. Their egregore protects them, influences them, and ultimately helps them achieve their goals. I have laughed at the idea of such a thought form existing somewhere on the astral plain as occultist drivel as soon as I read about it in one of the books I picked from a book shelf at Theodora's house once, and I only thought about it again once the final events of my life in London began to unfold. Remembering about the egregore, still unsure if I was prepared to give the theory any credibility, I thought that if there was any truth to it, rock musicians surely had to have one of their own, and probably a particularly powerful one too.

At the time when I first read about it, the whole thing seemed like something Tom would go on about during one of his spaced-out moments of New Age profundity, but what happened to me after a few weeks of being with Claire, told me that whether it's the egregore theory, or the karma principle, or simply the law of conservation of energy, the universe never lets our deepest, most desperate prayers go unnoticed. Like the ones I have unknowingly been sending out since I was thirteen.   Sometimes it just takes time to act on them.

Claire and I spent the next day looking for a flat to rent, first online at my place in Ealing, and then going out in the afternoon to actually see a few. Nothing that looked good was anywhere near our price range, and all the places we could afford given the money she was earning now and the money I was going to start making at the music shop, were so far away from any sign of civilisation, it took us over two hours to get to one of them from Ealing. That place was in SW16, a studio flat where most of the space was taken up by a bed which had to be folded away vertically into a wardrobe if you wanted to have any space to move in at all in this tiniest of flats. The prospect of living in a shoebox out in the sticks didn't seem too daunting though, neither to Claire, nor to me. So both of us decided to see if our parents would lend us money for a deposit. I was in a state of mind where all I cared about was the music that we were writing, and the fact that I was finally going to live with somebody I knew I loved. So I wasn't going to let household routine ruin how I felt about what I thought were extremely important changes in my life. I knew girls like Claire were one in a million and wasn't going to let anything to stand in our way.

As we sat in a pub near Streatham station talking about what we could do to make the place look more like our own, my thoughts began to drift, and in no time I suddenly found myself worrying about what would happen if something came between me and Claire, and we couldn't be together. Bouts of anxiety were something I was used to ever since I remembered myself, but the speed at which my imagination began to spin out all sorts of crazy scenarios where Claire was meeting someone else and leaving me, surprised me. The person who was taking her away from me was someone rich and famous, a magazine editor, or a record producer, or maybe even a rock star. Not only did I go through all the trivial

180

possibilities where she was taken away from me by money, power, or promises of stardom, but I also imagined her meeting someone utterly and irresistibly talented, much more so than I could ever hope to be. As I sat there frozen with fear, all I could do was smoke one cigarette after another, trying not to let show what was going on in my head, holding up my part of the conversation on autopilot. Those attacks of insecurity have never descended on me so unexpectedly and so ruthlessly before. Within just a few moments I went from being relaxed and happy into a sate of absolute misery.

After a few minutes our conversation drifted towards music. Claire was telling me what instruments we could use for the arrangement of the song we began writing the day before. I then slowly began to unwind. It dawned on me that the fact that we were sitting here unable to talk about anything else but music for longer than five minutes, showed that there was a connection between us that was extremely rare for any two people to share, the one where you trust each other to the point where you can actually write music together and feel amazing doing it. I knew this meant that what united us went deeper than vanity, pride, or narcissism. This was exactly what held Zara and Rich together, something that went beyond things that you can name. I suddenly remembered Tom and how he was talking about things beyond language at the time when I thought it was all incomprehensible rubbish. I now knew that as long as Claire and I had something meaningful to share and could write together, our bond would survive. And as long as that bond was intact, we would always remain intimately close. I leaned over and kissed her, suddenly feeling lifted and clear.

'Are you happy?' I asked her, looking her in the face.

'Yes,' she said, smiling. 'Are you?'

I didn't reply. I just grinned and kissed her again.

IX

DO WHAT THOU WILT II

I was in the shower when our land line phone went off, and then a few moments later heard Dave knocking on the bathroom door, yelling, trying to get me to take the call. I was going to ignore him, but his knocking and yelling wouldn't stop.

I finally popped my head through the door and saw Dave's excited face, shouting, 'It's Bob Ellis for you!'

'Who?' I yelled back, water still running, annoyed at being dragged out of the shower.

'Bob Ellis, you know!' Dave screamed, unable to contain his excitement. 'The producer!'

'Are you serious?' I asked, now feeling bewildered more than anything else.

Dave bobbed his head enthusiastically. I took the call.

Bob Ellis, the producer behind all the Seventies and Eighties musicians I admired since I was twelve, was calling from LA telling me he was putting a band together, and I was being recommended to him by Theodora as a rhythm guitarist. He said he heard some of my demos on my MySpace page and wanted me to fly to LA to meet him. I scribbled his number down on a piece of bog paper, and when I hung up, found myself standing in the middle of our living room, dripping wet, wrapped in a towel, and staring dazedly around me.

Dave was looking at me as if I've just reincarnated into of some kind of pagan deity right before his eyes.

'What did he say?' he whispered reverently.

'He said I should fly to LA,' I replied.

Theodora rang a few hours later.

'Have you spoken to Bob?' she asked, as if nothing had happened between us just a few weeks before.

'Thank you for doing this to me,' I said, trying to sound as sincere and humble as I could.

'When are you flying?' she asked in a business-like voice.

'I have to speak to my parents first about borrowing money for a ticket,' I replied.

'Don't ask your parents,' she said. 'You'll fly with me. We are still a couple, aren't we?'

'Sure,' I said, knowing that this was my only possible answer.

It all happened very quickly after that. In the afternoon I went to Theodora's to help her book our tickets online and to talk about the deal Bob Ellis had in mind for me.

The tickets were booked one way, and once all the details were entered, and our e-tickets printed out, we sat down in her drawing room, me feeling edgy, excited, and guilty about the way I talked to her the last time we saw each other.

Sitting next to me on the sofa, she suddenly stopped going through the printouts of our itinerary, looked at me, smiled, and said, 'You didn't think I could do this for you, did you?'

I shook my head. I didn't know what to say.

'I spoke to my father,' she continued, 'and he spoke to Bob. He doesn't really need to audition you. You are flying to LA to join a band that will be signing a deal with Global in the States later on this month.'

All this sounding like a fairy godmother tale, all I could do was begin asking questions, not because I was ready to take in all the answers, but simply because I thought that way I'd keep in touch with reality and make sure I wasn't dreaming or hallucinating.

'What kind of band is it?' I asked.

'I'll play it to you,' she said, getting up, walking over to her Bang and Olufsen and pressing a button.

What I then heard was loud, brash, polished hard rock which instantly reminded me of the stuff I was playing with the Storm Angels, but delivered to an entirely different level of musicianship – tight, practiced, and self-assured, with stickier hooks and better vocals – a high-pitched perfectly trained voice, the bloke sounding like a music college graduate.

'The bass player and the lead guitarist write,' she said. 'But they should be flexible about allowing you to contribute. At least when we told Global that you wrote, they were glad to hear it. But, again, it all depends on how well you are going to get along with the rest of them. So I'd say make sure they like you. How much money you'll end up making will depend on that.'

'How old are they?' I asked.

'Your age. The drummer is the oldest, he's twenty-five.'

'What if we don't get along?'

'Oh, you will! You have the right kind of personality.'

'Do I?'

'Of course you do! I know you, don't I? I told Daddy that you were a complete package – good-looking, a good musician, smart, and flexible.' She laughed.

'Wow,' I said, trying to think what she meant by "flexible". 'But wouldn't they mind someone they've never met before being hired to play in their band?'

'They are overjoyed they are getting signed. Global told them to get rid of the original rhythm guitarist because he didn't look the part. They were looking for someone to take his place, and Daddy told them you were a perfect fit. We are placing you there at exactly the right time.'

'That's amazing,' I said, very aware that this was the time for another "thank you", but unable to bring myself to say it. I didn't know if this arrangement was something to be grateful for or to be awfully embarrassed about. But my excitement soon made me forget about that.

'How much of your stuff will you be taking with you to LA?' Theodora asked.

'Well, at least my clothes!' I replied, surprised at the question.

'Your clothes are cool,' she said. 'Take them with you, but don't take anything else apart from your guitar.'

'Why?'

'You'll buy everything you need there. The advance is going to be pretty big. Which is, again, unusual these days.'

'How much is it?'

'Enough to rent your own place in a nice area over there,' she said. 'And you can drive one of my cars in the first few months.'

'Are they going to be recording any time soon?'

'As soon as you get there. They are going into the studio at the end of the month. Most of the material already has been written.'

When I got back to the flat, both Dave and Ben were looking at me as if I've just become a superstar. They asked me if I wanted some of their hash. They made me a cup of tea. They fussed over me, and they wanted to know every detail of what I was being offered. Even though I've decided some hours before that I wasn't going to let anyone onto all the details, mainly because I was afraid I'd jinx the whole thing, I ended up sitting on our living room sofa spending a good half an hour blurting out everything I knew so far about the deal to my flatmates who sat on the floor listening to my very own version of the ultimate show biz tale, wide-eyed, with awed open-mouthed expressions.

The next day the flat became besieged. The phone was ringing non-stop and people were stopping by all the time, the

186

kind of people I thought I'd never see in my flat. There were girls I knew from being in the Storm Angels, all feeling more amorous towards me than ever before, owners of some of the shithole venues I played in Camden at one time or another, bouncers from clubs I haven't been to in ages, and women I've never met in my life before, claiming to be photographers, fashion designers, burlesque dancers, writers, and Ayurvedic healers. Ed Sunders rang asking if I would do an interview with him, to which I said I'd call him back and never did, and, I couldn't believe it, but Tracy Huggins suddenly rang me too saying she was sorry to hear about Doug. She then asked if I would meet her for a drink, which really amused me, and which I politely declined.

'Anyway, the girls and I thought we'd stop by your flat,' she said. 'We have a present for you.'

'Which girls?' I asked, bewildered.

'Well, all of us from the Rocktastic Rock Review!' she said, sounding more enthusiastic than I ever heard her.

'And who's that?'

'Me and Emma,' she said, moody overtones beginning to appear in her voice.

'Who's Emma?'

'Emma drives me to interviews in her car sometimes,' Tracy said glumly, evidently resenting my questions. 'So maybe you'd give us a short interview as well, eh?'

'Sorry, babes,' I said. 'No can do. This week is going to be mad and then I'm off.'

'So what do you want us to do with your present? Do you have an address in LA we can send it to?' she asked in a voice that sounded utterly offended by now.

'You know what,' I said. 'Why don't you sent it to Global Rock, and they will pass it on to me?'

Then Sandy rang, congratulating me and asking if I had time to have a drink with him in Camden, which I didn't really want to do – there was nothing I could say to Sandy at that point. So I told him I'd ring him back, meaning to call him from the airport on the day of my departure to tell him I was sorry it didn't work out.

But, to be honest, even though I moaned to Dave and Ben about all the intrusion being a nightmare, I welcomed this bustle because it distracted me and gave me something else to think about instead of sharing the news with the one person who really needed to know – Claire. And then it occurred to me that I was lucky she didn't know anyone on the London rock scene. That way, I figured, I wouldn't have to tell her anything at all. Right until my departure. And once this thought fully formed in my mind, I had to sit right down on the floor – so horrified and disgusted I was with myself for even thinking of not letting Claire know. Of course I had to tell her. I just had to find a way of doing it and telling her exactly when I was coming back to London. But who was I kidding? I knew I wasn't coming back. Then I thought that I had to figure how to persuade her to move with me to LA. But I knew that was nonsense too because there was no way Theodora was going to let any other woman near me now. I knew all too well that I was her trophy she was bringing back to LA with her, a living proof to the fact that two years away in London weren't spent in vain. It wasn't the Courtauld diploma she was going to brandish and show off as an achievement to all her friends and enemies there, no matter how venerated the school was. She knew no one over there gave a fig about art history, or her studies. What everyone cared about was if she finally managed to get over her rock star ex and if she could still bag someone good-looking and talented. That was how I got my record deal and that was the game I was going to have to play for some time now – the role of Theodora's boyfriend. And I laughed to myself at the irony of it all. Now that I finally got what I wanted, there was nothing more I'd rather do than ditch it all and stay in London. I suddenly felt so rotten I felt like either crying or smashing something. I then turned my stereo on to play *Led Zeppelin IV* for some kind of release, but it only made things worse, pointing out what I have become compared to what I've always wanted to be.

Meanwhile hoards people continued to turn up. I've switched my mobile off a long time ago and told Ben and Dave not to answer the land line. The last message they took was from the features editor at Global Rock, and slimeballs at Global Rock were the last people on Earth I wanted to talk to at that point. In the end I couldn't take it any longer. I lifted the land line receiver, dialled Theodora's number and asked if I could come over and stay at her place for at least one night before I became mobbed to death by well-wishers, sycophants, small-time journos, big-time journos, groupies, and hangers-on. She laughed and said I could.

Tom was at Theodora's when I arrived, this time with his hair clean and looking all of a sudden rather handsome in his faded flares and his blue and white Wes Montgomery t-shirt. He was fiddling around with his Strat and a small Marshall combo in the drawing room, which sounded like he was writing a song, and while he was busy doing that, Theodora and I sat in the garden with a bottle of champagne she opened because it was "so hot outside". I was in the middle of telling her how the flat was invaded by people I hardly knew, when Tom finally joined us, sitting down on the wooden bench next to me, saying no to champagne but asking for a can of lager.

'I'd never be able to cope with being in such a regimented band like the one you're joining,' he said to me when Theodora went back into the house. 'I've always admired people who could make music and do business at the same time.'

'That's just something some people find easier to focus on than others,' I said, trying to sound genial, while thinking that he probably despised me for selling out and joining a manufactured act in LA.

'Every time I have a producer, or a manager, or a journo tell me I should meet so-and-so, or send my demos to so-and-so, or join such-and-such band here in the UK or over there, I know I don't have the time to deal with it all,' he said.

'How many bands have you been asked to join?' I asked with undisguised curiosity.

'Oh, dozens,' he said nonchalantly. 'Theodora got pissed off with me a few weeks ago for not taking up that offer to join some blues-rock outfit across the pond.'

'I heard about that.'

'Yeah. I'm just too busy writing my own music to waste any time on relocating and then explaining to a bunch of people I've never met in my life before how to play my music and what I want out of my band.'

'Right.'

'You know, I barely have time to write down and record the ideas I am getting all the time. I have no time for shit like dealing with business arrangements and all the politics. I'm lucky to have the band that I have now which lets me do what I want to do and which gives me basic instrumental support.'

'So you aren't really after a record deal or anything?'

'I just don't think about it. I know that something will happen sooner or later. I just don't have time to deal with it right now. Someone will come up with something at some stage that will suit me and won't be too hassling to sign and get into. I just can't deal with relocating, touring, and all that crap now.'

'What are you nattering about?' asked Theodora, smiling, having returned with a bottle of Stella for Tom.

'I'm just telling John, sorry, Joe, why I can't be asked to deal with the business side of things at the mo.'

'You know, Joey is getting completely mobbed right now,' Theodora said. 'He managed to escape from his own flat just before they were going to tear him to pieces.'

'Well, that just proves my point,' Tom said. 'You get nothing out of fame apart from hassle.'

I would have laughed at this bold statement coming from anyone else, but hearing Tom say it I knew he meant it, and there was no jealousy or resentment on his part. After all, I was

Theodora's second choice. Her first choice was Tom.

'Don't worry,' she said, smiling at him. 'One day you'll come to see me in LA. And you'll love what you now call hassle.'

I suddenly felt champagne go to my head and the return of a nagging feeling that I still needed to speak to Claire to tell her what was going on. But then Theodora made me forget about it again, asking us what we thought she ought to be wearing to tonight's party.

'Which party?' I asked.

'Ah, it's Sammy Robin's birthday party tonight,' she said. 'He's the Chairman of Global Union UK operations. Do you guys want to come along?'

'Nah,' said Tom. 'It's gonna be full of twats.'

'Not all of them are twats,' Theodora said, rolling her eyes. 'Joey, do you want to go?'

In fact, there was nothing I wanted more that evening than to go out, get drunk, and forget about things.

'I'd love to,' I said, grateful for a legitimate excuse not to deal with anything until at least the next morning.

'See,' Theodora said, turning to Tom. 'Joey's up for it. He knows how to be in a right place at the right time.'

Tom shrugged, swigging beer from his bottle.

'This isn't just another party,' Theodora said. 'Sammy's just turned sixty and he's planning something pretty extraordinary for tonight.'

'Really?' Tom said. 'Hendrix's gonna rise from the grave to congratulate him?'

'Not exactly,' Theodora said, 'but you are pretty close, actually.'

'Wow,' I said, 'Led Zeppelin are going to be there?'

'No, don't be silly,' Theodora said. 'Not them. But that's all I am going to say.'

A few hours later, as the sun was setting over Hampstead, the three of us climbed into a black cab that has been waiting outside of Theodora's gate. We were going to the Hyde Park Corner end of Piccadilly to a party that began half an hour ago and was supposed to go on until four in the morning. Theodora was wearing an ankle-length silk yellow dress, and Tom and I looked like dirty rock stars – jeans, t-shirts, shades.

Theodora spoke to the birthday boy himself, dialling his number from the cab and asking to put two more names on the guest list. She didn't sound exactly reverential, but extremely polite, calling him "Mr. Robin" and laughing seductively at what I assumed were some lame jokes the guy was trying to spice the chat with.

While I was trying to listen to Theodora's end of their conversation, Tom was looking out of the cab window, telling me how the greatest thing that had ever happened to him in London was going in a cab in the middle of the night from Victoria to Hackney once, passing down the Embankment lit by all the lights along the river bank, with Hendrix's *Electric Ladyland* playing in his Walkman.

'You mean iPod,' I said to him, distracted, not really following.

'No, man, *Walkman,*' he replied, reaching into his pocket and producing an object I've last seen eighteen years ago when I was four – a real Eighties Sony Walkman, a portable cassette player made of grey plastic, big, chunky, with a pair of cheap red earbuds plugged into a wide panel.

'This is amazing,' I couldn't help saying, staring at this museum piece.

'Yeah, man,' Tom replied, looking proud, 'Awesome, innit?'

He then began telling me how iPods were crap at reproducing the lower register, and how tapes sounded more "authentic", while all I really wanted was talk to Theodora about the people who were going to be at the party.

We finally arrived, getting off at the corner of Piccadilly and Old Park Lane. I was the last one to get out of the car, and was about to close the door, when I saw my mobile on the back seat. It must have slipped out of my pocket on the way. I was going to reach out to get it, but hesitated for a moment, a million thoughts racing through my head, then took one last look at my Nokia, slammed the cab door shut, and let it drive off. Moments later we were walking up a narrow side street just off Piccadilly, Theodora telling me to be nice to Sammy Robin and to avoid talking to journos.

A small group of people stood on the pavement outside of an open black metal door with bright light pouring onto the street from the inside, and two enormous bouncers guarding the entrance. A short blond girl holding a clipboard stood between them, who, I noticed, was exceptionally pretty, and could have been really beautiful, if not for her height and her slightly masculine-looking jaw. The young people who were about to get in looked nervous and excited. The older ones, in their early fifties, while looking pleased, wore a peculiar expression of self-pity mixed with sarcasm over having to deal with the guest list, while at the same time still deferential in their acceptance of this encumbrance. I guess they were grateful to have their names on the guest list after all.

From the outside the place looked completely anonymous – there was no sign above the door, and the brick wall which stretched for yards from each side wasn't giving away any clues. We waited for a few moments for the people in front of us to go in, and then Theodora told the girl our names.

We went through down a narrow carpeted corridor and in a few seconds found ourselves in a gigantic room full of people. A colossal ice sculpture at its centre sparkled under blindingly bright lights, and I realised it was a 3D carving of Global Union's logo – some sort of celestial goddess in a flowing robe and a star in her hand raised above her head. Her other hand was holding what looked like a harp. It was lit with red, blue, and green lights from underneath, giving the room a slightly bizarre, almost Christmassy feel. A smiling waitress in a tight Chinese dress holding a tray of Margaritas appeared in front of us. Those Margarita glasses were huge, probably three times the size of any cocktail glass I've ever seen before. I took one sip out of mine and instantly knew that it was the best Margarita I've never tasted. Not that I've had many before.

I downed my first drink pretty quickly, while staring around me and noticing that most people were dressed casually, apart from a group of amazingly tall long-haired young girls who looked like catwalk models and wore incredibly revealing clothes. One wore hotpants and a top with a v-neck that plunged all the way down to her belly button, while others wore skin-tight mini-dresses.

'Who are they?' I asked Theodora, not being able to stop staring.

'The silicone club,' she sneered contemptuously.

'Must be high-class groupies,' Tom giggled. 'Hey, you guys wanna try these blinis?'

An impeccably poised waiter was now standing in front of us, smiling, holding a tray with a mount of tiny pancake rolls which, as I found out a moment later, were stuffed with caviar.

'We should have continued drinking champagne,' said Theodora, studying critically her Margarita glass.

'Do you need to say hi to a lot of people here?' I asked her.

'Anyone I need to say hello to will find me,' she said. 'But we do need to find Sammy at one point.'

More people were now coming into the room, some of them looking shy and lost, some – brassy and over-confident, some – calm and assured. A tall, thin man in his late thirties with long brown hair, wearing threadbare jeans and a retro Seventies floral shirt came over to say hi to Theodora and talked to her for a few moments about some book he's written about the English Seventies Psychedelia, mentioning Sammy, and how grateful he was to him for helping with the research.

'I admit I feel a bit out of place here,' he said. 'It all seems very grand.'

Theodora gave him one of her sweetest smiles before he walked off, and then turned to us saying, 'This is the guy's only chance to market his book to all the right people, and I already know that he's going home empty-handed. A few people in this room would be interested in what he's written, he just doesn't know how to spot them or what to say if anyone introduces them.'

'Help the poor sod then,' said Tom, chewing on a sushi roll he's just picked from another tray. 'Or do you only help hot young studs?'

Theodora pretended she didn't hear him, or maybe she actually didn't, as she was now exchanging kisses with Arthur Molsey. I don't know how he managed to creep up on us, but as soon I saw him, my first instinct was to hide. He was with Don Blackman, which made matters worse, and I was now seriously thinking of disappearing into the crowd, until I realised that it was too late – they both saw me, Arthur grinning, and Don pulling an elaborate expression which was supposed to convey acknowledgement, indifference, and benevolence all at the same time.

'It's a shame no photography is allowed here tonight,' Arthur turned to me after exchanging casual pleasantries with Theodora. 'I'd have you on page three of our next issue with the headline "The New British Invasion". Or "Britain Does Have Talent", ha-ha!'

I smiled feebly.

'You owe us a *big* interview, matey,' he continued. 'We'll send someone over to LA to talk to you when your record is out, so no disappearing acts! You gonna need us when the record sales are slumping, ha-ha!'

Just when I thought I wasn't going to tolerate Arthur's thinly disguised insults for much longer, Theodora spotted Sammy Robin at the other end of the room, and dragged both me and Tom over to meet him.

Mr. Robin was an almost completely bald man, short and portly, looking every year of his age, if not older, and with a down-to-earth, sensible, rational air about him that gave away nothing about the sort of business he was in. He looked like a politician or a factory owner. He was wearing a perfectly tailored grey suit, had a glass of sparkling mineral water in his small tanned hairy hand, and was completely immersed in a conversation with a serious-looking guy about his age, whose face I recognised, but couldn't place. The guy had distinguished, intelligent features that expressed no revere, glee, or excitement, just pure interest in what Sammy was saying to him.

'Oh, there you are!' Sammy exclaimed when he saw Theodora approach him, smiling as she leaned over to kiss him on both cheeks. 'Andy and I were just talking about LA. What are you doing in London anyway? The weather is dismal here this time of the year.'

'I thought I'd say "Happy birthday" to you before going back,' Theodora said, smiling at him. I've never seen her smile so luminously at anyone before.

'That's nice of you,' Sammy said, now noticing Tom and me.

'This is Joey,' Theodora said, touching my arm lightly. 'He's flying to see Bob Ellis in LA next week. Bob is putting a new band together.'

'I know,' Sammy said, nodding.

'Hello, Mr. Robin,' I said, trying to project a respectful, sincere, and thoughtful tone.

'Hi,' he said. 'Good luck with the new band. We were going to sign your old one, weren't we?'

'That's right,' I said. 'But that band, unfortunately, split up.'

'Really?' Sammy Robin sounded mildly surprised.

'The guys were shocked over the death of our manager, and decided they couldn't go on.'

'Yes, the death of a dear friend sometimes makes it impossible for a band to continue,' Sammy said in a voice full of sentiment, if not nostalgia, but then assumed his earlier business-like tone, turning to Theodora, saying, 'Make sure you see tonight's show. A bunch of old mates are putting up a little gig here this evening. Go up those stairs in about ten minutes,' he said, raising his glass in the direction of a flight of stairs at the other end of the room. 'Or get there now if you want to be close to the stage.'

196

'I can't wait!' Theodora replied with what looked like genuine excitement.

Sammy nodded and signalled that we could now go, by turning to his companion again.

As we walked off, I noticed five or six people coming in our direction who have just spotted Sammy, all looking like they wanted to talk to him.

'This jumped up kid wants more than just his producer's fee, and I'm telling him that it's not him who's calling the shots here,' was the last thing I heard Sammy say to the guy he was talking to just before both of them disappeared from our hearing range. I then realised who the other guy was. He was the producer behind more classic British rock records than I cared to count. The last time I saw his face on TV was in a retrospective about the early days of glam.

'I don't see any musicians though,' Tom said, following us up the stairs and giving the room one last glance from the top.

Moments later we stepped into a space that looked like one of those small clubs in Camden, only cleaner and with a smart-looking bar facing a small stage.

'Here they all are,' Theodora said quietly.

She was right – the room was full of people I was only used to seeing either on TV, in newspapers, or in music magazines. People from bands I grew up listening to and obsessing about in my teens were having conversations with elegant women and relaxed, confident men in suits; people whose Eighties style I, until a month ago, was so desperately trying to copy, were here talking to TV presenters and record producers; Nineties Brit pop stars whose fame fizzled away as quickly as the alcopop fad, were here too, as well as guys of my age who got signed in the last couple of years, hanging out with talk show hosts, models, magazine editors, radio DJs, and people who I didn't know but who looked like they belonged – self-assured, well-dressed men and gorgeous women.

While I was staring around, failing to look cool and unaffected, helpless in my star-struck loss of nerve, Tom and

Theodora looked absolutely unimpressed. Tom pulled us to the bar to get more drinks, which we did, noticing more people appearing in the room while we were waiting to be served. When we finally got a chance to shout our orders to the barman, I heard a murmur going through the crowd behind our backs, and when I turned around to see what was happening, I saw four musicians walk onto the stage. A second later I realised that it was the band I thought I'd never see in my life. They were Sailcraft, the legends of British hard rock, apparently reunited to play at Sammy's birthday party for the first time after disbanding twenty-seven years ago. Even Theodora, who knew they were going to play tonight, looked stunned. Tom stopped babbling about how amazing it was that all drinks were free, and now stared at the stage, his expression shock-still, managing to nearly drop his whiskey glass, which he caught at the last moment, spilling half of it on the floor, and the other half – on my jeans.

He then leaned over to me, whispering, 'Is this who I think it is?'

Numb, I nodded slowly, almost paralysed, but at the same time aware that the only sensible thing to get as close to the stage as possible, to the front row, where the London show biz beau monde was scrambling for space.

'Come on,' I said to Tom, suddenly forgetting about Theodora. 'Let's go to the front.'

Making our way there wasn't easy, but once we managed to move through the crowd of awe-struck punters at the back of the room and all the industry big-timers standing by the stage, we could now see the band play less then two feet away from us. They were in their early sixties, all with grey hair apart from the singer who's kept his golden mane, the tiny stage not allowing them to move much but still giving them enough space to put up a dazzling show. There were no stage props or elaborate costumes that their performances in the Seventies were so famous for, but none of it mattered that evening. This time it was all about the atmosphere they were creating, treading the fine line between strong emotions and delicate nuances, light and shade, bravado and respect for the audience. They were just beginning to play their first song, an all-time hit from their second album released back in 1969, and it seemed that all I had to do was pinch myself for this dream to end. Spontaneous and emerging from several points, the song swung with breathtaking magnificence, tight, but at the same time lush and open. The guitarist was an awesome sight, chopping out rough, fierce leads with his guitar strapped at knee level, moving freely and impulsively, like any true guitar hero should, unaffected by time or any other considerations. The balance he was striking between the rhythm and the lead parts was remarkable – something you learn though years and years of playing in a band where you are the only guitarist. There was a sense of unsettling, restless urgency to the way everyone in the room sang along, partly because it was most people's first time they saw the band live, and, as almost everyone was realising, their last. Sailcraft have disbanded in 1980 because of the death of their manager who was their close friend, and have since then every year been declining offers of hundreds of millions to reunite for a world tour. But right now I wasn't thinking about their history. I wasn't even trying to draw parallels with the band's past and their Seventies shows I've seen on DVD. Any links to that would have been meaningless, as tonight they played with a purpose beyond legend and remembrance, with full consciousness of their true goal – to transmit the immediate impulse and the immediate sensation.

I looked over at Tom, and saw that he, in turn, was looking at me, trying to see if what was going on was having the same effect on me. Our eyes met.

'Here,' he said, taking a tiny piece of paper the size of a stamp out of his pocket, tearing it in two, and giving one half to me. I instantly knew what it was.

'Thanks, man,' I said, putting half of the acid blotter in my mouth, grateful to him for single-handedly allowing me to take my mind off so many things – any unnecessary comparisons my brain would start drawing between myself and the magnificent, dignified band on the stage, the fact that I haven't called Claire, and another, equally painful fact that I was given this incredible chance to watch my heroes only because a certain girl took me here, a girl I was now resenting more than ever before.

In a few moments sound became colour, and colour became a physical sensation. Sailcraft were now playing inside me, their music moving within my body in warm balmy waves of awareness. The bass was a strong, thumping spring wrapped in cotton wool, contracting and relaxing in time with the drummer's tickling pulse, while the guitar wrapped itself around its groove, now and then attacking it with sharp screams that I later managed to solidify into a monolith barrage of sound that abandoned its previous cowardly tactics and was now roaring over the bass and the drums in majestic anger, led by my fiery resolve and unbending will. Then I *became* the guitar and began spinning and whirling around the bass and the drums, piercing and puncturing their pace, merging with the vocals in an angry act of physical love, wielding revenge on the drums that were so desperately trying to control me. Then, with a change of strategy bordering on genius, I split the twin attack of the guitar and the vocals into five separate channels that were now beginning to slowly strangle the rhythm section, tricking it into dropping its guard by staying serene and mellow, only to explode again in a heated wave of revenge once the bass drum began to lose its vigilance. It seemed to me that I was now winning this battle. The trick was to know when to remain passive, play along, and when to attack the bass drum, which I knew was the root of all evil. Once I managed to disorient it, I could then mess up the whole rhythm section. Crash cymbals and the hi-hat were mere brown-nosing sycophants playing along to the malicious oppressor that was the bass drum. I finally realised how it all worked. It was all crystal clear, and I knew I had to win this battle because my future depended on its outcome. The guitar had to be liberated, and I was the one who was going to make it happen. No more control of the drum kit, no more tyranny of the bass, no more having to pretend or play along with all this evil. The shadows on the stage where

200

simply cartoon characters, crudely drawn one-dimensional cut-out figures that were put there to distract the crowd from the real events that were unfolding in this room – my battle against the dictatorship of the rhythm section. The so-called musicians in front of us could now finally be seen for who they really were – conductors and carriers of energies generated by their instruments. They had no will of their own.

In a cab back to Theodora's I was trying to think if we've really just had a conversation with Sailcraft over a drink and a spliff on the roof of the club, or if it was another vision of the many I've had that evening. I tried to ask Theodora if it was true, but instead of hearing the sound of my voice just saw a wave of orange smoke come out of my mouth and enter her ears. She turned to me, her lips motionless, but her voice resonating inside my head: 'Anything you want to happen is now possible.'

The next few days were a blur. No one could get through to me because my mobile was no longer with me, and I was staying at Theodora's, whose number, thankfully, nobody knew, apart from Dave and Ben. At first Dave would ring a few times a day to pass on the messages, but then I told him not to bother. He told me that Claire rang a few times and wanted to know where I was, but he kept telling her he didn't know. I then asked him to bring my stuff over to Theodora's, a request to which his reply at any other time would have been the standard "go fuck yourself", but which was now met with eagerness I never knew Dave was capable of. I asked him to bring down my clothes and my guitar, and to keep my Marshall combo, which he was extremely grateful for.

It was a miserable, grey, wet day. The three of us sat in Theodora's drawing room with a bottle of Chablis, Dave wishing me all the luck in the world and telling me how everyone thought I was a wanker for not throwing them a party and not leaving any contact numbers. I was grateful to him for not mentioning Claire.

Theodora then wanted to check if she remembered to pack her tarot cards, and as she left the room, the two of us sat alone for a while, before Dave asked me what I wanted him to do with the tapes Claire and I have made. I suddenly felt like telling him not to poke his nose into other people's private lives, but then realised this would have been a completely OTT reaction, showing how painful the subject really was to me.

'Give them to her, I guess,' I said, trying to hold back my anger at being reminded about Claire. 'Tell her she can come over and collect them.'

Dave was looking at me timidly, about to say something that I knew would embarrass us both, and most certainly make me say something I'd later regret. To prevent this from happening, I spoke first.

'Remember when Bob Ellis rang, and you dragged me out of the shower, and then stared at me like I was some kind of Egyptian god, when I told you what it was about?' I spoke slowly, slurring my words for a particular effect, while letting my head roll back on one of Theodora's silk Thai cushions, which seemed like I was looking down at him, although our eyes remained on the same level – Dave was taller than me. I knew full well I could from now on assume this kind of tone with him whenever I wanted, probably for the rest of both of our lives.

Dave nodded and giggled, like a kid.

'You looked at me like I've just died and reincarnated right before your eyes.'

'You can say that,' Dave said, smiling. Not exactly sycophantically, but with a certain degree of reverence.

'Well, why don't you tell Claire that I have really died and reincarnated in LA,' I continued slowly. 'And that if I ever return to London, I'm gonna die again, only this time for eternity. That having to live in LA is the unfortunate condition of my reincarnation. A curse.'

Dave nodded, smiling, hopefully picking up on the veiled threat in my voice which I deliberately chose to let him know I wasn't going to be preached to about my private life by a no-name sound tech.

'I listened to the tapes you guys have made,' Dave suddenly said, sounding shy, but at the same time weirdly excited, without realising that he was now being downright tactless, all my not-so-subtle efforts to shut him up on the subject evidently having gone over his head. He never must have understood what that girl had meant to me.

I got up and walked across the room to turn the light switch on – it was getting dark outside. It looked casual, and at the same time excused me from having to reply to his last remark.

'It's awesome stuff,' Dave continued, making my insides curl with pain.

'Right.'

'From now on, every time I'm gonna hear one of those acoustic Led Zeppelin tracks, I'll be thinking of you two jamming.'

I turned my back to Dave and stared out of the window. A lamp post with its light shining murkily in the descending semi-darkness, and a couple of miserable-looking passers-by, a man and a woman, both in their late fifties, was all I could see, as I tried to fix my stare on its dim yellow glow to keep my thoughts at bay. But it didn't help. All I could hear in my head was the last song Claire and I wrote, her high-pitched voice sounding so clear it was almost as if she was in the room. My memory suddenly resurrected the song in my mind, each detail sharp and clear, magnified by my misery, making it the first time I ever regretted having perfect pitch which was making this flawless recollection now possible. I suddenly began to doubt the sanity of my decision of going to LA. I thought that I had probably underestimated my ability for erasing people and events out of my memory. It suddenly occurred to me that I was either going to end up in a psychiatric institution, or become an addict if I did go to LA right now. And then I thought that it still wasn't too late to change anything. All I had to do was repay Theodora for the ticket and ring Bob Ellis to tell him I couldn't make it this time. But I knew it couldn't be done. Not only because a chain of events has now been set in motion, but because of the way my mind has been set, and such a long time ago too, that it was not only too late now, but impossible to change the path I have chosen for myself. I didn't have any options now apart from doing what I grew up believing I was born to do. My love for Claire, and even my love for music weren't going to change things. Whatever it took, I was going to follow through with what I have embarked on when I was thirteen. Blame Big Roar magazine and its posters I used to rip out and stick to my bedroom walls – the first images I saw every morning when I woke up and the last I saw before going to sleep. Going to LA now wasn't even what I wanted to do, but something I *had* to do. Otherwise I'd betray my younger self. Those, anyway, were the things I was trying to convince myself of while turning away from the window and looking at Dave, whose face, I now saw, expressed nothing but pure simple-hearted adoration. I've never encountered anything like this unquestioning devotion until this week, and I knew that Dave was one of the potential millions. And seeing people react to me like this for only a few days has convinced me that more amazing things were about to start happening.

'It's late,' I finally said. 'We've got an early flight tomorrow. Cheers for brining my stuff over.'

'No worries, mate,' Dave said, getting up. 'Drop us a line when you get there.'

'Will do,' I said, 'Definitely will do.'

'Oh, stop bloody sulking,' Theodora said to me half and hour into our flight, as she saw me put my Ray Bans on and turn permanently to the window where thin transparent clouds sprawled under the airplane's rime-covered wing. She hung on to her Britishisms even more now that she was leaving England for good, making me fear she would end up adopting a fake English accent once she arrived in LA. I was feeling so rotten all day, I felt like lashing out on her, about to tell her that her English jargon sounded endearing but unnatural, when she added, 'You're not the only one flying to LA with a broken heart.'

'Eh?' was all I managed to utter, taking my shades off and turning in my seat to face her.

'Yes, you heard me right,' she said, fixing her gaze on a whiskey glass on the fold-out table in front of her.

'What's that supposed to mean?' I asked, trying to decide if I was supposed to sound offended or indifferent.

She didn't reply, but pulled at an almost invisible chain around her neck, producing a small silver (or was it platinum?) locket from underneath her silk brown shirt. She pressed it open, and I leaned over to see what was inside. Once I saw the miniature black-and-white image, all I could do was stare. Inside Theodora's locket was a picture of Tom, smiling with an open, unguarded smile, his long blond hair in his eyes, looking straight into the camera with a mixed expression of confidence and childlike vulnerability.

Theodora's face was expressionless as she snapped the locket shut and hid it under her shirt.

'Don't tell anyone I wear a locket,' she said. 'It's the height of bad taste.'

'Wow,' I said, feeling something akin to pity for her, and forgetting the resentment which began mounting in the taxi on the way to the airport, all the way during the check-in, while boarding, and then sitting next to her for the first half an hour of our flight. I even wanted to say something to comfort her, but couldn't think of the right words, so I ended up sitting there staring at her, unable to articulate anything meaningful.

'I would never have thought someone like Tom would get to you,' I finally said.

'It's the talent, stupid,' she replied with what sounded like spite in her voice.

'What do you mean?' I asked, not quite getting whose talent, and for what.

'It's not the looks, it's not the money, it's not the power people fall in love with,' she said tersely, her cheeks turning pink.

'What is it then?'

'It's the brilliance everyone loves. The inspiration that's behind any great talent. It's always an artist who gets to you, not a moneybag or, god forbid, a politician, or a model. Art and talent go straight for the spirit, bypassing the brain.'

'Oh, I see,' I said, pretending not to care, but at the same time thinking glumly that I was the last person she should have been explaining all this to. 'I remember you telling me rock stars married models and millionaires' daughters. So maybe when Tom finally makes it, you could still have your chance.'

Theodora gave me a short look full of disgust, took a sip out of her whiskey glass, flung back her hair, and finally replied in an aloof voice, 'Those who are truly great don't seek greatness in their lovers. Tom is talented enough not to long desperately for someone whose brilliance would illuminate his life. His own light is bright enough. Great men are content with the mundane and the banal in their women. But those who are ordinary will never stop wishing for an extraordinary lover. Someone who'd make their life worth living.'

'So when I'm a star I'll be looking to marry a checkout girl,' I said, trying not to let too much sarcasm seep into my voice.

'Stardom and brilliance are two entirely different things,' she said.

We sat in silence for a few moments while she drank her whiskey and I continued watching the sky and the clouds.

'So how did your girl take it?' Theodora asked after a while.

'What girl?' I said, looking her in the face, and suddenly feeling nothing but hatred for her. 'There was no girl.'

206

EPILOGUE

I am writing this on the balcony of my apartment in Brentwood, Los Angeles. The sun is setting over the skyscrapers in the Southeast, and I've just finished a bottle of Chablis and my second packet of cigarettes this evening. Our manager says we should all keep diaries. First off, it's supposed to help the creative process, and, secondly, it could sell well some ten years on.

I thought I'd be living on Sunset Strip when I signed the contract and got my share of the advance payment, but it turned out that nobody who's anybody really rents or buys on Sunset Strip. A lot of it, apparently, is a dodgy area. So Theodora helped me find this apartment. We decided we weren't going to live together, but as far as the outside world is concerned, we are a couple. To be honest, I don't care as long as neither of us is seen openly going out with someone else. She now has her own art gallery in the fashionable part of Westwood, not that far from my place, but we don't see each other that often – maybe two or three times a month. We tell the press that we are a very private couple.

My bandmates turned out to be reasonably cool guys, all apart from the lead guitarist who, from what I can tell, probably secretly resents me, or maybe he's just a moody bastard, I don't know. To tell the truth, I couldn't give a flying fuck about what goes on inside his head as long as he allows me to write.

I ended up contributing to four out of twelve songs on our debut album, which isn't that bad, but I still wish I'd written at least one song of my own, which I somehow couldn't focus on, or couldn't find the right groove for.

The record came out last month, did very well in the charts and got some good press. A few web sites have panned us, but I don't care as long as all the big mags have given us a thumbs-up.

Zara moved to New York soon after I moved to LA and married Rich Mills a month later. I was at their wedding in Saddle Rock and brought with me a silver cocktail shaker our publicist helped me pick at Tiffany's on North Rodeo Drive. From what I sometimes read in Rich's blog, they seem to be happy and still in love. Between his ramblings about the US being besieged by its enemies, complaints about increasing food and gas prices, and general misgivings about the state of the music industry, he talks about traveling with her to photoshoots and both of them spending most of their time hanging in the photo studio which he built in the basement of their house. There was recently a spread done by Zara in one of those arty fashion magazines where Rich looked like an eighteenth century pirate, shot in a half-lit room with his tattoos, long hair and goatee making him look like a bona fide A-list celebrity. There isn't much chance for Silver Cats of getting back into the charts, but they continue to tour in the States, as well as once every two years in Europe, and seem to be making some sort of living out of it.

I sometimes check MySpace pages of some of the people I used to hang with in London. The only person whose page I haven't opened once is Claire. The last time I saw her and spoke to her was the day when we went flat hunting in Streatham, which was the day before Bob Ellis's phone call.

The Storm Angels have disbanded right after Doug's death, just like everyone has expected them to and have all deleted their MySpace accounts. Not that I give a damn. As far as I'm concerned, they could have followed Doug to the grave for all I care. And in my mind they have. I have completely buried all memories of that band. It's not like I am ever going to have anything to do with losers like the Storm Angels again. If nothing else, moving to LA has allowed me to cut all ties from fuck-ups like my former band

and the scene they belong to.

Sandy, as far as I know, is still struggling in London. He e-mailed me once asking if LA was any different from London, and if chances of getting singed were better over here than there, but I still haven't found time to reply.

Dave's been fired from the studio in Primrose Hill for moonlighting, and Ben is now in Japan working for a studio set up out there by some Americans I speak to him occasionally and he says he's learning Japanese. I should hang with him when we're in Japan next year. Next year is the year of our first world tour.

My parents say I should come home this summer but it doesn't look like I'm going to make it, now that we have US tour dates scheduled for the next three months. I've always dreamed of going on the road with the band we are going to be supporting, so it's a thrilling time for me. The money, the TV appearances, the parties, the posh groupies, I am slowly getting used to, but what will never stop giving me the kick is meeting all the musicians I idolised when I was younger, and still look up to now. I've met almost all of my heroes, and it's the greatest buzz in the world, apart from the attention you get from the fans, of course.

Fan mail has been coming in like a flood since our first single came out. If being in an unsigned London band and getting a few dozen e-mails through MySpace a day seemed like stardom at the time, this is an entirely different game. A few club dates that we played in LA so far went down a storm, the fans mobbing us and making it almost impossible for us to leave. If signing autographs was all we were going to do each of those times, we'd have to spend the entire night doing just that after each show. Some chicks were outrageous – willing to do anything, some of them pretty, some of them – stunning. And most guys look at you like you're a higher being. Sometimes it gets creepy, sometimes it feels a touch embarrassing, but overall it's an incredible high.

We are going to be playing some big arenas and a lot of

festivals this summer, and once we posted our tour dates online last week, the response was bigger than anyone's expected.

The label runs our MySpace page, but I check it sometimes, and some of the messages people send are mind-blowing. A lot of people basically think we are gods. Grovelling messages that convey nothing but blind worship arrive en masse every day. Those are the people who are prepared to do anything for your attention. If we ever wrote personally to any of them, receiving our reply would have been the most important event of their lives. Some messages are up to ten pages long, people telling us their life stories and looking for some kind of guidance or spiritual help. Some messages are from people truly obsessed and begging to meet us. Contempt is just one of the possible reactions you can have to this, but in reality it's exhilarating. Those people could be morons, by they are *our* morons.

Most letters though are from regular people who think that our music kicks ass. Thousands of women write to us saying that I am the hottest guy in the world. It's crazy and it's astounding. To think what fame can do, especially given that our band's balloon still hasn't gone up properly yet. Our fan club has one hundred thousand members, and it's only been a few weeks since the album came out. I can't wait to hit the road. I know I'll come back home an entirely different person. It scares me and it excites me at the same time. I don't know what to expect. I just really hope I'd be able to finally stop spending my every waking moment thinking about Claire. I hope it will make everything worth it.